THE BEST OF THE WEST 3

THE
BEST OF THE WEST 3

NEW SHORT STORIES FROM THE WIDE SIDE OF THE MISSOURI

EDITED BY JAMES AND DENISE THOMAS

PEREGRINE SMITH BOOKS
SALT LAKE CITY

First edition

92 91 90 3 2 1

This is a Peregrine Smith Book, published by Gibbs Smith, Publisher, P.O. Box 667, Layton, Utah 84041

Design by J. Scott Knudsen, Park City, Utah

Printed and bound in the United States of America

Library of Congress Cataloging-in-Publication Data

The Best of the West 3 : new short stories from the wide side of the Missouri / edited by James Thomas and Denise Thomas.
     p.   cm.
ISBN 0-87905-320-8
1. Western stories.   2. American fiction—20th century.   3. Short stories, American—West (U.S.)   I. Thomas, James, 1946-   II. Thomas, Denise, 1954- .   III. Title: Best of the West three.
PS648.W4B472   1990
813'.087408—dc20   90-6917
                                    CIP

For Jesse and Christopher

CONTENTS

INTRODUCTION

Th(T)here are several pleasant chores associated with making this book each year, not the least of which is notifying the authors that we would like to include their stories. Almost always they are surprised and grateful (I will leave it to you to imagine the exceptions). Surprised because they hadn't *submitted* the story to us, so didn't know we were considering it (we "find" the stories by reading all the fiction in the hundreds of magazines and journals sent to us); grateful for the celebration and the extended readership that comes with anthologization of the story.

But in order to get to the author with our happy news, we always first contact the magazines where the stories originally appeared, with congratulations to the editors for having had the good sense to print the story in the first place. And to tell the truth this correspondence is every bit as satisfying, in fact *particularly* satisfying, in its opportunity to applaud both the fine writing and the fine publishing of fiction that is occurring in this country, especially in the "little" magazines. Each year for the past several we have noted a muscular expansion of the number and quality of pages and publications—and certainly not just in the West, although we are pleased to note a recent and vigorous flourishing of fine literary journals among the desert cacti and in the mountain valleys.

Certainly the little magazines have always been a first front for the promising writers of important literature in this country, a tradition which reaches back to its founding (with such magazines as *The North American Review*), and only rarely have they been regional in their editorial interests. Indeed, it has seemed to be the province of the journals to foster a fascination of literature that is both national (the

"American short story," for example) and avowedly international (in the past ten years especially, an astonishing amount of poetry and fiction originally written in languages other than English has been translated and printed in the pages of these magazines—especially that from China and eastern Europe).

And so it really comes as no surprise that these serious, literary "western" stories were first published all over the country—in New York and San Francisco, in Ohio and Virginia and Tennessee and North Dakota, and in Washington, D.C. Nor is it a surprise that at least a simple majority of them were first published in the West, since any publication's familiarity and visibility—for the submitting writer—still has a bit to do with proximity and geography. The stories in *Best of the West* owe their appearance to these magazines, both small and large (as well as audio), and this year we would like to take the time to publicly commend them. Congratulations especially to *Sonora Review, Puerto del Sol,* and N.P.R.'s "The Sound of Writing: The PEN Syndicated Fiction Magazine of the Air," each of which has contributed two stories to this year's *Best of the West.*

Also, and because we would like it noted that we do not make the final selection of the stories alone, we would like to acknowledge and thank our associates who helped in the final shaping of the book: Madge Baird at Peregrine Smith Books in Utah, Evelyn Belcher, Darin Cain, and Kirk Donnan in Ohio, and especially Dan O'Brien in the Black (and spirited) Hills of South Dakota. Tough and talented critics, their astute reading made our job a little easier.

Still, as always, there were a number of fine stories set in the West and published last year (our tripartite criterion) which we were unable to include in the book. With that in mind we would like to introduce a new (small, but we think important) feature of *Best of the West:* a listing of additional stories which we found to be distinguished, of great interest and high merit. This year the number comes to thirty, and the list follows this introduction. Congratulations to those writers and the magazines which published them.

James Thomas

Distinguished Western Stories Published in 1989

Lee K. Abbot, "How Love Is Lived in Paradise," *The Kenyon Review*, XI/4

Phyllis Barber, "Criminal Justice," *Crosscurrents*, 8/3, 1989

Will Baker, "Field of Fire," *The Georgia Review*, XLIII/2, Summer 1989

Bruce Berger, "Of Will and the Desert," *Sonora Review*, 17, 1989

Carole J. Bubash, "The Turkey Stick," *North Country Review*, May/June 1989

François Camoin, "Lost in the Desert of Love," *Colorado Review*, Fall/Winter 1988

François Camoin, "The Natural Condition of the World," *Manoa*, Fall 1989

Ron Carlson, "A Thousand People Later," *Manoa*, Fall 1989

Louise Erdrich, "Potchikoo," *Granta*, 27, Summer 1989

Mark A. R. Facknitz, "Las Golondrinas," *Shenandoah*, 39/2, 1989

Nancy Gage, "A Room on the Other Side," *Sonora Review*, 17, 1989

Katherine Haake, "All This Land," *The Minnesota Review*, 32, Spring 1989

Katherine Haake, "The Laying on of Hands," *Mississippi Review*, 17/13, 1989

Dan Hall, "Wolfy," *Carolina Quarterly*, Spring 1989

Linda M. Hasselstrom, "The Price of Bullets," *Missouri Review*, 12/1, 1989

Maria Mitchell Hayes, "The Ethro Plane," *High Plains Literary Review*, Fall 1989

Pamela Houston, "How to Talk to a Hunter," *Quarterly West*, Fall 1989

Walter Kirn, "Yellow Stars of Utah," *Esquire*, July 1989

William Kittredge, "Three Dollar Dogs," N.P.R.'s *The Sound of Writing: The PEN Syndicated Fiction Project of the Air*

Eugene Kraft, "We Gather Together," *New Mexico Humanities Review*, 31, 1989

Karen Latuchie, "The Simple Truth," *Southwest Review*, Summer 1989

Don Lewis, "American Mercury," *New Mexico Humanities Review*, 31, 1989

David Long, "The New World," *Antaeus*, 62, Spring 1989

Bret Lott, "Brothers," *Iowa Review*, 19/1, 1989

Kent Nelson, "Wind Shift," *The Sewanee Review*, Summer 1989

Lisa Poneck, "Touching Chavela," *Indiana Review*, 12/3

Ron Steffens, "Stories from Tuba City," *Sonora Review*, 17, 1989

Christopher Tilghman, "Loose Reins," *The Sewanee Review*, Summer 1989

Judy Troy, "Accident," *The New Yorker*, July 19, 1989

Chilton Williamson, Jr., "Death Do Us Part," *The Sewanee Review*, Summer 1989

DAGOBERTO GILB

THE SEÑORA

The view from the señora's building was handsome. Below its height on the Franklin Mountains sat a wide, manly expanse of land, from the buildings downtown, over the river to Juárez, past its colonias, to the emptiness of the Chihuahua Desert. In the day, in the summer, the land below never budged, and the blue sky would hang above it without end, everywhere, while in the evening the same sight was an ocean mirroring a black, starry air above. No doubt it was this which attracted the señora to the spot here on the mountain so many years ago when she was young, when she and her husband, who survived only a year back on this side, moved north, wealthy from Mexican mines. So maybe her building wasn't the most plush in the city, but expenses weren't spared either. This could have been a matter of chance — that is to say, a matter of history, because it was built in the days when property and labor were especially easy to come by — though it could equally be argued that for someone of her wealth and position, life had always been cheap in El Paso.

Maybe cheap, but never easy. Anyone who had lived here knew this. Jesus knew, and Jesse had come to. They both knew that this woman — the señora was all they ever called her — wouldn't for one moment let them think it could have been another way. Not that they would

mention this to her, not that she'd have to remind them
of it, or even bring it up once. Not that they thought
about it at all.

They thought about her, though. Maybe for the
obvious reasons. Like that Jesus, a national without doc-
uments, often got work from her, both here and on her
ranch in New Mexico, and that his wife, who was also
undocumented, was her maid. Like that Jesse rented one
of the guest houses (in these times called a "furnished
apartment") for practically nothing, even when he paid,
which he hadn't every month because the señora didn't
always notice. But there was more to it than that. They
thought about her because it would be impossible not to.

In the four months he was a tenant, Jesse seldom came
out of his apartment. When he did, he always had his
shirt off and dark glasses on. There was no one around
to ask him what he was doing in El Paso, why, how; no
one but Jesus made a question of anything, and his only
one had been where Jesse was from. California, Jesse told
him, the Bay Area. And even that was answered with a
caution Jesus could read. But despite first appearances,
Jesse was gentle and soft-spoken, friendly toward Jesus,
who was as kind as the name of the village he'd come
from, La Paz.

"Coffee?" Jesse asked with a leg outside his screen
door. His shirt was not on, and a blue tattoo of an eagle
spanned his hairless chest.

"Of course," said Jesus, pleased. He rested his roller in
the bucket of white paint and wiped his hands on the
brown cotton pants he worked in. Then he adjusted the
paint-splattered Houston Astros baseball cap, and waited
at the steps near Jesse's door.

Jesse came back and stepped outside with two mugs
of hot instant coffee he'd already sweetened. "You keep
going as fast as you are and you'll paint yourself out of
the money." The arm with the black widow tattoo held
out a mug for Jesus.

"The señora told me when I finish with this she has
more for me, like the rooms inside, and some other

things too." Jesus had been defensive ever since he per-
ceived that Jesse didn't approve of the wage he'd accepted
for the work.

"It's a little hot," said Jesse.

"I think it's just right," Jesus said, referring to the
coffee.

"I'm talking about the sun, the heat. That it's already
hot."

"Oh. Yes. A little." He hadn't thought about it.

They drank the coffee under the wooden eves of the
building while the chicharras, the cicadas, clicked on and
off like small motors.

It was always quiet when the señora wasn't there. She
wasn't physically loud when she was around, but even
her unseen presence filled what was silence otherwise. So
the noise she made the day she died wasn't surprising.
Both Jesus and Jesse heard it from the beginning and
neither thought anything peculiar about it. She was
throwing a tantrum at a nurse—the woman, anyway,
who wore a white uniform. The señora fired her,
screamed at the woman as she was helping the señora
into the wheelchair. The señora told her to get back in
her car and to go and to not come back. The nurse
obliged and drove down the unpaved alley, popping her
tires off the rocks, dusting the air. The señora rolled herself across the rocky path until she got to the smooth
cement sidewalk. Neither Jesus nor Jesse moved to help
her, instinctually knowing better. When the señora got to
her door she began screaming about that nurse still having the keys. She stood with her cane, then standing on
her old legs, heaved that cane into the glass panes of the
door. That's when Jesus came over. He couldn't understand all she was wailing about in English, but he broke
out a square of glass and reached inside and turned the
deadbolt. When the door still didn't open, the señora
tensed again and screamed more. She was not sweating,
but she was breathing with a loud hiss. Jesus couldn't get
it opened, and the señora hollered. That's when Jesse
came over. He positioned himself, then kicked the door.

It splintered the jamb and sprang into an arc. The señora did not thank them as she went inside and left behind the wheelchair and the two men. She screamed and complained from within her home. Jesus and Jesse returned to what they were doing after a few moments, which is to say Jesus rolled white paint onto the plaster walls and Jesse went to the other side of the screen door where he couldn't be seen.

It got hugely quiet. Jesse stepped out of his apartment, and Jesus looked over to him.

"We better see," Jesse told Jesus.

"Yes. It's what I'm thinking."

They entered the señora's home, the mahogany and crystal and silver sparkling with cleanliness. She was sprawled on her rug, the stem of a rose in the carpet's pattern seeming to hook between her teeth. Her eyes were closed, but an ornery scowl kept the señora from looking peaceful. The combination suited her death. There was nothing at all sad about seeing her like this, and neither man felt a twinge of sentimentality. They simply respected the finality of it.

Later, after people had come for her body, Jesus tried to finish the section of wall he'd started, while Jesse went back to his apartment. In those hours, the chicharras, hundreds of them, drilled without pause at the sky. They were the reason the memory of that day became so inexhaustible, and they were what both men, in their separate lives, talked about from the moment they moved on and told this story.

CHRISTOPHER TILGHMAN

HOLE IN THE DAY

Six hours ago Lonnie took one last look at Grant, at the oily flowered curtains and the kerosene heater, the tangled bed and the chipped white stove, at the very light of the place that was dim no matter how bright and was unlike any light she'd ever known before, and she ran. She ran from that single weathered dot on the plains because the babies that kept coming out of her were not going to stop, a new one was just beginning and she could already feel the suckling on her breast. Soon she will cross into Montana, or Minnesota, or Nebraska; she's just driving and it doesn't really matter to her where, because she is never coming back.

Grant sits in the darkened parlor room, still and silent. He's only twenty-nine, but he's got four children. It's five-thirty, maybe six, in the morning. He's in his Jockeys, and his long legs and arms are brushed with the white of his blond hair. He feels as if the roof of his house has been lifted, as if he's being stalked by a drafting eagle high above. Straight ahead of him on the other wall, above the sofa and framed in weathered board, is a picture of mountains, of Glacier Park, but Grant isn't looking at the picture; it was Lonnie's. He is listening to the sound of the grass, a hum of voices, millions of souls, like locusts. Outside there is a purple dawn over the yellow land, reaching toward this single house, and a

clothesline pole standing outside casts a long, heaving
shadow. There is a worn lawn between the house and
garage, and beyond that in the rise and fall of Haakon
County there is nothing, but still always something,
maybe just a pheasant or pronghorn, or maybe something you don't want to stare hard enough to find; it's
like swimming in the river and looking straight down
into the deep.

Grant shifts his weight off the thigh that's fallen
asleep on the wooden edge of his sagging easy chair.
He's got his twenty-gauge bird gun at his side, but it
isn't loaded, it's just there. The grass tells him to forget
her, *Forget Lonnie the Whore.* There is a sigh from the kids'
bedroom, a sigh and a rustle. Through the half-opened
door of his bedroom Grant can see the tangled sheets
where she stopped him last night a few inches away, left
him hunched over an erection dying in its rubber sheath,
a precaution taken too late and too sporadically to save
her. The white dresser on the far side is now empty, the
small bottles and pink boxes swept off the top into a
duffel bag that she shut with a loud snap from the clasp.
Grant had watched from the chair, and his mouth had
settled open. *Lonnie the Whore,* sings the grass, and Grant
cannot resist the song even though he thinks she's never
been unfaithful.

The kids' door opens and five-year-old Scott comes
out, sees Grant, comes over and stands at his father's side
for a minute or two, until he understands there will be
no response. He goes off to the kitchen hoping to find
his mother, and does not come back. Grant hears the rest
of them stirring, but he cannot help them; he's not sitting
there. He's out on the plains, swooping low over a pack
of coydogs, looking for the bitch Lonnie; he's up on the
light-brown waters of the Cheyenne, waist-deep and
getting ready to launch out naked into the passing root
clumps and cedar hulks. He's standing on a four-corners
in the middle of the grass, underneath the solid dome of
silver sky, and he feels the hills dark in the west, and he
knows that is where she's headed.

Grant looks at Leila, his oldest; she's eight, sandy and freckled, already almost as tall as her mother. Grant understands that she has been talking to him, remembers that she has just said they are out of milk, Dad, the kids are hungry. In the kitchen the baby wails as he is passed around; the sun is now high outside, dropping across the draped window casings. Grant cannot answer, even though he knows she is very frightened and wants to know what is happening and where her mother has gone. After a while, Leila shrugs bravely and says, "I'm takin' us to Muellers'."

He looks through the window and watches as they settle the baby in his stroller, Scott holding his bear, and the four of them head down the shoulder, clumped together like the grass.

Grant's open mouth is caked, his lips tight, his teeth glazed like china; he feels as if he's got no defense against the hot air, as if his mouth and nose are just holes in his skull. He moves finally because his bladder is full, has been full for hours, but he's afraid to stand up because of what she might have taken away: she's hollowed him out from the very point of his penis right up into the hard knot of his gut.

It's noon now, twelve hours since she backed the old Buick out onto the county road. She's a small woman, she's thin and taut; pregnancies have made her stomach wiry, not loose, but wiry like long scars. She's a fine-looking woman, but her teeth aren't good. The big car makes her look foolish, but there's no room for him as she throws it into reverse. She is crying the whole time, but she's also gone. Her breath is always stale from smoking, and when she's in Philip she goes to her friend Martha's room and they drink Canadian Club. She has a good time, but she comes back just the same. She's sleeping somewhere now, maybe at a scenic turnoff with the doors locked, or maybe she's driven down into a creek hollow where there are trailers beached like rafts on washed stones. Maybe while she sleeps there will be a flood of yellow waters under a cracked sky.

Grant is back in his chair, but now he's thinking about his dead father, and before long Grant sees him. The whole room smells like him, of the cold cattle blood he brought home under his fingernails every day from the yards, ten crescents of decay. He's wearing his overalls, worn to the white warp everywhere but the pencil pocket. His neck is long and bunches into dark sinews as it slides into his shirt. He walked five hundred miles in the furrows before he was fifteen. They changed teams at either end, but the boy held the reins all day and he walked alone so long that he learned to hear the voices in the ripping sound of parting roots; he walked in the furrows so much as a child that he tripped on smooth floors as a grown man, even years after the farm was lost.

Seems to me, boy, you got some things to attend to.

Grant nods; he'll do anything not to meet that gaze of the father he loved. When he seemed beaten by life and by cancer, his look burned with the coal fires of the other side, as if he'd been there before and would come back again. Grant would do anything to finish it, to be done with him for good.

How long can you last out here like this? A couple of days? A week?

He gets up finally and looks at his watch for the first time of the day; it's almost three. He's hungry, and he goes into the kitchen and tries to find something to eat — not just something, but something good to eat. There's nothing — just some American chop suey left over from the night before, a few hours before she opened her thighs for him and then stopped him and then was gone. He steps through the back door and out into the dusty yard. He doesn't know who owns this place or any of the land around it; the owner probably doesn't know he owns the place; Grant sends his rent to a lawyer in Pierre. It doesn't matter, the place is Grant's, and could have been always, but Lonnie missed the birds out here, that's what she said. She missed the sound of people just passing the time.

He goes back inside to the bedroom, gets dressed, and then walks back outside to his truck. He pulls around halfway into the garage, and then crawls under the camper top to off-load his welder and his tools. He brings one of the mattresses from the kids' room and lays it out in the bed of the truck, and follows with a pile of blankets and pillows. He makes up a box of canned food and juice from the pantry and throws in a handful of knives and forks. He doesn't really know what clothes the kids wear, but he does the best he can, stuffing four shopping sacks. He gets his razor. He gets his gun. He takes one last look around the house and then drives off.

Muellers' is about two miles down the road, in a hollow that shields the place from the worst of the winds but gathers the frost like low fog. It's a big house, two floors and a porch, built by a farmer back when it was thought bluestem grass could survive the winter. Grant drives up and Tillie meets him on the porch. "They're havin' supper," she says.

"I'm leaving Leila with you."

"I cain't take no babies," says Tillie. She's not as old as she thinks, but she's telling the truth.

"That ain't the plan," Grant answers. "Just my oldest." Tillie nods and the flesh bunches around her chin; she's gotten fat out here; that's what happens to good women when the kids are grown—they just keep cooking the same as before.

"I'll explain myself to Hans," he adds.

Grant waits on the porch. He listens to his children finishing their supper and tells himself he's got nothing to be ashamed of.

"Evening, Grant," says Hans, passing him a bottle of his best ale.

Grant takes it and takes the plate of pork chops that Tillie brings out to him. They sit on the porch; it's good to the west, clear and bright.

"I need a hundred, Hans," says Grant.

Hans goes back into the house and brings back three hundred. It's not kindness, it's just what it takes. Inside, Tillie is running a bath.

"This happens out here," says Hans. "Sometimes the women can't see beyond the day-to-day. I can't tell you why."

Leila comes out to the porch; she's got too much burden on her just now to cry or be frightened. "Tillie wants to know if you want them in p.j.'s," she says, and Grant nods.

Grant sees Tillie walking over to the truck from the back door, and watches as she gathers the four sacks of clothes and carries them back to the house. She's getting a limp and Grant knows it's her hip, just like his mother. He hears the washing machine start up, and sits while Hans smokes his pipe, and then hears the clanking of overall buckles in the dryer. Pete and Scott come out, and they're excited about sleeping on a mattress under the pickup cover. Scott has his Teddy bear, and he's telling Teddy all about it, about how maybe they're going to Disneyland, which makes Grant think he may cry yet in front of Hans. Instead, it's Tillie, on the lawn, who brings a Kleenex to her eyes, and she draws Leila back, right under her bosom, and crosses the loose flesh of her biceps over the girl's soft cheeks. The baby is running hard back and forth over the lawn, and each time he makes a circuit he pats one of the truck wheels. "My turk," he says.

Leila helps them pack the clothes up again, and Hans brings his Coleman stove from the barn. They get the baby into the car seat in front, and the two big boys onto the mattress. Grant hugs Leila, but she's too brittle to let herself bend and she knows it, even though Grant's been good to her and will always be. He starts the truck up and sees Hans listening carefully at the engine until he's sure he likes what he hears, because everything has to be smooth out here.

"Sometimes," says Tillie, "God just wants to make sure He's got your attention, is all."

Grant nods and backs out. It's a clear night, but there's enough rain in the sky to bring out the musty acid of the grass. It's sharp on his nostrils, but clean; he thinks he can trust it. He turns for Nebraska, even though the hunter in him shouts, *Why are you going south? She went west; she's trying to outrun us to the mountains.* Grant looks back through the sliding door into the camper; the two are asleep now. It's in their blood to feel comfortable on the road, like Grant's great-grandfather, who left his first, maybe even his second, family and jumped off from St. Louis and went all the way to the Pacific before he turned around back to Nebraska. He arrived in time to gather in the farms the first wave had won and lost, the wives mad, the husbands strangled with worry, the children sick and ancient.

Grant is tired but the baby is alert in his car seat, his large blue eyes shiny. "See big turk," he says as a triple rig blows past. They've come down the interstate to Murdo and are now heading south again toward Rosebud. Grant doesn't want to camp in the reservation; he's hoping to get across the border and stop outside Valentine. He's nodding a little, so he says, "Lots of fun," to the baby. "See Auntie Gay."

"See Mommy."

"Well, that's the thing," he answers, and he realizes he hasn't, in all this time, really thought about *her*, about Lonnie. He can't start now; he can't think of the sharp line of her chin, or her easy laugh in bed. The baby is asleep now, his lower lip cupped open like a little spoon. Grant crosses the Nebraska line, and he pulls over into the first creek bottom he finds. He finds a level place to park under the steep sides of a sand hill, and carries the sleeping baby around to the back. He pushes Scott and Pete to one side, takes a moment to piss, and crawls in beside them. He can feel their three hot bodies, Grant and his boys curled together. He doesn't know if this will ever happen again, or what will see him through the next few days, or whether his family will ever again be whole.

Everyone wakes crying, even Grant. The baby is soaked, and the air in the camper is strong with the smell of urine and shit. Scott is whimpering for Mommy. Grant sets up the Coleman stove and starts to warm up two cans of corned-beef hash, and Pete says, "Where's the ketchup? We always have ketchup."

"There ain't no ketchup," says Grant.

"I don't want to be here," the boy whines, and that starts another round of tears from the other kids. "I want to go home."

They eat, even without ketchup, and that makes everybody feel better. Grant sends Scott and Pete off to the small creek to rinse the dishes and the frying pan, and when they come back he leads them off a bit behind an outcropping of sandstone and tells them to squat and poop. They think this is funny, and so does the baby, who joins them in the line and pretends to push as the other two drop hot brown fruit onto the dry soil. They're back on the road, all four of them in the cab, a few minutes later, driving down the wide main strip of Valentine, a big city in the boys' eyes. They turn east, through Brown County, then Rock, and Holt. There are so many cars and trucks on the road that the baby kicks his feet with excitement; the boys keep asking him what color they are and he says red, and they laugh. There are so many pheasants along the road that Grant thinks for a moment of his shotgun, almost as if this were the hunting trip he'd always planned to take when they got older.

They pick up the Elkhorn River at Stuart and follow it down into O'Neill, where they stop and eat at McDonald's. It's as good as Disneyland for the boys; they each come out holding the plastic sand buckets and toys that came with the Happy Meals; by now they've figured out they're going to Grandma's. Grant wants to tell them what his father said years ago: these places suck the spirit right out of you. Grant was an eager boy then, but he knew his father was telling him this because they'd lost the ranch and now they were moving back to live with his mother's family.

It's Grant's sister Geneva who comes to the door when he rings, and she tries not to look surprised. His ma used to say to him, "It ain't Gennie's fault she was born without the gift of laughter." She's so slow unlatching the screen that Grant thinks maybe she isn't going to, but Scott and Pete have already run around to the tire swing they remembered in back, and it's just Grant, holding the baby.

"We didn't hear about this new one," she says. She doesn't ask about Lonnie; just the sight of Grant tending the youngest tells her she isn't with them.

"I'm leaving the kids here for a few days."

Grant knows she's about to say he can't leave no baby with them, but just then his ma comes around the corner, pushing her walker. She's shrinking, as if she's just folding together through her disintegrating hips, but she's tough; she's sheltered Geneva all these years. Grant leans down to give her a kiss, and she smells like ashes.

"Where's Lonnie?" she asks.

"She's left me. I'm taking the baby to Gay's," he says.

"That ain't going to work," his ma answers. "She's alone now, too."

The baby squirms in his arms, and finally works himself upside down, reaching for the floor.

"Put him down," his ma says. "There's no fire in the stove. No one delivers coal anymore." The baby comes over to the walker and slams his small hand on the tubing, and then starts to climb.

His ma brightens, but this gives Geneva her chance. "We can't keep no baby."

Grant goes out to the truck and brings back two of the remaining three bags of clothes. They still smell fresh from Tillie's dryer, all folded and carefully placed, even though they've been knocked around some. He looks to either side, at the other green lawns and pleasant houses on this quiet, tree-lined street. He doesn't know how his ma did this, how she kept the house after the meat-packing plant was locked one night without word from the owners. Two days earlier the steers had stopped coming in, and when the men had split and carved their way through the emptying stockyards there was nothing more to kill.

Grant takes a nap in the back room, the vacant sleep of townspeople; his dreams are wild but they don't mean anything. He wakes drugged but rested, and he eats supper with his ma while Geneva gets things ready for the boys to stay. "Go home, Grant," says his ma. "Go home and wait. You can't take the baby with you. Gay can't and Gennie won't keep him."

He knows she's right. He can't take his baby with him, but he can't wait either, because there is another baby that will need him when he finds Lonnie, a baby that may have to die anyway, but will most certainly not live if he waits for her at home. He says his goodbyes to the boys and gives Geneva fifty dollars. His ma works her way out to the truck and watches him put the baby back into the car seat. She's standing there as he drives away, with the baby waving both hands, fingers straight out and spread like two small propellers. "Bye-bye," he sings. "Bye-bye."

They're back out into the farmland in a few minutes, retracing their way toward Valentine. Grant is still fevered from his nap, and even though he keeps shaking his head and has the windows wide open to the chilly air, his eyes feel puffy and heated. The baby is content to ride high in his car seat, looking around at the land as they begin to roll into the sand hills. Grant doesn't know how he's going to work this: when he finds Lonnie she'll see the baby and that may be the end of it right there, because two hours before she left, the baby had brought her to tears, had finally made her understand that never again in her whole life would something happen easy, that she would forever be fighting just to get through the day. And Grant had tried to comfort her, first with love, and then sympathy, and then passion, and it had not worked.

"Piece of milk," the baby sings. Everything from him is melody.

Grant reaches down for one of the bottles he filled at his ma's.

"No one wants you," he says to the baby.

"O-kay," he sings back unblemished.

"No one but me," says Grant finally, and he gives him one of his large round fingers to hold, and the baby drinks his bottle and falls asleep like that. When Grant gasses the truck in Valentine he puts him in back. The little warm head rolls into the soft of Grant's neck; there's a firmness about the baby's body, an energy even when so completely at rest. This time Grant remembers to put on a dry Pamper, and then checks to make sure the screens on the sliding windows are strong and secure, and locks the tailgate from outside.

It's two in the morning when he crosses back into South Dakota. The grass doesn't speak to him anymore; Grant's at peace in the cab with his sleeping baby behind him. He knows Lonnie can be saved, he knows this now, for the first time, as he and the baby dart back across the Rosebud Reservation. He sees the contempt that comes to his sister Geneva's eyes when she thinks of Lonnie, and he knows why he loves Lonnie—because she's chosen the living, the light. She's not a whore, she did not become a whore on the plains; she became a mother. And she was not a whore when they met, in Pierre—just a nineteen-year-old who had enough fire and humor not to panic when she was dropped by her boyfriend hundreds of miles from home. Grant was twenty: what difference did it make that they left the Elkhorn Bar an hour later and he wasn't even trying to cover up the erection stretching his jeans? What difference did it make that she was pregnant with Leila when they got married in the Gem Theatre? After the ceremony, if he wanted to call it that, they went to Marston's store and were invited to pick a few things off the shelf, free, and all Lonnie wanted was a giant-sized box of Pampers.

Grant pulls over finally behind the fairgrounds in White River, and wakes up the next morning to the baby's big grinning face. "Daddy, Dad-dee," he says, pounding on Grant's back. They stop at a café for breakfast—he doesn't have enough time now to cook out—and Grant feels a little funny there with the baby among the farmers and the road crew, as if they thought he was half man, and it hasn't really occurred to him he'll need to bring or ask for some kind of special seat for him. But the waitress is older than she looks; she gives the baby a handful of coffee stirrers to play with, and they are back on the road fast and up on the interstate by ten, heading west.

He hopes to make Sheridan by midafternoon, then up into the Bighorn and through the Crow Reservation before he sleeps again. In front of them the grassland buckles and slides, building for the Black Hills. The baby gets restless and starts to cry, and then to scream, and Grant lets him out of the harness. It's the tourist route, and there are billboards for Wall Drug and Reptile Gardens and exit signs for the Badlands and Mt. Rushmore. He knows she's been this way, he knew it before he started, but now he feels it.

They're in Wyoming, coming first into Beulah and now into Sundance. Grant wonders what the people who started this town were thinking of when they named it Sundance. He knows what it stands for: he's heard the stories about ghost dancing and the sun dance, about men stitched to buffalo bones with pegs through their breasts. He knows what it stands for, but he doesn't know what it means; no one does, maybe not even the Indians, maybe not even the Indians who danced. It was something for the spirit, not the body; it was too powerful, and forbidden, nothing like this town that is so quiet a generation could live and die before anyone noticed.

He has to stop a few times at rest areas to let the baby run around, and at Gillette he buys a grab bag full of small toys, and a long tube of Dixie cups that he hands back one by one through the window for two hours until the whole camper is covered with them. " 'Nother cup!" squeals the baby with delight and surprise each time. Grant has begun to catch the rhythm of the two-year-old. He wishes he didn't have the baby with him for this last dash to the mountains, but as long as he's got him he's grateful for the company, for a pal. Grant's got his friends stretched across the plains: they'll never leave the plains. But maybe he's never had a buddy, and maybe he's never guessed that a baby could be a buddy, willing and cheerful to go along, always surprised by events. The land is getting drier, baked hotter over the shining stones and the white rim of alkali at the waterlines. Lonnie is headed for the mountains, just the way the wagon trains yearned for the mountains ahead of them, no one worrying about snow in the high passes. Nothing was more foreign to them than the plains. At night, the Lutherans, Calvinists, and Methodists sang their hymns and hoped the sounds carried beyond the glow of the campfires. They knew they were up against something on the plains. He drives past a car wreck and it's a terrible one, two bodies laid out under tarpaulins, casualties on the way to the Bighorn. This is how it was told to him, like every schoolchild, that Custer would be alive today if he had stayed in South Dakota, but he was teased deeper and deeper into the grass. And it was the same for Lewis and Clark, led by the trapper Charbonneau, but they had a girl with them, an Indian girl, a sign of love and the promise of a gift, because she was pregnant — just like Lonnie.

In Sheridan, a long hot strip, they stop and he buys them a meatloaf-and-gravy supper at a café and then gives the baby a bath in the men's-room sink of a gas station next door. Grant has never before seen how that skin shines like silk; he traces a line down the flexing back and it feels like powder. Grant uses every muscle and nerve ending in his own body, as if keeping the baby from falling is the one job in his whole life that truly matters. He's toweling him off on the curb outside when he breaks away, naked and round-bellied, to the front, and three high-school girls who are gassing a big new Pontiac catch him and bring him back. All three are a little too heavy, and Grant thinks of them as pregnant. They're giggling with the baby and he's giggling back, but when they try to flirt with Grant they read something on his face that chills their laughter, and they hand the baby back to him and leave fast.

That night Grant and the baby sleep in Montana under a few cottonwoods that have found water somewhere deep. He's so tired when they pull in he doesn't notice a small house not much more than a hundred yards away. In the low yellow light of morning an elderly Indian couple appears at his side, just as he and

the baby are finishing breakfast. He's made a kind of
high chair out of rocks with a scrap of sheet iron as a
table. The Indians don't say anything, and Grant guesses
this means they're still inside the reservation. Off in the
distance a dove is cooing and there is a flapping of laundry in the very slight breeze. It's a little chilly and Grant
has on a sweatshirt, but the Indians are bundled up as if
for winter, the man in an orange nylon parka shiny with
dirt, and the woman in a heavy blanket jacket over jeans.
Grant wonders why they're out at this early hour, but he
straightens from his kneeling position in front of the
baby when he notices them and goes over to join the
man at the truck while the woman comes over to the
baby.

The old man points with a stubby damaged finger
toward the baby; the woman is poking at him, taunting
him with a piece of bread in a way that is not cruel but
not kind either: a test, more like—the first of many. The
baby laughs, and the woman swats his head. Grant stiff-
ens; any more of this and he'll spring.

"Yours?" asks the man, and it is as if they're going to
fight over the child, not because the Indians want him
but because he's theirs anyway.

Grant looks hard into the old man's face. "That's my
boy—my youngest."

"Where's his mama?" the Indian asks. "Where's his
grandma?" It's the right question to ask, Grant can't fault
it. By now, the baby has finished his breakfast. The
woman has freed him from the pile of rocks and they're
pitching small pebbles at each other. She's keeping him
on the very edge between delight and fear, on the blade
of some plan.

Grant doesn't answer; he looks over the Indian's
shoulder at the house. There's an old tractor, a Ferguson
or a Ford, painted hunter green, and it's plain it hasn't
run in years. A sprinkler is watering a brown patch of
grass.

"We're going after his mama," says Grant, finally. "I
can't tell you where she is."

The Indian nods, and then does something that takes Grant by surprise: he picks up Grant's box of Frosted Flakes and eats a couple of large handfuls. Grant doesn't know if he's being robbed somehow, but it doesn't seem necessary for him to say anything. The woman has taken the baby's small hand, and she's leading him down the road to the house. It's flatter here than home, and drier; it's sage country, not grass. On the horizon he can see a straight line of trees, aspens waving a silvery flash of leaves, and he knows it's the Bighorn, where the brown trout are big as salmon, where the rainbow males fight each other for the hook. Grant and the Indian follow along, because the woman's now in charge. They go into the small house, two worn steps off the prairie, a shell of gray asbestos shingles, and it's clean, spare, and dark. The baby lets out a squeal of joy when the woman shows him a toy box in one corner filled with trucks and alphabet blocks. They drink coffee.

"How long you planning to look?" asks the man.

"She's headed for the mountains. I'm not far behind."

The woman holds out her arms toward the baby; she thinks he's going to leave the baby with them. She thinks it's her duty; she thinks Grant hasn't got the right to refuse.

"We'll be leaving now," he says. He looks over at the baby in the corner and gets ready to cut off the woman's approach.

The man looks at his wife; this isn't his affair, it's up to her.

Grant hears the laundry flapping outside and thinks the pulse of his blood is pounding as loud. He knows he could leave the baby with these people. He's lived his life believing that he could ask anything of plains people, white or Indian, just the way he knows he'd do about anything if another asked him. He could leave the baby and know he was safe. But he also knows now he can't go on alone. He's too frightened of failing: how does he expect to find Lonnie, a single lungful of air in a sandstorm? How does he think he can do it alone?

Grant pulls out his wallet and gives her a ten. He means "Thank you," and he means "No, thanks." He's not at all sure that she will take it, but she does, and then she and the man watch as he goes over and picks up the baby. The baby's having fun with the blocks and he starts to shriek, beating his arms and legs so fast that for a second Grant almost loses his grip. He's reaching out over Grant's shoulder for the toys; he wants those more than anything in the world. He screams, "Want Mommy, want Mommy," and Grant knows he's just saying this as a way of getting the toys, but still it helps, because they *are* going to find Mommy. Grant jogs down the road toward his truck without looking back for the Indians, and he has to fight hard, harder than he would have imagined, to get the baby buckled into his car seat. He's still screaming; it's been twenty minutes. If Grant tries to keep his children together by himself it will be Leila, the oldest, who pays the price, but he hasn't asked himself those questions yet. He's only marvelling at the noise the baby can make when he opens his cords, and trying to figure out how he'll bring his mother back.

But now they are out on the road, gathering speed. That's all the baby wanted, just some action, something to see or do. Grant feels light, as if they have made an escape, have just weathered a close call together.

"You and me, boy, almost got scalped."

There's something about those words that sets the baby off, laughing and laughing. The sound fills the cab, and for a moment they're not in a Ford truck anymore, but Grant doesn't know what it is; he's into his fourth day beyond tired, but he's sharp. He knows he can find her. He feels low and close to the ground, the way a hunter wants to feel when he's caught up at last to the buck in the brush. There's a voice in the deer that tells you where he's going, said his father; it's the way of nature. Close your eyes and listen, that's what his father said, reminded him, on cold fall mornings. But be wary: there are voices outside that are not to be trusted.

Lonnie is running to the northwest; she's a creature of hills and mountains and trees, doing anything not to get caught flatfooted on the plains where the dogs, those endless, nameless dogs, can pull you by the hamstrings. Grant pushes down on the accelerator and the Ford buckles and gulps. He wonders about the old Buick; how long before it dies? He's been looking for it already by the side of the road, in the repair yards of the gas stations, behind the bait-and-tackle shops. He can picture it halfway into the parking lot of a bar at a place where the men fan out to give her advice with their eyes all over her ass and crotch, and he knows she feels them looking and it gives her a dot of pleasure and a line of wetness. Maybe she'll decide Screw it and they will all head back in, and even the last of the men funnelling in the door six, seven behind feels as if he's got something loose on the line. Grant can picture all that because he's never known anything in his life better than Lonnie asking him to turn off the radio and come in and fuck her.

He's looking for her already; when her face comes out to him he won't be surprised. She's stopped running; he knows that because he feels the tiredness in his own body. They come into Billings, past the refineries and tank farms. There is a whole yard full of silver tank trucks, and he says to the baby, "Trucks. See the bi-ig trucks." Grant looks over and sees a wide smile, pure wonderment on the tiny face, and he cannot resist rubbing the back of his fingers on that round cheek. He thinks if he finds Lonnie and she comes back with him, looping around through Nebraska to pick up Scott and Pete and then up to Mueller's for Leila and then home— if they all come back to that empty house tired but glad to be off the road, they all will have won.

They come to a stoplight in the center of town, and now he's got to make up his mind: west or north? He could head west on Route 90 and hit Bozeman and Butte and Deer Lodge and Missoula, one after another. For this reason Lonnie might have taken this route, but the voice inside him says, *No, she went north,* and anyway if she has a plan it's to get up to Glacier and look for a waitressing job where they wouldn't suspect or care that she'd run out on a husband and family. That's what she was doing nine years ago when she stopped in Pierre, on her way to Glacier, and the thought never died.

So he heads north out of Billings toward Roundup, and in a few minutes he knows he's done the right thing, because the road's begun to climb, not steep and quick like the push over the Black Hills, but patiently, cutting through the choppy sides of the buttes and the caked bottoms of the valleys. He's crossing the Musselshell and the Flatwillow, and he sees they're faster and cleaner than the rivers of South Dakota and he feels their tug back to the east. He is so glad now that the baby is with him that he starts singing "Wheels on the Bus" to him. He doesn't know any of the words, but he's listened to Lonnie sing this song to four different babies and he's got a general idea how it goes. The baby falls asleep. He drives past the town of Grassrange and sees three women tending thrift-shop tables in the swirling red dust of the roadside. Each hill rising carries him away from the real earth. Grant feels no mystery in this land, just danger. At home the yellow grass smooths the hills like velvet; here the rocks thrust into the plains; the creeks rip their course; the land is damaged, not shaped. And when finally, about eleven in the morning, he turns west out of Lewistown, he thinks first that it's clouds he's seeing, or a streak of grime cutting across his windshield, but it's neither. He follows the shadows to the left, and to the right, and they're everywhere, mountains rising out of his life. He feels the pain the mountains cause, and he knows now that he must find her soon.

He pulls over and slides out of his seat onto the narrow shoulder; the road is high here. There is no traffic, no sound of engines, nothing except for a gusting wind that pulls at his shirttail and chills the moisture of his sweaty T-shirt. He starts to eat a sandwich he bought in Billings, but he is suddenly too tired to chew. He moves around to sit on the front bumper, out of the wind, and stares west. Maybe Lewis and Clark sat on this spot. They too would have been afraid, because in all this thrusting rock what they had to find was a single drop of water, a single drop that would become two, a puddle, a pool, a stream, a creek, a tributary, and finally a river flowing west. They found it, Grant is certain, because they listened to their fear, and the sound that came to them was a waterfall.

She's frightened now, and so is he. He imagines the deer, steamy yellow froth dripping from his sharp lips. He listens for the voice through the whimpering of the grass, through the deep pounding of his heart. She's tired now, he knows that; Lonnie's getting to where she thought she wanted to be, and she's missing her babies, and she knows she lost part of her mind back there on the plains and can't trust what's left. He stands up. He shouts, the words breaking off from the very bottom of his throat, "Where is she?" but this time there is no sound from the grass, just a steady wind. "Where are you?" he yells. The shout is cut off clean; it doesn't even stir the baby. Grant is in the hills now, listening only to the fear that he may have lost Lonnie for good.

Lonnie's purse and wallet are emptied into a small pile in the center of a stained knobby bedspread. Outside her motel window there is a gas station, and then a lube shop, and then the whole long studded string of Tenth Avenue South. It's Great Falls, and she can no longer believe she has come so far for this, a baked island of neon on an immense high plain. The boys she saw last night, bunched into small packs outside the bars, wore the look and hair of the Air Force. Some of them spoke to her as she walked into what was left of the old cow town, past nameless markers and corners that were nothing but numbers. She can get work here; tonight she can be inside some bar wearing a white cowboy hat and fringed hot pants, and, if that's all she does, it will last for two or three months, until one late afternoon the satin waistband no longer closes at the snaps. Already she feels the force inside her, sooner, more powerful, more demanding than any of the others, so strong that it pushes the others aside, her real babies, whose soft skin and voices she misses so badly that her arms ache.

She could get work here, and she'd ask the other waitresses who to talk to about fixing everything; maybe it wouldn't cost anything, maybe the state would pay for it. She could do this; it's what she planned. All the way from home, eyes on the mirror for the growing red dot of Grant's truck, she pictured the nurse, bored maybe and unforgiving, working through a list of questions as if it was a driver's-license renewal, or one of those customer-service interviews in the IGA. And then there would be a white room, and a white sleep, and it would be done. It wouldn't be so bad, really. In a few days it would all be over and then, then she might think about going back.

She counts sixty-four dollars and change. She has a full tank of gas, and even though the Buick has started to skip a little and lose power, she knows enough to think it is just the altitude, the thin air. Her clothes are clean; earlier that morning she met a woman at the motel's coin-op, a tourist from Oklahoma washing out a few kids' T-shirts, and she offered to let Lonnie throw in her things because the machine wasn't hardly full. She was the kind of person Lonnie had often wished could be a neighbor, in a house that didn't exist and that would never, she knew, have a reason to be built.

Grant may still be back home; if he is she hopes he's thought of Tillie Mueller to help him, but it's all just wishing. He's hunting her because he thinks it's his duty, and she's not afraid of what will happen if he finds her, she's just afraid of being hunted, the seeker already tugging on her from the other side of the plains.

She leaves her motel and begins to walk. She tries not to see what she's seeing, to see any landmarks through her own eyes, because Grant will see them, too; she tries not to say the name of this city because Grant will hear it. When she married him she didn't ask for this, except maybe by wanting something different as a teen-ager, something with mystery. He has powers. People laugh at her when she tells them that, but it's true—it's always been true. Grant is so thin and blond that people think he's nothing but a kid, until they look him in the eye.

She has lunch — a salad at Burger King. It's her first meal of the day, and the memory of the morning sickness she endured with Leila, and then less with Scott, churns at her stomach. If she wants to find work tonight she'll have to start in a couple of hours, by four at the latest. She doesn't doubt that he knows where she was headed: when she left him she turned without even thinking, and didn't realize she'd turned west until she began to see the signs for Rapid City. She told him she was headed west the night they met in the Elkhorn Bar; her boyfriend got scared and turned back after a last beer together, and then, at that second, the goodbye wave she gave to the boyfriend turned into a hello to Grant as the two men passed in the bar doorway. But even if he knows she is in Montana, where will he start? Even if he knows she is in the city whose name she doesn't want to say out loud, can he find her? Even if he knows what block she is on, a block made of avenues and streets that are just numbers, no names at all, what is the chance he'll spot her?

She looks up from the counter in sudden fright and quickly scans the restaurant. She has to stop thinking these thoughts — they're energy flowing out of her, a beacon for him. She's giving herself away. She runs outside and cuts off Tenth Avenue, back toward the old city. She walks until she comes to the deep chasm of the Missouri, and she reads a sign that says "GIBSON PARK." She brings her hands to her face, because now those words are out on the line and maybe he knows them, maybe he's heard of this place. The grass is green, and there are children in the play yard, and then, beyond, there is the river, full and wide. She doesn't think of the trees or the statue she's standing in front of, or the white, freshly painted bench she has to sit on for a minute or two because her legs are fluttering. Why wouldn't he let her be? Why couldn't he give her some time, such a small amount of time?

She's walking again, and now she's got a new plan: she'll blank her mind to the details around her by thinking about home. She's going through the drawers of the steel kitchen unit and she's picturing the knives, the forks. She's counting the spoons, including the baby spoon with the chipped plastic handle that has a line of ducks on it, except the yellow paint they used for the beaks washed off. She's trying now to count the floorboards in the kitchen, but it isn't working; she's still on that baby spoon. She has held that spoon for four babies, scooped in the first mouthfuls of pears and custard, given those four babies their first tastes of everything on that single spoon. Even now she can feel through the handle the tug of the baby's lips when he's hungry, and the resistance of the tongue that moves her hand aside when he's not. She's given her children life on that spoon, and now she wants it, she wants to hold it and look at those beakless ducks.

When she gets back to the bars, the neon is bright, not because it's dark or will be for three more hours but because the watch has changed at the Minuteman base and the boys will soon be there. She's standing there, just one of the girls, and a big red pickup goes by and takes a wide U-turn back, and she looks away and says to herself, Please, let it be some ranch hand looking for a whore, but it's not, and she does not ask herself any more questions about how he did it. He has dropped on her through a hole in the day, a parting of clouds straight up to the sun. He parks alongside her and comes forward halfway and stands crazy, so spent that she thinks he will fall, and they look at each other until it seems that he has started talking without making a sound.

"Lonnie," he says, "I won't hurt you." There's gravel in his voice; he's hoarse, and it makes her think he's been crying.

She looks into the truck and sees the baby, who starts pumping his arms up and down in a little dance, even though he's still strapped in. "Mommy," he shouts. She can't help smiling; the baby makes her smile and laugh for the first time in five days. She can feel the tug to him—powerful, intoxicating. He's every bit as demanding as before, as merciless, as selfish, as he reaches, but there's a sweetness now; the difference is she wants to give it to him, to all the kids, to Grant. Her body starts flowing toward the baby, her breasts heavy.

"Oh God, Grant, you brought the baby." As she says this she pictures the two of them riding in the truck together, side by side, and remembers how so long ago she loved to think of him and the kids together.

"I didn't have no choice," he says, but she sees through it—she knows he couldn't have found her alone.

"Where are the others?" It is suddenly agony to be apart from them.

"Carry!" yells the baby from the truck. "Carry!" he yells again, reaching out, and she can feel herself open for him, a torrent now, a burst.

"They're safe. Do we still have another coming?"

"I can't have another. I can't do it. You can't make me."

"I want you back. I need you back."

"You can have me back, Grant. I want to come home. I miss my babies." She's trying not to cry. She is Lonnie, she is only twenty-nine, she has come to this place and cannot escape. "But this child will kill me."

And Grant has known for five days that he can come this far and no farther. He'll choose the living; he'll choose Lonnie. And Lonnie has known for five days and whether she likes it or not Grant and her babies are everything for her, that she may want something more but needs nothing else. She is crying now as she passes Grant, going toward the truck. She picks up the baby and he feels like satin, and the three of them stand on this spot in this city beside the Missouri River. Lonnie thinks of the river on the map, flowing north out of Great Falls almost to Canada before it begins to drop southeast, straight back home through South Dakota. They could almost ride home on a raft.

LESLEY POLING-KEMPES

MY SISTER AND HER VISIT WEST

My twin sister died in the same town where she was born, raised, and married within the borders of the upper class. It is one of those towns rich in fine houses and very green lawns, big mimosa trees and lots of rain to keep the well-kept rose gardens watered and thriving. I was also born and raised within these same borders, but I left when I was seventeen, I have no roses, and I have never married, even way out here, as far west and south as one can go on the desert.

She died on a Tuesday. I knew the end was near those few days before because of urgent notes from back home requesting my return. I did not return. Instead, on one of those last nights, I dreamed my sister came to visit me.

My sister never visited me. She never left the immediate vicinity of that same lush town, never saw sand that wasn't beach, or trees with thorns for leaves, or a sky that could glide by for days without a single cloud interrupting it.

I never encouraged her to visit. I do not believe I ever invited her to come west.

I had not seen my sister in twelve years when she died. We spoke on the phone now and then, usually about estate matters, or someone's wedding, or someone else's funeral. I never told her, or anyone back home, about my success — my serene adobe home on the edge of the desert, my dress studio and clients. I wanted the details of my western life to be mysterious and hardly known. The vast space between my dry, dusty patio and their wet, lacquered verandas meant I was — heart, soul, and way of thinking — a different species of person from what I was born into.

After my sister became ill, I called home more often, although we did not enjoy one another's conversation anymore than before, nor find a new depth to our relationship after the illness became permanent. I called home because a tightness moved into my stomach while I was trying to work in my studio — a tightness that solidified my feelings about illness and a sister's impending death, about the years between me and the past coming to nothing.

The dream was one of those that takes just enough of the natural elements, the real environment of one's thinking, to fool the dreamer of her dream. I lay on my bed in the dream, in my bedroom, every detail just as it is when I am awake: huge windows facing west, the end of the patio wall seen through thin, white curtains. Even the bureau with my carved jewelry box, the ceiling made of split cedar branches, forever dusty because I have not yet found a cleaning lady who will climb up and wipe them off with a cloth after a dust storm — all were in my dream just as in life.

My sister floated into my bedroom through the large western windows. Her body blocked my view of the western sky which was just then the most perfect peach as dusk came to me from the desert of my dream.

I know the sky well from this place in my room. I wanted the color of the sky to fill my room, and although I was enchanted at the sight of my frail, naked sister, a wispy cloud floating in from the patio, I was annoyed that she was here, uninvited, in my western life at all.

She smelled like the old rose garden our mother
tended with the servants back home, and she hummed a
song just enough out of tune to be irritating. I had dis-
liked her humming and the smell of that garden—both
reminded me of old women. And now my sister, forty
years later, had brought it all back: roses and servants
and a song of old women in my western bedroom.

I left the bed in an effort to look past her out the
windows, but I could not see around her. I began to
reach for her, hoping to pull her down; I jumped at her
body, now rising towards the ceiling, swinging my arms
in an effort to hit her. But she was out of my reach.

My sister stretched out a thin, transparent hand and
examined the dust on the ceiling wood. She inspected
my room. She touched each object as she floated past,
felt the plaster of the old adobe walls, the cloth of the
curtains, the skirts hanging in the closet. And then she
turned and drifted back out the window, dissolving into
the now gray sky, the soft and lovely peach of only a
moment before gone. My sister dissolved into the desert
air as if she had always known it, as if it were all hers for
the asking.

I woke crying in the early dawn.

I called her the morning after the dream on what
was to be the day before she died. I knew she was about
to go—a telegram from her doctor and her husband both
had come at breakfast. I called before beginning work.
We immediately fell into the conversation we had had
last time—about the garden and how difficult it was to
get good help these days, someone who really knows
roses, who didn't complain or steal.

Back home just wasn't the same, she told me again. I
did not say it seemed very much the same to me.

I wanted to tell her, just as she began to relate the
redecorating plans for the living room, that I was nothing like her and that I detested her garden and her
yellow carpeted bathroom. But then I remembered the
dream and the way she had drifted over the desert, a
little cloud, my twin sister, a lovely mute breeze lifting
the curtains of my favorite windows. I drawled

something about the summer ending, the heat almost over, the dry air lifting, instead.

I said goodbye without once pursuing the paths that were our lives, the rhythm of our thoughts that had nothing and everything to do with being twin sisters. I sat in the studio thinking how I hated her garden and how I wished she would not die because it threatened to age my idea of myself; to change my belief in my own immortality.

After I left home I went west—far away where I sought unpaved streets and houses without grass between them and the road, and people who were proud of their differences. I was determined to like everything about this new home—not only the wide open beauty of the blue sky and the rose color of the sand at sundown; but the sandstorms of early spring, too, and the loud, repetitious and somewhat off-key music that beat incessantly from every bar and apartment window on a Saturday night in town. Even the plastic flowers bought at five and dime stores used to adorn the graves at the local cemetery: I even learned to like those flowers, although I could never quite imagine my own headstone covered with them.

I could never quite imagine my own headstone.

My sister died on a Tuesday and I did not go home. I sent flowers. I thought about sending something that would tell them all back home how different I was—like a huge wreath of those fake flowers, a real prize in the eyes of my neighbors. But I sent a standard bouquet of roses and a card embossed with silver, nothing that spoke of deserts or sandstorms or ceilings made of cedar branches.

It had been a predictable dream in content and emotion. I figured it was a textbook example of a dream about a sibling's death. Even so, after all the telephone calls and wires and letters to and from home, after all the death stuff was finally exhausted, the sister of the dream changed her mind and, instead of drifting out into the desert, turned around and came to my house as a visitor.

My sister came to visit me.

Oh, I knew it was because of the dream, this feeling
that she was visiting. She had never visited here, not
really, not before in real life. She couldn't tell an unfed
dog from a coyote crossing the road. But as sure as I
woke in my favorite room, opened my curtains towards
the western sky of early morning, my sister came to visit
me.

It was not a ghostly thing; not a feeling of a dead
person over the shoulder, of spirits whisking about the
house. No, this was like having a visitor. This was the
feeling of my sister and her visit west.

Maybe she wanted me to ask her during one of
those last phone calls, just ask her, to come west. Even
knowing, both of us, and never saying, that it was
impossible. Maybe she died wishing it and now I was
left wishing it for her; for both of us.

Maybe we both knew that it would be easier this
way, her floating in off the desert instead of driving all
those hot, sandy miles in a car, even an air-conditioned
one. We knew it would be more enjoyable a visit if we
couldn't talk about anything. This way, she could watch,
observe, sit about the house oblivious to the heat and
dust, the glare of the sun at noon.

I went about my days as always. I sewed in the
studio most of the morning, walked the road in the
evenings, had tea with a good friend on Wednesday
afternoon, baked bread and read magazines on Saturday
morning. My sister met my friends, listened to the loud
music in town on Friday night, ate quiet suppers with
me on my patio in the peaceful desert evenings.

It was actually very enjoyable, my sister's visit west.

One afternoon in the second week, I packed a lunch and
went to see a favorite old cottonwood tree that grew a
far ways out on the desert. I took a lot of water so I
could hike and a book to read in the shade of the old
tree's branches. I drove the little car.

I had never mentioned my big car. It was one of the
few real luxuries I had allowed myself. The car was
white and huge and had every convenience known to

man built into it. I never used it to drive the four miles from the house to town, nor did I use it for errands or quick trips to clients. I had the little car for these, dented and dusty and exposed to the weather of the driveway. I kept the big car in the garage, behind locked doors. I brought it out only for long drives across the desert to the city, or for vacations to the mountains or excursions south of the border.

I remember thinking when I stood in the dealer's making the final arrangements that my sister would love this car. I remember thinking those very words: my sister would love this car.

I never mentioned it on the phone. She would drawl on about her husband's business expanding all over the state and the kids going to fine schools and how she drove up to see them in the company limousine and I didn't say one word about the long, gleaming car in the garage.

Now she was here and I guessed there was no hiding it. But I did hide it that day, taking the little car out to the desert.

It was nearly autumn and the shadows were becoming long again, the sand still hot but the sky a clearer blue. The chamisa flowers were in bloom, and flocks of piñon jays and other desert birds flurried and scuffled noisily about the scruffy bushes that grow here and there in the sand. Dust devils swirled up and around the arroyos in the afternoon wind. Before we left, the mountains of the eastern horizon gathered the falling sun into their sides and turned the desert shadows into shades of peach and rose.

My sister and I shared an intense dislike for housecleaning. Even living way out on the edge of the desert, I managed to find someone to come and clean the studio and house every week. I usually hired the same people again and again, but with my sister around the house, I decided to try something different and hire someone from the plaza.

The plaza in town is known for such workers— young girls in from the outer villages seeking day jobs in town; a few young boys from south of the border who cannot find permanent work because they do not have the necessary papers. Many of my friends hired these young boys and girls but until now, I had never considered doing so. I didn't like the necessary questioning, choosing, the looking over the young people. It didn't bother my friends—they said the boys and girls needed the work and were there of their own free choosing.

With my sister visiting, I found new courage. I drove the small car to the town plaza and surveyed the group standing and sitting about the curb and sidewalk. There were no girls. I inquired about this and one boy, thin and poorly dressed, with beautiful dark eyes, said he didn't mind doing some housework, just so he didn't have to iron. I assured him I did all of my own ironing. He climbed into my little car and we drove out of town.

I was very relaxed with the boy around the house. I worked in the studio after he had finished cleaning there, and offered him iced tea mid-morning. I made a cold lunch at noon and we ate together on the patio. I even showed him my projects and some of the finished clothing stored in the studio closets. I told him I would pay him well, at least twice what he was used to.

We became friends.

His English was broken but carefully pronounced. I asked him if he had a family and he said he had six sisters and one brother and a hillside of goats back home.

In the afternoon I fell asleep on the studio couch while he finished cleaning the bedroom. I woke and found the boy standing at the kitchen door, looking out the screen at the road and the desert beyond. He was startled when I asked if he were finished? He nodded that he was and then turned and limped to the table where he set down the rag and spray wax. I had missed the limp— all day long and I had missed his limp. I decided to pay him even more than I had intended.

I went to the bedroom to get my keys and his payment from my desk drawer. The room was clean but I would have to wipe the window ledges, and then there was the old dusty ceiling.

I looked for my jewelry but it was not where I had placed it in the carved box on the bureau. I had one silver ring, two bracelets, and a set of earrings that a friend had given me years ago, back when I could not afford to buy anything for myself. They were worth a good deal now.

I looked through each drawer of the desk, in the bathroom, even on the floor by the night table.

I stood and looked out the clean, wide windows at the blue sky above the patio wall and knew my jewelry had been stolen. It was four miles to town: four miles of open mesaland, sand arroyos and old cottonwood trees with a few houses in-between. If I lost the boy now, I would never see him, or my jewelry, again.

My jewelry was in his boot and I could not possibly wrestle it out of him. I had to get him into my car—the big car. I could lock all of the doors with one switch of a button and he would be unable to escape.

I settled my nerves, gathered my purse from the closet, and returned to the kitchen. The boy watched me. I avoided his eyes and said how much cooler the evenings were, like autumn, all those subtle changes in the desert air, and that I would drive him back into town.

He watched me with those dark, careful eyes.

If I ever needed my sister it was now. She must have known. My sister must have gasped with delight, leaping right in, for I am certain it was not I who urged the boy into the front seat. It wasn't me who started the big engine with a long, confident roar, backed easily down the drive, and locked all of the doors with a loud snapping noise that caused everyone in the car to jump.

The boy reached slowly for the door. I watched him out of the corner of my eye as he slowly pulled the handle and found it would not move.

Four miles to town. I talked easily about the summer behind and that one dry spell that nearly killed the tamarisk and browned the sage. I casually mentioned the number of stray dogs seen recently along my road, and the absence of my jewelry in the carved box in my room at home.

I drawled on in my most nonchalant voice how we would first have to stop at the police station and file a report. I explained to the boy that this is what we do here when something is stolen: we go to the police.

The boy began to fidget with his right foot. He followed the right side of the road with exaggerated interest and his hands gripped the edge of the white leather seat as if he were losing his balance.

I went directly to the police station. To a young boy without papers from south of the border, trouble with the police is a one-way walk. There is no returning to the plaza. There is only jail, and then a trip back home where there is probably more jail. I knew this. I knew he ate one meal a day if he was very lucky. I knew he had no future here and even less of one back home on that hillside of goats, especially if he got into trouble with the authorities.

I parked the car in front of the town jail and turned off the engine. We both looked at the police cars parked around us and at the policemen coming in and out of the station door. I glanced over at the boy. He was sitting very low in the seat. Tears rimmed his dark eyes.

I took a deep breath to gather my own courage and then he began to cry. He bent over onto his knees and with his head in his hands, wept like a child who cannot find a friend in the world. The tears soaked his old pants and the tops of his boots.

His boots were torn to bits around the sole and I saw he had no socks.

I was terribly shaken.

There had been this awful night.

It was not a dream.

My sister had had the most terrible row with a girlfriend who had taken some of my sister's doll clothes home after playing on our veranda after supper. The neighbor girl said it was a mistake, but my sister called her a liar and a thief and a terrible, evil person who God would punish one day soon.

My sister screamed terrible words from the back of the garden where our yard met the neighbor girl's yard; where our rosebushes met her rosebushes. That evening I sat on the veranda in the dark, on the big wide steps near the mimosa trees, and listened to the neighbor girl's weeping. She had been sent to her room and she cried that night until she fell asleep.

No one ever really knew the truth. My sister had boxes filled with doll clothes. My sister's dolls had more clothes than the cleaning woman. I could not imagine how she had ever missed those that were said to be missing. The neighbor girl was never allowed into our house again. I hadn't known her well—she was my sister's friend—but sitting on the dark veranda, I missed the days, now suddenly passed, when we all played dolls on the porch after supper.

Dolls. Doll clothes stolen. A neighbor girl crying in humiliation in her room. My sister yelling into the dark of the rose garden terrible words about old women and death, about being buried without friends to bring flowers.

Later that same evening, my sister had played the piano and hummed senseless songs to herself in the house behind me.

This is the stuff of dreams.

It was only for a minute or so that we sat like that, the weeping boy and I, people walking by, looking in through the tinted glass of the huge, white car. And then, still sobbing and now blubbering apologies, the boy emptied his boot and my jewelry spilled onto the white leather seat between us.

I placed the jewelry in my pocket and started the car. The boy remained bent over his knees, his head in his hands. I drove past the plaza and the few remaining workers waiting on the curb, and stopped on a side street where we could not be seen. Before I unlocked the car doors, I held out the money I owed him.

He tried to refuse. It was a sincere effort. He wanted this one bit of dignity, this refusal through his streaked face, his wet pants, his lips shivering with humiliation. He needed the money. He was only fourteen. I shook my head and I think I smiled. I insisted again and he took the money and stuffed it into his boot.

I unlocked the car doors. He fled the car and disappeared into the nearby parking lot, lost like some fragile bird into the vast air above the desert.

I sold the car that afternoon. My sister protested all the way to the dealer's, talking my ear off in a final effort to change my mind. I was glad that she liked the car but I didn't want it anymore. When the final papers of the sale were signed, my sister departed. I knew it, standing in the dealer showroom, the visit was over. It wasn't because she was upset; I think she even understood. But it was time for her visit west to be over.

I began to cry and had to stop and sit on one of the plastic chairs in the showroom. I remember thinking how my sister would think I was crying about the car, and the dealer would think I was crying about my sister, and how the boy from south of the border would think I was crying about my jewelry. But I knew, weeping into the Kleenex, rubbing my eyes raw in the waiting room of the car dealer's, that I was crying about me and my western life, and how a chapter was ending. The chapter about having someone come and clean my house; the chapter about my sister and her visit west. I could feel it closing, feel the present becoming the past. I would clean my own house from now on until forever and I found myself floating through someone else's bedroom window at dusk.

After a long, slow walk across town to the bank, I headed out to the south road where I hitched a ride from some hardly known neighbors. I told them I had sold my car. My eyes were raw and puffy. I also told them I had just said goodbye to my identical twin sister. Identical. I told them how she had fallen in love with my desert home, just as I had years ago.

It had not been an easy day. I was thinking about getting home and climbing into a bath before eating a light supper on the patio, when one of those stone memorial markers on the last mile of road caught my eye. I yelled Stop! even before thinking it. The car skidded to a halt. Everyone turned to look at me.

As I climbed out, they asked if I knew the person that had died here? Just to make them leave I said that I did. They drove on, leaving me to walk the last half mile to my house.

The sun was nearly down for the day, a relief truly known by those who live in desert country. Up close, the marker was very crude, with someone's name scrawled badly into the stone. And then all those cheap, plastic flowers faded from a thousand sunsets, dirty and shredded from a hundred sandstorms sweeping in from the desert that seemed to begin just over the barbed-wire fence. This was the true western memorial for a universal tragedy.

It was not a grave. This place had no body, only the memory of someone gone. The memory was enough.

I tried to straighten the plastic flowers but they were too stiff now to be changed. They were somehow beautiful, way out here on the desert where everything either becomes raw with the struggle, or gives in and becomes lovely. I left them as I had found them and walked home.

I reached my house in the early dusk. I sat on the patio holding, but not drinking, a glass of lemonade. During the two weeks of my sister's visit, I had often longed for this feeling of complete and utter solitude as the desert over the wall became peaceful with night. Even so, I missed her.

I miss her.

There was a soft ache in my belly from some overlooked but suddenly seen finality, the sort of understanding that makes one's opinions seem thin and intangible, half-hearted at best. And it was in this mood on the patio after supper, the candles long burned out, counting shooting stars like hours passing noiselessly through the dark of the desert, that I remembered, clearly, the smell of roses; I clearly remembered the heavy scent of mimosa, and heard the shared songs of childhood drifting by.

RICK DEMARINIS

DESERT PLACES

Fred Ocean wrote to his wife Sara twice a week — amusing, energetic letters meant as much to cheer himself up as to entertain her. He made the stark Arizona landscape bloom with Disneyesque exaggerations: "It's so desolate out here the red ants look up at me beseechingly when I walk to the post office. They want me to kill them." He described with good-natured cruelty the geriatric midwesterners who came here to Casa del Sol to retire among the scorpions, lizards, and black widows. He assembled the details of the daily skirmishes between their sixteen-year-old daughter, Renata, and his mother. "So far it's a bitchy little war of hit-and-run raids and long-range sniping," he wrote. "But it's going to escalate into a full-scale nuclear exchange if we don't get out of here pretty soon." He didn't tell her that his panic attacks had returned full-blown since he and Renata had arrived in Casa del Sol, or that because of them, he'd started drinking again. Nor did he mention the woman in Tucson, Germaine Folger, who had become his de facto drinking partner.

The high spirits he mustered for his letters home did not extend to his daily life. He was exhausted from being on edge most of the time, anticipating the inevitable snide remark from his mother, Mimi Ocean, and the wild mood-swings of his daughter. He felt like a tight-rope walker, his mother and daughter sitting on opposite

ends of his balancing pole. Renata hated the desert retire-
ment community and begged at least once a day to
return to Seattle. "I need *green*," she said. "Nothing's
green here. I've got to see a green tree, green grass, green
water. I feel like I'm stuck in a million square miles of
kitty litter." But he had promised Sara to keep Renata
here for at least a month. What had been a close mother-
daughter relationship had become a contest of wills beginning about the time Renata started high school.
Renata hated high school and wanted to quit. Both Fred
and Sara believed that a month of exile would give
Renata the perspective she needed to take stock of her
life and reconsider.

So far the strategy was a failure. The hoped-for tran-
quilizing effect of the remote desert community did not
materialize. The opposite happened. Renata had become
more hostile, more headstrong in her poorly-thought-
out plan for total independence. She wanted to go to
work as a gopher for a rock band, eventually breaking
into the management side of concert tours—all this on
the basis of having talked to one of the Eurythmics for
three minutes in a Portland hotel lobby. They had tried
to force her back into school, but neither Fred nor
Sara—only too aware of what went on in big city high
schools these days—had the necessary belief in the quality of the education Renata was receiving to give their
efforts moral authority. In any case, they would have had
to tie her hand and foot and deliver her to the school
grounds, but even then she'd eventually walk away, refuse to do the work, or find some other way to defeat
them.

Fred's mother hadn't seen Renata for three years. In
that time, Renata had grown to adult size. She was five
feet ten inches tall with a strong, wide-shouldered build.
Her only interest in high school had been the swim
team, but that hadn't been sufficient to hold her. Her
punk costume and hairstyle—a collection of colored
spikes that made her look like an old representation of
Miss Liberty—put Mimi Ocean off immediately. "Good
Christ, what in the hell did you let her do *that* for?" she

said to Fred at the airport, well within Renata's hearing.
"She looks like she's on leave from some halfway house
for mental cases." His mother, who had just had cataract
surgery, inspected Renata at close range through special
eyeglasses that looked like goggles.

"Luckily," Fred wrote, "Rennie finds the wildlife
around here interesting. For example, there's a swallows'
nest in the entryway to my mother's house. It's tucked
up in a corner and has three or four baby swallows in it.
Rennie checks on them every morning, fattening them
up with toast crumbs. There's a big, aggressive road-
runner that passes through the backyard every afternoon.
He pokes around for a while before moving on. Rennie
calls him Big Bopper."

It struck him that his letters to Sara were a kind of
espionage, treasonous to both his mother and daughter.
For that reason, he had to write them late at night in the
privacy of his bedroom, or at the local cemetery where
his father was buried. Needing an afternoon escape, he'd
drive his mother's white Cadillac convertible out to the
local "boot hill," the grassless, hardpan graveyard that
had once served the adjacent, nineteenth-century mining
community of Doloroso. Doloroso had been partially
restored into a certified "ghost town," the owners of
which had their cash registers primed for the permanent
tourists of Casa del Sol. "I like this cemetery," Fred
wrote. "It's filled with the bones of miners, gunfighters,
and Civil War deserters — a worthy cast for a big budget
western. I think of Dad and the other retirees who are
buried here as sort of underground tourists, mingling
with the local color." He wrote his letter seated on a
bench-high stone next to the flat, concrete slab that
marked his father's grave. His father's slab looked —
appropriately, Fred thought — like a section of pre-
stressed concrete used in bridge construction. It was
more of a barrier against burrowing animals than a
memorial.

Renata hated the cemetery and would not accompany
him here even though it meant that she'd be in the house
alone with her grandmother. She liked Doloroso,

though, because it had a cafe, and this was where Renata
took most of her meals. She couldn't bear her
grandmother's cooking. "Mother is essentially blind,"
Fred wrote. "All kinds of debris winds up in the food—
hairpins, buttons, even animals. Last night—I swear to
God—something crawled out of the *paella*. It was
cricket-size. Rennie and I watched it drag itself across the
table trailing a saffron slick. It moved badly, as though it
had left a couple of legs back in the casserole pan. Rennie
retched, excused herself, plunked down in front of the
TV with a can of cashews and a Pepsi."

The stone Fred sat on marked the grave of one
Henry Phelps, a man killed in something called "The
Arrowhead Mine Disaster of 1912," according to the in-
scription on the brass plate attached to the front of the
stone. He imagined that Phelps and his father would
have had common interests—Ivan Ocean had started out
as an iron ore miner in northern Michigan back in the
1920s. The notion that the two men were somehow
compatible satisfied a relic religiosity in Fred. Perhaps
they were sharing a mild and unharried eternity, trading
memories in the closeted earth. Why not? If the
Mormons could give their dead entire *planets* to rule,
why not this simple and unembroidered afterlife for the
bones of Henry Phelps and Ivan Ocean?

When Fred wrote his letters in the cemetery, he felt
as if he were addressing both his wife and his father. He
whispered each word aloud before committing it to
paper, even though he knew his father wouldn't appreciate his humor, or more accurately, the whimsical melan-
choly in which it was couched. He remembered how his
father would sit behind his no-nonsense steel desk, his
barrel-like torso erect, glancing at his watch impatiently,
only half-listening, picking out a phrase now and then to
single out as evidence of his son's faulty and perilous
grasp of reality. "Life makes no apologies, son," he once
said. "And self-pity is the *worst* reaction to hard knocks."

The mottoes of rust-belt capitalism had always been
easy to make fun of, but Fred had come to understand
that, hokey as they were, these mottoes aptly represented

his father's honest strength, his untethered spirit. Ivan Ocean had risen out of the iron ore mines of northern Michigan to become the owner-manager of Decatur Metal Fasteners, Inc. "Rennie is Dad all over again," Fred wrote, "just as stubborn, just as smart, hating all forms of dependence, waiting for her chance to cut the ties. No wonder she wants out of high school. Yesterday she called it 'a day-care center with team sports.' Dad quit school when he was fifteen — did you know that? Ran off to Escanaba, lied about his age, got work in a nearby mine, worked his way through Michigan Tech, bought his ticket for the capitalist gravy train. He doesn't know it — " He scratched that out and rewrote: "He didn't know it but he was never able to accept discipline, either. He was a wild mustang with frontal lobes. They say character traits leapfrog the generations. Think of the Fords. Henry was the mustang, his son Edsel a sweet old plug — nice guy, but he went swayback under the saddle — but Henry the Second, the grandson, was the mustang reborn. So it is with Rennie, me and Dad. (Hey, am I leaving you out of this formula, darling? But you've always said that Rennie is one-hundred percent Ocean.) Mother can't see the similarities, but I can, and they are real, even to the physiognomy — the big, peasant build, the tough jaw, the unblinking eyes. I'm the Edsel of the clan, honey, the rageless caretaker, the nice guy with a music box tinkling where there ought to be a snarling dynamo. I'm just the conduit for the genetic fire."

Whoa, he told himself, dropping his writing pad and pocketing his pen. He didn't like the drift of this letter. He didn't like the metaphors, the deft but unconscious switch from witty reportage to dark confession. (He could almost hear his father coax, "Don't stop now, Freddy, you're on the right track. You're headed for a solid dose of reality; go for it, boy.") "Reality is overrated, Dad," he said aloud. A sudden gust of wind, a dust-devil, sucked a plastic rose from the grave of another retiree, carrying it high in a violent spiral. He watched the dust-devil vandalize the old graveyard, scattering the unwilted artificial bouquets. It rocked the

Cadillac as it crossed the road that paralleled the cemetery and moved toward Doloroso, where it seemed to
lose interest, allowing its hoard of fake roses, bits of twig
and litter, to settle back to earth.

That night he dreamed of dust-devils, grown to
tornado size. They were coming for him. He drove the
Cadillac into the desert, trying to escape, but the engine
gradually lost power and finally quit. He put the top up,
rolled up the windows, turned on the air-conditioner,
the radio, the tape deck, but nothing worked and the
wind chuckled insanely against the rocking car. He woke
up sweating, sick to his stomach. He reached for the
Rolaids on the night table then realized that the nausea
was from adrenalin, and that he wasn't sick but frightened, the fear coming to him disguised as an idea that
could be worked out or ignored, and he rolled over,
pulling the covers up, thinking to find refuge in sleep,
but the adrenalin kept coming and he began to shake. He
got up, moved down the hall toward the living room,
switched on the lights. His mother kept a stock of gin
and tequila in a cabinet against the wall. He took down
the gin from the top shelf of her liquor cabinet, poured
himself a quiet glassfull, drank half of it down. He went
out then into the patio, under the night sky that seemed
blistered by a million stars. He sat in a deck chair and
gulped gin. "Jesus, Jesus," he said, rocking back and
forth.

When he went back into the house it was nearly
dawn. His mother was already up, making coffee. He
tried to slip back into his bedroom unnoticed but she
saw him and called him into the kitchen. "You're drinking again," she said.

"Medicinally," he said, not wanting a lecture or an
argument, but she was a drinker herself, well into her
cups early every evening, and did not press it.

"When are you leaving, Freddie?" she said.

"Eleven days," he said—too quickly—and he realized
that he'd been marking time.

His mother's eyes without her goggles seemed
unnaturally dark and liquid, capable of absorbing more

of him than ordinary sight would permit. "Eleven days won't change anything," she said. "Eleven hundred days wouldn't be enough."

"Oh, mother, come on," he said. "Rennie's not that—"

"Rennie's not the problem, Freddie. *You* are. You're afraid of your own daughter."

"Brilliant," he said, turning away from the black, unfocused eyes.

"Say what you want, it's true. You're afraid of her, afraid she'll not love you. But you're fooling yourself, Freddie. Rennie's a whole lot tougher than you are. She's a steamroller and she knows it. As long as you treat her with kid gloves, she's going to walk right over you."

"Fine," he said. "I'll take the belt to her."

His mother sighed. "No, you won't. You couldn't. And even if you could, it's far too late. Let her do what she wants. She will anyway. "The coffee finished perking and she poured out two cups. After taking a small hissing sip, she said, "Freddie, I'd like you to leave. I'd like you to go back to Seattle as soon as you can."

He almost took advantage of this remark. It was an old habit. He put on a wounded look, the phrase he wanted was on his lips, but he saw a tear start out of an old ruined eye and he held back.

"You miss Dad a lot," he said.

"I do," she said. "I really do."

When he went back to his bedroom, Renata was sitting on his bed. "I want to burn down this house," she said.

"You can't," he said. "It's made out of clay. Adobe."

"Then I'll turn the hose on it and dissolve it."

She was actually smiling. "Brat," he said, slapping her lightly on the thigh.

"I want to go home, Dad," she said, her voice small, like a remnant of childhood.

"So do I, baby," he said.

He sat next to her on the bed. Renata put her arm around his shoulder. "Dad," she said, "you're out of your envelope, you know that, don't you?"

"What?" It was hard to keep up with teenage jargon. He wasn't even sure that it was jargon, since Rennie tended to invent her own.

"You're over the edge, out of your element," she translated. "You're red-lining, Pop."

"Look, Rennie—"

"I heard you talking to grandpa yesterday. You were in the bathroom, shaving. I think you're weirding out. Daddy, I want to go back home for your sake, too."

"I'm surrounded by wise women," he wrote, later that morning in the cemetery. "I guess I'm either lucky or cursed." He started to cross that sentence out but dropped the pen. Sara had been after him lately to "rethink his situation." He was in a dead-end job, but it was secure and he liked it. He'd been a technical editor for Boeing for twelve years and he'd reached the ceiling as far as promotions and big salary jumps were concerned. He didn't mind—he liked the job well enough to excuse himself from the lures of ambition. He had no desire to climb the corporate ladder. He was paid decently, he was well liked, and he had managed to make himself as indispensable to his unit as the man he worked for, maybe more so. He had what all reasonable men wanted: security—and this long leave-of-absence bothered him. Sara thought the time off would make his boss realize just how important he was to his unit, but Fred was uneasy. His work would pile up or would be done poorly by someone else. But more than that, he missed the job itself. He actually relished cleaning up the strangled prose of engineers, who, left to their own narrative devices, could make the operation of a pencil sharpener seem as arcane and as potentially dangerous as the operation of a breeder reactor. His was a small job in the great world of jobs, but it was what he wanted. He was content. At forty-two, life had become pleasantly fixed and unchanging for Fred Ocean.

"You're an old man already," he heard his father say. He could see how his father must have appeared to the other retirees of Casa del Sol: the big, sturdy peasant features, battered but unhurtable. Ivan Ocean: even the name was strong, suggesting both the Russian masses and the sea. Ocean was a retooling of a difficult Russian name, Ozhogin, which was a bit too slushy for the parochial phonetics of American rust-belt English. Ivan Ozhogin, son of Vladimir. Born in the U.S.A., in post-frontier North Dakota, moved out of his home after knocking his father and older brother down a flight of stairs, rode the rods to Escanaba, buried himself in the red rock of iron country, emerged as a man with a slashing, take-no-prisoners vision of America. He was a happy man, but not a content one. Never content. The content do not contend. The happy people of this earth are the fighters, the conquerors, the risk-takers. Fred, lovingly, put a Mexican wedding shirt on his father, white slacks to match, *huaraches* on his big wide feet. He saw him tanned Apache brown, saw his white teeth flashing as he shouted, "You think you've got it made. Let me tell you, you don't deserve what you have. You don't deserve Rennie, or a wife like that Sara who only wants you to do your best. You're going to lose all of it. You'd let the world go to hell and not blink an eye as long as you were content. Men like you can't hold onto anything except by luck." Even in death his father was full of instructions and warnings. The trouble with such advice was that it only made sense to those who gave it. Crazy mustangs did not travel with dollar-a-ride ponies. Advice from his father, he always believed, was like clothes handed down: you could wear them only if they fit. His father's instructions fit him like a shroud. "Back off, Dad," he said, gently. He watched his father, as if on a freight elevator, sink down into the hard ground to resume his reminiscing chats with Henry Phelps, a man more to his liking. Fred picked up his pen and pocketed it.

He drove into Tucson, ostensibly to make reservations for weekend tickets to Seattle. But he didn't drive to the airport. Instead, he stopped at The Conch where Germaine Folger would be waiting for him.

"Well, gracious," she said, "look at you, tiger."

He glanced at himself in the smokey mirror behind
the bar. He'd driven in at high speed with the top of the
Caddy down. His hair was wild and his eyes were
spooky—wide and wind-whipped red. His heart was
tripping along at highway speed, and he was very
thirsty.

"What's been chasing you, honey?" Germaine said. "A
ghost?"

Judging from her cozy slur, Fred knew that she'd
been here for a couple of hours already. Germaine was
older than he was by at least ten years. She was a tall
woman with a doughy but still pretty face. She had a
small mouth. Her lips seemed like the lips of a child. He
liked her looks. He liked the wet brown eyes that
seemed to have been evolved specifically for barroom
light. And he liked the way an old torch song could send
her gaze into the middle distance as if revisiting scenes
from a bittersweet past. He'd never seen her in sunlight,
and could not imagine her squinting her way across a
sun-bright parking lot. She was a barfly. He smiled at
the old-fashioned phrase. She was half-ruined but not
destitute. She dressed well, her credit was good enough
to allow her to run a tab, and the stones in her rings
looked genuine. Her husband sold real estate in Scotts-
dale. He'd made a fine art of keeping his distance from
her.

"It's been a hard week, Germaine," he said.

"Could be a trend, baby," she said, patting his hand.

Fred ordered a bourbon and soda. The juke box in
The Conch specialized in ballads from the 1940s. Dick
Haymes was singing *All or Nothing at All,* saturating the
dim air with a dangerous nostalgia. Everyone in The
Conch looked on the verge of making a serious,
life-upsetting error.

"Maybe you ought to start thinking about heading
back to Seattle," Germaine said. "This country can be
tough on you webfeet."

"That's for sure," he said. "In fact, that's why I'm in
town. To make reservations."

"But you came here first."

"I didn't say I was in a hurry," he said, clinking her glass with his.

She smiled—bravely, he thought, because her eyes seemed resigned to a future measured in hours. She still had the power of her former beauty, and though the reason he was attracted to her was not that simple, he didn't try to find a deeper motive. He'd wanted her strictly as a drinking partner. That was safe; anything beyond that could be avoided.

"Hell, webfoot," she said, recklessly. "Maybe we ought to say goodbye in style."

He sipped his drink as if thinking it over.

"I've got to get to the airport," he said.

"The airport isn't going anywhere," she said. "Besides, there's a travel agency around the corner from me." She put her hand on his, a proprietary gesture that took away his right of withdrawal. "Listen, Freddie," she said. "We're friends, aren't we? My apartment's a minute away. I think I know what you like."

Fred believed her. He believed that she possibly knew what he liked better than he did himself. She was a student of the small variations that made one man different from another. It accounted for her wrecked life.

"My Dad says what I like isn't good for me," he said.

"Then it's time your Dad minded his own business, I'd say."

They went outside where the sunlight instantly betrayed her face. Her eyes tightened to leaky slits, and her chalky skin, blasted by the desert sun, became mottled and rough. She looked permanently angry, as if deeply wronged by unforgettable abuses.

He walked her to the parking lot. "I'll follow you," he said, and he did, for five blocks, where they were separated by a red light. He saw her pull over on the other side of the intersection to wait for him, but when the light turned green he made a hard right and headed for the airport.

"Well, *say* it, Pop," he said as he eased the Cadillac onto the freeway.

"There's nothing to say, Freddie. I would have done the same thing. You have to weigh the consequences."

He gave his father a diction in death that he didn't have in life. It was easier to talk to him that way. The blunt homilies and warnings needed a good technical editor if they were to be taken seriously.

"Did you ever play around, Pop? Did you ever find a woman who knew what you liked?"

It was the sort of personal question ghosts can't answer. Fred found one of Renata's tapes in the glove compartment and plugged it into the deck. The flogging beat, the tortured guitars, and brainless lyrics eliminated the possibility of further conversation.

At the cemetery the next morning, Fred added a paragraph to the letter he'd been working on the last few days. "You'll probably get this after we're home, but these communiques from desert places are habit forming. I'll probably continue writing to you twice a week for the rest of my life. Proximity is our most deceptive enemy, I think. Distance is more than simple geography. Ask Rennie. I'm closer to Dad now than I've ever been, and he's somewhere across the universe. He thinks I'm incorrigible. It's true. But so is he. So is Rennie. We all are. Just like the tarantulas. We've got them, you know, big across as tortillas. Early this morning I escorted one off the premises. He'd done an incorrigibly tarantula thing. You know that nest of cute swallow chicks Rennie's been monitoring? Well, Nature's got no use for cute. The tarantula got them. I found him, after noticing the empty nest, sitting fat as a cat among a litter of darling little feathers. I eased him out of the entryway with a broom. He was so bloated on infant swallow meat he could barely waddle out of there. Then I dutifully swept up all the feathers. I pinned a cute note to the nest: 'Bye, bye, Rennie. We've flown away to become rock-star swallows. Thanks for everything. Wish us luck.' Dad would say, 'No one was ever hurt by a light dose of reality.' My answer to that would make him slap his forehead in disgust. Reality, Dad, is public enemy number one. It's the bottom line we can't deal with, truth be known."

When Fred got back to the house it was still early. Rennie was asleep and his mother was sipping warm gin in the bathtub — her arthritis was acting up — and his father was whispering sharp warnings in his ear. As a concession to all of them, he took the note off the empty swallow's nest and threw it away.

LISA SANDLIN

CREASE

Six months or so ago, about the time Ray and I split up, Livvy sent me to a palm reader. She was not in the least exotic. A bit overweight, with straight brown hair, she was as ordinary as a house shoe. Her apartment was filled with plants and as she grasped my hand, a quiet current passed. She said, "When people like you come, I tell my plants . . ." here her voice piped up to falsetto and she confided to a schefflera, ". . . don't worry, she'll be gone in an hour." I wasn't insulted. I once boarded my plants with a friend who commented, "You should run a plant concentration camp." So she was right on, just with a handshake.

She made all sorts of positive predictions, although it's difficult to remember them precisely. Things like: "You will live in the country," "You will meet your mate in three years' time," "It is possible that he will have money."

She gave me practical advice. The absence of moons in my fingernails proved I should eat more protein; she pointed out only one, mostly submerged moon. Actually only the halo of one submerged moon. Anyway (now I sound like Ray) she did tell me some good things. But what I remember best are the bad ones.

The first thing that made me feel bad was when she found Ray in my right palm. He was a crease about three-eighths of an inch long, so faint that if I tilted my palm toward her candle, he disappeared. The palm reader was disturbed, at a remove, of course; her voice registered the kind of irritable disbelief people express when they say "What will she do next?"

"You married him?" she asked me. I didn't say anything. I had already told her I married him. "You married him?" she insisted. "You weren't supposed to marry him."

Well, I did. But the thing that shook me the most was when she inspected my left palm. That one, she informed me, mapped out the history of my past lives.

"Will you look at that," she said. "You've never been old."

The dangling lines, the isolated Xs, the dead ends in my left palm upset me more than Ray's invisibility. I could have taken it, I suppose, this way: I've had a natural taste for blazes of glory. For lifetimes, I've left a good-looking corpse. But that's not how I took it, concerned, as I am, with the task of the life at hand.

As a child, I dogged my grandfather, Daddy Arthur. I puzzled over his stories, his skills, his tricks, and poked at the mysterious caving-in of his body. Daddy Arthur could shuffle and deal with one hand; he could make the cards stream like water or sift out onto the table like cake flour drifting into a bowl. Daddy Arthur knew things. He knew why hell was hot—not naturally, no, hell is naturally cold. But every Friday, the jaybirds dip their beaks into steaming sand and carry the sand down to hell, scattering it all around. His mouth would work in and out, in and out, until it was loose enough to smile, and he would croak out a secret laugh. Daddy Arthur's shoulders got thinner and thinner, my teeth fell out and grew in, but I was still his shade: for him, I was like a shadow that bumped into you when you stopped. It was because I felt he knew something he would never tell me.

So when the palm reader said to me "You've never been old," how I took it was as a handicap: here I am, yet again, without the stored wisdom that will allow me now and then to intuit either disaster or a lucky break.

She was telling me mine was a raw soul. And why I felt so bad was that the second she said it, something shifted in my chest, and I knew it was absolutely true.

Recently, as she tapped a cigarette on the table, Livvy asked me, "Why Ray? I don't mean to say 'How could you take it all those years?' but why Ray?"

But that was what she meant to say and all I could think of was that by the time I couldn't take it anymore, Ray was home. I am a rooted woman. I can make homes out of motels and sleeping bags; they assume, in an hour, the sentimental aura of my territory. Livvy said, did I know the story of the Archangel Gabriel collecting everyone's troubles and dumping them in sacks? He lined up all the sacks on a fencepost and told everybody to run get one. And they all raced as fast as they could to snatch their own troubles back. Was that what I meant?

That's one way of looking at it, I said.

I was new to Santa Fe when I met Ray. Out job-hunting, the last place I tried was a small bar with a giant harlequin snake painted directly onto the wall. Purposeful as a divining rod, its thick tongue forked toward a row of glittering bottles. It was 11:30 in the morning, and there were only the bartender, one customer and me. Prying the completed application form from the sticky rings on the small table, I began to half-listen to the story the bartender was telling his only customer. The customer was half-listening, too, while he tossed cherries in the air and tried to spear them with a tiny plastic sword.

". . . so I asked him to move his chair. He won't. He's a young guy, a real hard-case Chicano, got the bandanna, got Guadalupe on a chain. Got the red ass in general for the whole Anglo world. Anyway, he puts his feet up on the table, won't let me by. He's staring out the door like I'm the Invisible Man. Hey, scout, I tell him again, I gotta get by here. He's looking at me, you know, but he's not seeing me.

"So I'm standing there getting mad enough to dump the whole tray on his bandanna when Benny Duran comes over. You know Benny? Works downtown at Kraft's selling shoes."

The customer said, "Guy with one shoulder lower than the—"

"Yeah, that's Benny. He's not Superman, know what I mean? Anyway, right away I see this is a scene. Benny's walking Pachuco-style, kinda loose and swinging, like he's got an hour or two to cover the five feet up to the guy's chair. He gets there, he just stands there. Both of them, not seeing the other.

"Everybody gets real quiet. I know Benny fifteen years, he always comes to hear me play the guitar. But even I'm looking at him, wondering what's up."

"Benny Duran, got one shoulder lower . . . Hey, all right!" the customer lurched forward, a cherry stuck on his sword.

"*Madre de Dios,* some people's kids. Anyway, Benny kind of straightens up, gets both shoulders real even like they're carrying something. Then he bends down. He grabs the arms of the chair and picks the guy up, picks up the whole goddamn chair and sets it down out of the aisle. Makes a big thump. The guy's looking at him now, and I guarantee you, he's seeing him.

"So Benny leans over and in this real quiet voice, he introduces himself, he says 'Capitan Benjamin Eduardo Antonio Duran y Salazar, *a su servicio.*' I'm thinking, Benny, where the hell you getting this rank, but mostly I'm thinking Benny my man, you are gonna get your throat jumped. But the guy sweeps off the bandanna like it's some kind of cap and says 'Tenente Juan Diego Vigil y Romero, *a sus ordenes.*' They look at each other for a minute and nod. Then Benny walks off. Mr. Pachuco again. Guy was polite as hell for the rest of the night."

"Give me another Manhattan, over easy," the customer said. He wasn't impressed.

But I was. Maybe lots of people could fail to be charmed by a story like that, but not me. I love seeing people swell into themselves. I watch for it.

I handed the bartender my sticky application form.
By then he had a toothpick in his mouth. He took it out.
"Hi, I'm Ray," he said.

Ray is a little man with beautiful hands and tiny terrier
eyes. His being little never bothered me. I could put my
arm right around his shoulder and look straight into his
eyes. In our moments of harmony, we could walk the
earth that way, two little people locked at the shoulders
striding down the street on a snowy day.

Just today I remembered a conversation that took
place years ago. It was with a vacuum cleaner repairman
who assured me that my husband had a heavy burden to
bear in this society. The vacuum cleaner repairman was
from Oklahoma, and little. He let me know he earned
$50,000 a year, enough to support two ex-wives and a
penchant for gambling. He stared at me hungrily when I
told him that size didn't mean anything.

"Don't you never believe it," he warned, pointing a
miniature screwdriver at my young face. "He's on the
lookout all the time. He's gotta be." Well, I don't know,
but the man fixed the vacuum cleaner in five minutes
flat. He made me think.

How Ray expanded himself was by talking. Early on
he told me, with the sort of odd, downcast pride you
might feel if you discovered your backbone was double-
jointed, "I can sit down at a table and within ten minutes
I can dominate any conversation." Ray told stories,
segueing one into the next, to the bar at large. The
painted snake behind him was a fitting decoration. There
was Ray, there were the customers: charmer and snakes.

On a Saturday night, still jobless, I took the last seat
at the bar without one intuitive twinge that this was the
evening that would etch Ray faintly into my palm. As I
sat down, Ray dropped a glass. Two minutes later he
served a Bud Light to a regular whose drink was Scotch
and milk. Red-faced, he apologized and gave the guy a
Bloody Mary. The people at the bar all knew Ray, and
they were getting a big kick out of his being so
flustered.

Finally he came over to me. He wiped his hands on a
bar towel and took one of my hands in his. "I'm glad
you came in tonight," he said, and paused, looking back
over his shoulder to the row of heads turned toward us.
He started to say something else, but he was interrupted
by a commotion at the back table.

Two drunks were pouring beer on each other, trying
to fill up the pockets of their denim shirts before the beer
seeped out. Angry, Ray walked up and jerked his thumb
like an umpire. "You're eight-sixed, both of you! Useless
as balls on a priest!"

They snuck around to the back. Ray knew they were
coming. They were stumbling around out there, knocking over empties. Just as they kicked the back door open,
I saw Ray do something that made me fall in love with
him. Very carefully, gently, he removed his glasses and
laid them on the bar. They were big guys and Ray is a
little man. The moment seemed infinite to me — the back
door flying open and Ray, with exquisite resignation,
setting his glasses on the bar. Then he was sitting on top
of one guy with his thumbs on the guy's eyes and the
other one had tripped over a chair and was moaning on
the floor, his hand to his stomach.

I saw reluctance in Ray's gesture with the glasses; I
saw willingness, too. The look in his bare eyes went past
the calm of a man preparing himself; it was a look of the
deepest understanding, the kind of understanding that
means forgiveness. He forgave them, he forgave himself;
he owned the moment absolutely. Unhampered by even
a feather's weight of premonition my soul welled up: I
saw a man who knew something.

"So why don't you come over and bring your guitar
after work?" I asked him. Ray wiped his glasses and put
them back on. "Okay," he said.

We built a big piñon fire. Ray unsnapped the case,
lifted the guitar, and set a chair out of range of the flying
sparks. He tuned, patiently. Then he played, not a slow,
warm-up piece, but a surging, hundred-mile-an-hour
rhythm. The guitar and the leaping fire filled the room
with motion. I felt I was watching the rhythm, like a

train with glinting windows, rush by. The flamenco music was terrible and wonderful and despairing and joyous. That's all I could make of it, all those contradictions.

"Do they sing to this?" I asked.

"Oh yeah," Ray said, "it all comes from the *cante,* the singing. A guy out plowing his field and singing. Beating an anvil with a hammer and singing. Listen." He sang a verse. It sounded drawn-out and chopped up and very sad.

"That says something like 'For every step forward, I take two steps back.' And this one, I love this one. Listen now." Since I couldn't understand the words, I followed his hands. His long, elegant fingers had a life of their own. He never attended to them. They flew gracefully, from fret to fret, as he sang.

"That one says, 'My mouth hurts me, gypsy girl, from asking you if you love me'." We looked at each other for a while. "I love that one," Ray said, finally.

So I began to learn flamenco when I moved in with him, into his one room with the painted iron bed and the TV set that had to be turned upside down two or three times to get the sound to work. Ray sat in a wooden chair and played the fast rhythm — *bulerías* — while I danced a series of short steps that joined each other in a circle. My teacher had taught me these steps so that we could practice without stopping, on and on in novice infinity until Ray got tired of playing. Around and around I went, passing myself briefly in a Woolworth mirror we had hung on the wall. When I faced the mirror, my arms arced out of its borders. Ray played, resting his cheek on the guitar. When he was tired, or I had got it right enough times in a row, he nested the guitar in its case and snapped the locks. His terrier eyes lit up. I was very happy, I was. With my arm about his shoulder, we walked downtown to get a coffee.

I see what I'm doing — explaining to Livvy and the palm reader that faint crease that should have been outside my destiny. Now that I put it down, I see Livvy still tapping her cigarette. Here in my room, I tilt my palm under the twenty-five-watt bulb and find only a patch of unmarked skin. I wasn't supposed to marry him? Well, I did.

It is because of Ray that last night I dressed in a long, ruffled skirt and a fringed shawl and went off to dance at the Sheraton. Livvy came over, too, to dress, and to warm up before another night of hometown flamenco. We performed, enacting the torture of human misfortune, while the Jaycees ate and drank and slid their arms around giggling wives. It went okay, mostly, but it doesn't always. Inappropriate things happen. We take them in stride, that being the one condition of continuing to do jobs like these.

One night, as Livvy intoned the notes of the *tientos,* pulling the audience by the hair into the mood of the song, a waitress walked by her shouldering a tray of food. She stopped to ask Livvy if she knew which was table fourteen. Another time an old man whipped out a violin and fiddled along with our guitars. In between numbers, he jumped in with ancient jokes. We've danced on stages like trampolines, under latticework that snared the fringe of our shawls, on particle board set on a slope so that we had to dance uphill, heaving like wrestlers with the effort.

But Ray and I had a dream. We would live in Spain for a year so I could study there. I would learn to dance with all the *gracia* of the village flirt, the girl by the fountain with eyes like honey and a soul as deep as a well. Then what? He would play and I would dance. It didn't go any further than that, but it was a dream of remarkable buoyancy. It lasted well into the years when we only remembered what the dream was, and not how it felt. Misfortunes intervened, of course; they ravaged our savings like bears at a campsite: an emergency appendectomy, a car, unemployment. I haven't been old. I wasn't prepared for the way our dream broke up, in big bits, in little bits. I think now that that was one of the ingredients of Daddy Arthur's secret croak. He'd sift out the cards and grab me by the waist and laugh, a rooster in a pen, cackling at the inedible feed he knew was coming.

I envy Livvy not because she has the rugged, gold look of a lioness but because she remembers past lives and so cannot be as unequipped as I am. When she was little, she said, she drew pictures of elevators. Not plain boxes ascending in larger boxes, but lacy, wrought-iron cages with attendants in uniform. She was an old lady in Paris and the wrought-iron elevator went up to her penthouse apartment.

"What did you do up there?" I wanted to know.

"Oh, I think I watched people. I spent a lot of time watching people on the boulevard and in the park. I was very old. My family and friends were gone, so I adopted strange faces from my window." I was afraid she was downplaying it for my sake, but just then, with all the voluptuousness of a woman slipping a silk strap from her shoulder, she opened a fresh pack of cigarettes.

"I dipped snuff, too. From tiny lacquer boxes." After Livvy brought an imaginary pinch of snuff to her nose, she tapped a cigarette on the table and pursed her lips lovingly to receive it.

Her other drawings were a source of consternation to her parents. They were of breasts. They came from her life as an African Bushman, a hunter who fed his family with a spear.

"So why didn't you draw lions or gazelles or spears?" I pursued.

Livvy flicked her lighter; the flame hissed between us. "They were my wife's breasts. I can see them—they hung low on her chest with nipples like black beans. I must have loved her very much."

Now maybe breasts and elevators don't add up to a big advantage in life, but I'm not so sure. I think of what Livvy's Bushman knew of love and what her old lady made of the faces performing daily under her patient gaze. And that is much more than I can claim—a virgin in a hand-planed coffin, her lily eyes directed only to heaven.

*　*　*

We took the TV and the painted iron bed and moved to
a bigger place, a house on Cold Water Street with
startling floral linoleum. On the way, our car stuffed
with boxes, Ray decided that this move was so official
we might as well get married. We were at a stoplight.
His eyes were very bright and he shot me a look, side-
ways. He slipped his hands in his pockets.

"What do you think?"

"Ray, you're driving," I reminded him, thinking that
when we drove on he would say something more.

"Oh yeah," he said.

"It's a green light."

He grinned. "I'm glad you feel that way."

We got married at the courthouse. Judge Archuleta
asked me did I take this man Ramon to be my wedded
husband. He should have said Raymond, but I stared
into Ray's bright eyes and took him. My mother sent a
silver heirloom, Daddy Arthur's pocket watch, as a sym-
bol that I was now bound into the generations. Its small
oval case sparkled. But the fat Roman numerals which
had taught me time had faded to the breadth of eyelashes, as though in a decade without Daddy Arthur,
someone else's anxious glances had worn them thin. For
weeks I wore it on a ribbon around my neck, until Ray
convinced me to stash it in a drawer and not ding it up.

There on Cold Water Street, on the tappy, rosy linoleum, two other kinds of practices developed besides the
one which ended in a stroll downtown for coffee: bad
and solo.

I am stepping and clapping on our red floor with its
pattern of massive yellow roses. I'm barefoot, in a limp
polyester nightgown that has worn clear in patches, like
panes of glass. One step, then a clap, step, clap, over and
over until some semblance of a counter-time emerges.
My heavy hands are cold and they sting, the cold linoleum burns my feet. I have one good long run before I
mess up — ticka-ticka-ticka-ticka.

"That's it," Ray says, clapping out the *palmas* and using his tongue to sound the clicks in a syncopated roll. "Only fifty times faster."

Ray loves to coach; he's too into it to stop and get dressed. He's hunched on the edge of the couch wearing only the holey T-shirt he sleeps in. When he coaches, Ray is the bad cop. He rattles me. I step again.

"Jesus, you're not gonna break," he barks. Part of me escapes out the window, out to where snow is falling from a white sky, where trees and power lines are traced white.

"Play," I urge him. "I do better with the music."

"Look, I know it's not your culture. The Spanish learn it as babies. Hell, the kids count eggs to *bulerías* rhythm. Listen now. *Uno dos* **tres** . . . *cuatro cinco* **seis** . . . *siete ocho nueve* **diez**. . . . Don't fling yourself around like that!"

Half-naked, he hops over the freezing yellow roses to tuck his feet into the rungs of the kitchen chair next to the heater. He grabs the guitar, rubbing his hands, talking, talking. Like toffee between my teeth, Ray's voice is pulling at me.

"Listen now . . . *uno dos* **tres** . . ."

The solo practice is very different. Ray's at the bar. I am watching a late movie and dancing around the living room during the commercials. As soon as Robert Mitchum and Susan Hayward fade away in their sports car, I bang the TV and flip on the record player. A fast *bulerías* charges the room. I dance with a Goodwill lamp as though it were my iron-spined partner. Often, carried away, I dance through whole sections of movies. Something—some heavy, wild sediment—is being stirred up from the bottom of me. The lamp and I forget the late show. We cast passionate, bobbing shadows, shadows that inhabit the room as satisfactorily as company.

Then I hear Ray coming. The dogs start up. The one at the corner barks and, like a song sung in rounds, the next dog takes it up and the next one. When Ray is far enough past the corner, the first dog drops out, then the second one, until they are all quiet. There is a jingling, and Ray's key turns in the lock. He hangs his cap on the nail and is filling me in on his shift before his bomber jacket has quite slipped off his shoulders.

"What a night. You should of been there. This nut with a blond wig came in. Guy must have been six-four and the wig is supposed to make him into a girl. He went into the ladies' john and when I went in to get him, he's combing his pubic hair. *Madre de Dios*. Maybe I could join the civil service."

In between sips of tea, he lays out the rest of the night. After a while, I interrupt to trot out my inarticulate evening. "Ray, let me tell you. I danced all around the living room. Watch this step." I show him.

"Oh, good one," he says, nodding. "Anyway . . ." He presents me with the information he collected from various customers. This information could be anything—the derivations of words, civil war strategy—but tonight it's about remittance men and Elvis Presley. I'd like to talk about something else, something silly and important, but we don't. Ray preferred to leave those subjects alone when they applied to the two of us, untouched, stashed—like Daddy Arthur's wedding-silver watch, too rare to use everyday.

These days, with Ray gone, I walk through the house as though through water, cutting a temporary wake that seals behind me as I pass from the room. When Ray was not practicing, bent over the guitar in the kitchen, he kept the house filled up with theories, opinions, jokes, stories.

"Do you realize," I asked him when we'd been married a while, "that you talk like an essay?"

Ray leveled his eyes with mine. "Hey, I'm sharing things. Things that mean something to me because they're weird or enlightening or just go to show how stupid people are. Stuff like that's as good as a ten-dollar bill to me. Remember the guy I told you about the other night? The one who wanted to axe his sister-in-law because she had a nervous breakdown? He didn't believe it was real. She's an actress, he said, everybody's got problems. God only gives you more than you can handle, *once,* he said. Now that's worth talking about. He stiffed me, the bastard, but he dropped that little insight on the bar. So I brought it home to you. Anyway, you're certainly welcome to join in. A conversation implies two people. Is it so hard for you to say something at the end of the sentence?"

But by then I was unalterably in receiver mode. "At the end of the paragraph, Ray," I replied.

The semantic problem there is "sharing." Ray was giving. He brought information back to me like a retriever — gossip, obscure facts about Sicilian bandits, the workings of cranberry bogs. Sharing, no; Ray never left a space for me to share back. He finished a story with "Anyway . . . ," flinging out that stopgap word like a portable bridge, clicking his teeth to reserve the next block of time while he organized his thoughts to fill it.

The change that came was like the stretching of children's bones — as an event in time, inevitable and common, but in itself rather magical. He wasn't at all ready for it. Ray wanted to go on and on, me and him and the Woolworth mirror.

One August evening we performed for a fiesta on the Santa Fe Plaza — Ray and I; Frank, the second guitar; Cynthia, a dancer; and Livvy, our singer, in a long black shawl. It was a lovely mountain night, starry, with a light wind carrying the tang of two seasons.

Ray played the slow, compelling introduction to the *soléa.* Frank joined in. Scanning the ring of upturned faces, I lost them. I saw only the late summer night with its air of a last invitation. As Livvy sang the first sad notes, I rose from the chair as though lifted. I turned toward her, but she disappeared. Only the night was there. I let it in — the stage was gone, my feet and my twisting hands were gone. For all I knew, I was still sitting in the chair, a faint, awkward ghost waiting for the summer night to return my borrowed body. Livvy told me later that, when I'd finished, the audience was silent

for seconds before they began to applaud. I don't know.
I didn't hear anything until I was off the stage.

Ray was waving his hand. "Christ, I broke a nail! I
didn't know what the hell you were gonna do next!"

A woman from the crowd pushed past him. "That
was wonderful!" she said to me, "it was incredible what
you did."

When, from surprise, I didn't respond, she was confused. Looking me up and down, she suddenly smiled.
"Oh, you're from Spain, aren't you? *Habla ingles?*"

Ray stared at me, too, like I was something new.

A month later, it happened again. I danced at an
exhibit of Spanish pictures, across a polished gallery floor
lit with strips of late afternoon sun. The only real thing
to me then was what was inside—some part of me that
knew something—and it wanted to get out.

We had a turning point. It was invisible then, but
now, looking backward, I can see it, insignificant but
rebelliously upright, like one of those roadside crosses
the Spanish people here use to mark a violent death.

We were dancing in a bar. After the show, a drunken
Englishman brought a round of drinks for the whole
troupe. He caught me before I could disappear into the
dressing room, a dusty storeroom at the back of the bar.
"I bought them for you, actually," the Englishman said,
his eyes luminous. "You've got such sorrow in your
face."

When he walked away, rather unsteadily, Ray
grimaced. "What a bozo," he said. It was that, as much
as anything, that set the end in motion; that Ray had to
refuse me such a small moment of distinction.

Now I wanted to talk back to Ray when he came
home, I wanted to share. Ray listened, but he walked
around while I talked, polishing the telephone with a
dishrag. I followed him around the kitchen with new
thoughts.

"Uh huh, uh huh," he muttered, chipping black off
the burners with his fingernails. Then he put his hands
on my shoulders and seated me gently at the table. I
liked his hands there; they made me feel warm. He sat

me down like I was a guitar, and breakable. He had something curious to say. From habit I listened.

I began to have black-and-white dreams of laundromats. I was forced to do endless loads of laundry for unnamed persons. The dreams altered my dancing schedule. I danced during "Hawaii 5-0," and on into "Quincy." By the time the late movie came on, I was tired, and went to bed. Ray complained about coming home to a dark house, but I couldn't seem to help myself; I was overcome by sleepiness. It relaxed my knees, closed my eyes by 10:00 P.M. Ray shook me awake to tell me about the evolution of hard-shell beetles or how the median IQ of licensed drivers in Boston is eighty, but I drifted off between sentences.

His voice rolled into my dreams as a sound track. I was alone in a night-lit laundromat in New Orleans, stuffing wet sheets into an oversize dryer. Suddenly his voice ran along the edge of the dream like a banner of words at the bottom of the television screen.

"This guy told me hard-shell beetles have come a long way," I heard. "Did you know they started out with really flimsy coverings? Thin, like negligees." Pulling out a load of billowy sheets, I was horrified to see beetles marching up them, an invasion of hard-shell beetles. "Call them back, Ray!" I yelled from the dream, but probably I was only shaping the words with my lips.

One night I was shaken awake to find the light on and a suitcase by the bed.

"I'm moving out," Ray said. "But I want you to know that I know you moved out first." He jerked the quilt I was folded up in and I tumbled onto the floor. I sat in the corner, watching him dismantle the iron bed with a hammer.

"There was love here," he said between blows.

I was pinching the skin of my forehead. "Could you please just say that another way?"

Ray took off his glasses and wiped them with his shirttail. I couldn't read his eyes; he kept them closed. He threw back his head and sang a flamenco verse, beating the iron with his hammer. Halfway through, I recognized the words: my mouth hurts me, gypsy girl, from asking you if you love me. He carried out all the bed pieces and the suitcase. When I got up a couple of hours later, I found he had taken his TV, too. It was a pain, that TV with its tiresome ways, but when you get used to something, you miss it when it's gone.

Sometimes, now, I talk to Ray, to the kitchen chair where he would be running down his scales. Ray, I say, I bought a dress today. It's the color of a winter sunset on the Sangre de Cristos; it's the color of blood. Ray, I saw Benny Duran today. "*Como te ha ido?*" he greeted me. "Do you know why Espanola is covered with shards of glass?" No, Benny, why? "It's for the Penitente break dancers, man." We laugh like crazy, Ray, and you are with us, a white, peeling, live, roadside cross.

Livvy showed up last night looking like the mindful Russian peasant she is. She wore a long Russian blouse over a taggy print skirt and her sharp face stood out in gold relief from her tangled golden hair. "So what'll happen to us tonight? We'll fall off the stage? Frank'll miss all the chord changes? What?" Lifting the print skirt, she did a flourishing *remate* step. She was in a good mood.

"Frank's done mostly okay without Ray. It's hard to just jump in there as first guitar. It's been hard . . ."

Livvy shut me up with a look. I ironed our shawls while she transformed herself before the bathroom mirror. She hummed in her throat. In half an hour, the lioness was hidden. Blue-lidded, black-lashed, fuchsia-cheeked, she had a luscious red mouth and a red dot at the corner of each Tartar eye. "Ámanos, chica," she said, snaking a black and green polka-dot dress up her hips. She winked at me, her painted face merry as a carnival.

We met Frank and Cynthia at the Sheraton. Frank wandered over to the bar. We headed upstairs so Cynthia could wipe the lipstick off her teeth. Livvy stood at the door to the ladies' lounge, absorbing the gestures of a short, handsome Jaycee in a white suit.

"Think you could stretch it out a little?" He gazed nervously up to Livvy.

"Uh oh, we'll do what we can, but stretch it out how long?"

"Say twenty minutes, something like that."

"Uh oh." Livvy was shaking her head as though some unfortunate mistake had been made, but certainly not by her. "I think you should have paid us more."

"We've got a delay," she told me. "They've bungled their guest speakers. Naturally. The committee chairman says he can't speak after the Archbishop, he'll stutter or something. I'm going to check out the mikes."

I sank into a fat armchair and drew the shawl over me like a sheet. Cynthia was busy at the mirror with a Kleenex. Slipping out my right palm, I examined it in the dim light. It was wet. Sweat sparkled in the creases. I didn't look for Ray; instead, I followed my life lines. That was another thing the palm reader showed me. I have two life lines; they run in unbroken parallel from the veins of my wrist to the base of my middle finger. "Well, what does that mean?" I asked her. She smiled, getting up to move an African violet farther away from me, to a bookshelf.

"It means in this life you'll live to be old. It means there's a hell of a lot going on there." Bending over, she whispered something to the violet. She shrugged, such an easy shrug, but then it was me and not her with these endless lines. She sat down again, her brown eyes inert as buttons. "It means you're learning, dear."

"Thirty more minutes, *chicas!*" Livvy strode into the lounge. "Definitely time for a cigarette. The Archbishop is warming up." Carefully, to avoid smudging her gorgeous mouth, Livvy inserted a cigarette, puffing with puckered lips.

I hauled myself out of the armchair and walked into the bathroom. I began to do footwork patterns on the black-and-white tile. Though I was not dancing lightly, the sounds were sharp, weightless. I went on and on, doing step after step from my *soléa*. Ray has an original *Queen of the Gypsies* album, the one on which Carmen

Amaya recorded her inhuman *alegrías,* rolling rhythm after crushing rhythm, counter matched by counter-rhythm to the sole accompaniment of clapping hands. No guitar, no song, just the steady palms and an occasional shout of encouragement. Carmen Amaya danced the *silencio* for an eternity of fourteen minutes. I stopped to take a very deep breath. Then, gathering the skirt to my side, I cradled the ruffles and started the footwork again. I was realizing that, while she danced it, it must have felt to Carmen that that *silencio* could go on forever.

All in all, it was a fairly good night. Frank caught the chord changes. Cynthia and I didn't mess up. The Archbishop thanked us himself; that was nice. But near the end a mike gave out, and Livvy had to climb off the stage and circle the room as she sang, in order to be heard. The handsome little Jaycee, motivated by taste or by pique, leveled his spotlight on the dancers' chests, abandoning our sorrowful faces to the dark.

MICHAEL DELP

DRAFT HORSE

When he was a kid growing up in Fargo, he used to walk from the barn to the house, thirty below, his breath steaming out and then flowing past his face. On those mornings he could hear the way the cows seemed to brush together in the cold, and imagined he could hear them at night when the temperature dropped even lower. From his bedroom it sounded like their hides were made of metal, how each hair had frozen on their backs and was rasping against the others.

And he remembered the way the sun used to look coming in through a quarter inch of frost on the single pane window. It would break up, splashing into a prism on the walls. He would wake and hold his finger to the cold window, then come back later in the day from school and find his fingerprints perfectly preserved in ice.

Each day in the cold, each month when it never got above freezing, he wondered how the sun could shine and not warm him. He would stand for as long as he could and watch his shadow move in an arc in front of his body. The cold would begin in his shoes then work its way up the inside of his legs. Then his fingers would go numb and he would be dancing in the January sun, his shadow cavorting on top of the snow.

Each morning he would have to go to the cows. There would be the smell of heat rising from their bodies mixed with the smell of hot manure, steaming below them. He shoveled, the warm odor sifting like mist into his nostrils.

Sometimes when he shoveled, he remembered the old stories about the cold. Men freezing in their sleep. Or how the water would freeze in mid-air after you threw it out of the bucket. He had heard of a woman up north who had wandered outside during a storm and fallen asleep in a snowbank. In the spring they found her cut in half by a snowplow.

After he washed the manure smell from his skin with pure castile soap, he would always go back into his room and look for a long time at the photograph of his grandfather on Rogers Lake. It was 1925. There were several men standing around a burning horse carcass on the ice. The flames rose black and thick into the February sky. The faces of the men were contorted with the sudden heat. The horse, a huge Belgian mare, had slipped hauling ice on the lake.

He remembered the way his grandfather described bringing the horse down. How he slipped the barrel into her ear as if it were a finger, he said. He had wanted to leave her on the ice, let the cold take her but his brother had insisted she be shot and burned on the spot where she failed.

So they put her down. One shot. Then Uncle Ike doused her with gasoline. Someone, perhaps his grandfather, had touched the match to the mottled hair and the horse rose in flame like a storm. When they all stepped back someone took the picture. In the right corner of the photograph near the wagon you could see small icicles beginning to form on the ice blocks piled four high, the men holding their arms to shield them from the heat.

For many nights he had a dream of walking to a black spot in the ice, poking through the remnants with a pitch fork, how the silver bridle ornaments still glistened somehow. He could hear the sound of hooves, which sounded like ice breaking up. Now, every spring, when he drifts over that spot where they did the burning, he looks down over the edge of the boat and imagines the bones resting on the bottom, the horse in full gallop, her breath streaming out like clouds of snow underwater.

ROBYN OUGHTON

CRAZY RIVER

I tried to be a nurse, but I couldn't stand touching people. That was what the tribal council agreed to pay for when I was in college: nurse, or schoolteacher.

I'm a good teacher although I can never prove it. There's only so much anyone can do teaching Indian children. One chance here is cancelled out twenty times after they leave the school grounds.

Even my first year, I was a good teacher. By good I mean my kids don't waste time fighting me. With most of them I just let them know what I want and they do it. With some I have to make fools of them first, and then they do what I want.

I was back after the summer my second year, and in the classroom only two hours, when I looked out the window at the plain and saw nothing but brown to the end of my days — brown grass, brown earth, brown walls and desks and faces — and I thought to myself — this is exactly what I thought: I'll die here.

I can remember I actually got dizzy, sick to my stomach; I had to sit down. They all looked at me. Then I thought to myself: I'll go up the Crazy River tonight with Jen. I'll go up the Crazy River tonight. And just like that I was on my feet. I was writing on the chalkboard like nothing had ever happened, turning the fraction two-thirds into a decimal with a tail as long as the future.

While we walked up the river that night I told Jen I'd try to make as much money as I could since there was nothing else for me; I would substitute teach in the white schools.

They didn't know I taught full time in Duck Creek, of course. They'd call me up and I'd say I'd be right in and then I'd call Duck Creek Reservation School and tell them I was sick. They'd have to call in my substitute, a white girl who hated teaching and the reservation but who needed to make money if she was going to keep on living with the public health nurse.

I could only keep it up for three years. Nobody found out; I just got tired: there were too many lesson plans in my head.

I tried to get permanent work in the white schools in Santo Tomas but they wouldn't take me. I really tried, too, but I shouldn't have put so much stock in it. I almost took all the extra money I'd made and spent it on a trip someplace, to Europe maybe, to Paris where if you had brown skin and black hair you can be from India, Thailand, the Yukon, or Duck Creek.

At the last minute I ran over to Jen's and handed her my bankbook. She hid it in her mattress and took out a little of the cash money she kept there and said to me: "Let's go up the Crazy River tonight."

She saved me that time, like she'd done before.

I loved Jen like we were sisters, which I think is the closest love of all. People thought we were sisters even though she looked so different from me. We're bony and narrow from this part of the country. Jen was from the north and her face was broad and flat and open like she had room for a lot in her head.

When she died it broke my heart.

Over Christmas that year she was yellow and sick as a dog. We all figured it was cirrhosis from her drinking or hepatitis from cleaning up the infirmary, but we were wrong. She had a cancer on her bowel and it went to her liver and by spring she was gone. Her body went home to her people at the Warm Springs Reservation in Oregon.

That summer was bad. I stayed in my house and slept until I couldn't stand the heat any longer, then I got up and went outside and sat on a lawn chair under a tree until I fell asleep again. I stayed there until I got cold and had to go back inside.

That was ten years ago.

Nothing much has changed for me since then, except that I go alone on Friday nights when I go up the Crazy River.

I get home from school. I wear white blouses and by the end of the day there's a brown shadow across my shoulders. I always feel like I have to shake myself off at the door. My head hurts like it always does at the end of the day. I can't wait to take all the pins out of my hair and brush out the dust. I climb into the tub and wash off the smell of children.

Then I put on a dress I never wear anyplace else. It's smooth on top, with two tiny straps, and full below. It's turquoise blue.

I walk up One Tree Canyon to the road that goes to Santo Tomas. In a mile there's a bridge high across the Crazy River. I don't cross it. On the other side is Senecu Falls, but this side is Venetia; and this spot here is called Little Venetia. And this is Jolene's place.

I walk up here in my sneakers. I always come in the back door. I leave my sneakers and my bra and whatever I brought to keep me warm on the walk in Jolene's bedroom.

I use her brush to brush out my hair. It's got the hairs of a dozen women in it: red and yellow and brown and black. Every once in a while one of us will comb it out and leave the hair in the blue glass ashtray on Jolene's dresser.

I leave my money in the jar on the windowsill. I always like to look out the window one time: the sun is setting on rocks that are every color of red. There's nothing moving except a bird or two flying small and black across the rock and out over the river far below.

Then I go into the hall, past the kitchen and the toilet and through the swinging doors.

"Larkie! Here's Larkie."

That is Eunice who's been coming to Jolene's for more years than I have. She is blond and has skin so tough she breaks the needles when they give her the test for TB.

She holds out her hand with her fingers dangling down so she can handcuff me. She smells so sweet I can only stand to be near her because I love her so much.

Just behind her is Marie. Marie's hand is on Eunice's shoulder and she's whispering in Eunice's ear. She is black and claims to come from New Orleans although Eunice told me she's really from Chicago. I love Marie less than Eunice, mainly because she complains a lot.

Eunice draws me in. She laughs and buries her face in my neck. She lifts her head to whisper in my ear. Marie hooks her chin over Eunice's shoulder so she can hear, too.

"You can't believe it, Larkie," she says. "He came after the children but they were at my mother's, so he couldn't get them. And Fritz moved back in. He told me he missed me."

Marie says, "Fritz is back and you're here? Suppose he finds out?"

"He won't. Not this time. Anything new with you, Larkie?"

"Not a thing," I tell her, as always.

We've got a lot of ground to cover in a short time; Eunice has to catch me up on everybody in the room. It helps to know how people are getting on, so that if they do something spiteful to me I'll know whether it's something I've done or just the mood they're in.

The sun comes in low through the dark green curtains and the smoke hasn't come down so far yet to make seeing hard. There are not so many people here that I can't pick out a new face or two.

"That fellow there," says Eunice, "He was with the rodeo but they laid him off. No money, but the face of an angel and hair on his chest like hay in a field. What do you think, Larkie?"

I look, and look again. "No," I say, "but who's the little one behind the cowboy?"

"Oh, he's just a baby," says Marie. "He showed his license but I think it's borrowed or stolen."

I tell them he is a sweetheart, and he is. A pretty little boy, no taller than me, with soft, light hair standing up to an electricity that's bothering no one else. He has eyelashes like a foal's and a little blond mustache and a sweet, deep cleft in his chin.

"What's his name?" I ask Eunice who knows every-one.

It's Ford, like the car. I watch him a few moments longer. He only looks out at the room when he takes a drink, and then he peeks over the rim of his glass.

I have some more hellos to exchange, including one with Jolene. Jolene and I are related through my mother's people, but because our mothers are both dead we're not sure how. Like me she's dark and little. She cuts her hair short and wears a heavy line of eye makeup that makes her look oriental. We don't have a thing to say to each other since we know each other's mood by looking. I shift my eyes to this Ford child and she knows I'm feel-ing an old fire.

"You want me to introduce?"

Jolene talks like a movie Indian for several reasons I think. She loves her friends to tease her is one; another is that she makes people who don't know her think she's stupid so she can outsmart them. Late at night by the light of the cash register with only one couple necking in the back booth and two or three of us sitting on the stools, she'll drink a shot of tequila down, lick the inside of the glass with her long, pointed tongue and say, "Sisters, let me tell you the story about a gentleman who ventured in here Friday last and for one hundred and fifty dollars bought a worthless string of shells right off my neck."

Right now she's cocked her head in the direction of this boy. I shake my head. I want to work for this one. I smile at her.

I dance a little, I drink a little. We sit in a booth, Eunice, Red Bone and myself, and tell stories about Jolene's to a newcomer named Katherine.

"Everyone knows you lose your mind when you're on this side of the Crazy River," says Red Bone. She's so dark she looks like she comes from south of the border, but she's really from Jerome, Arizona, and her daddy was half white. "What they don't know is that if you live here you grow it back in a different place."

"And where's your mind, Red Bone?" asks Eunice.

"Between my legs," she says and laughs like she's never said it before.

We tell Katherine about the night Horace Smith took his shirt off and danced to rock and roll. He asked his partner if she wasn't too hot and wouldn't she like to get undressed, too.

"Not fair," she said. "You're only showing a chest everybody's seen before while I'd be showing what I never show in public."

This was Irenie Ortiz, a big, tall woman who was about forty-five at the time. She's dead two years now from stroke.

Horace says the music isn't right. He wants something slow and pretty. So Jolene skips the jukebox over a half dozen songs until she hits a waltz and then Horace takes off his boots and his jeans and his underwear and starts dancing around the floor stark naked, all by himself, as smooth and steady as a boat on calm water.

Irenie beckons to Jolene, takes off her little jacket and hands it over. She backs up so Jolene can get the zipper on her dress. The dress falls to the floor and she steps out of it, naked except for a black garter belt and stockings and high heels. She just waits until Horace dances up to her and then off around the floor they go.

Now what was everybody else doing while this was going on? Well, they were laughing and giving a few whistles to Horace until he started to dance and then they joked him about his steps a little, but when Irenie stepped out of her dress they got quiet.

I'd say every man and woman stayed on that night. Jolene even had to put a few of them up in the barn. Everybody just had to fuck the beauty right out of themselves.

Katherine listens hard to the story. I know she'll be good to have around.

Now I'm going to get busy, so I say my excuses and move on. I go talk to Laughing Man who's standing right behind my boy. From here I can see when his drink runs down. I take a step or two closer. I wait until he looks up.

I say, "When you get your drink, will you bring me the same?"

He blinks his eyes and says, "Yes, ma'am."

I could kill for this one, I think to myself as he walks away.

He's back real quick with our drinks. I start to talk to him. His eyes open wide and he sniffs the air—I swear I can see the tips of his ears quiver.

Then I leave him for a bit, and come back again. I tease him and he looks down as if he might have come unbuttoned someplace. Then he starts to talk back.

"Where do you come from?" he wants to know.

"Why do you ask?"

"I don't know."

I tell him: "I came out of a crack in the wall. At least that's what my mother said. What do you think of that?"

"I don't know," he says.

"Where would you like me to come from?"

He paws his foot over somebody else's cigarette butt. "I only want to know what town you're from. I've been all over these parts and maybe I've been there."

"You're not old enough to have been all over these parts."

"Yes, I am," he says. "And I bet I've been to your town."

"No, you haven't, or you'd have seen me. Once you'd have seen me, you'd have stayed on a while."

He grins. "I'd have stayed a little longer. If your town has a movie house, I'd have taken you there."

"It used to," I tell him. "Where else would you take me?"

"For a walk, maybe."

I ask him: "Do you dance?"

"Not really. I'm not very fast on my feet."

"You don't have to be when the music's slow. You can just stand there."

"All right," he says.

It's always a little strange, the first time I stand up close to a man in a public place. It's the smell that knocks the wind out of me. The aftershave they slap on over the leather and horsehide, diesel fuel and gear oil; it's so thin and hopeful. I love knowing that they put the sweet stuff on just for me, but I want to tell them right then that I won't mind when they start to sweat and stink.

Then there's the first time I touch them: out of the blue it seems, and it's usually just their clothes. This boy's shirt is so new it hasn't been washed yet. It's prickly. If I were to take off my dress, like Irenie did, and dance with him, my breasts would go red with rash.

I put one hand on his shoulder and the other in his hand. His palm is hot and wet.

Then we stand and sway some while he finds the middle of my back. I don't hurry him: we can make as much time as we want. I only wonder when he'll get over his worry to his wanting.

When he moves it's so nice a move he catches me by surprise. He puts his arms up high across my back and hugs me like I'm his sister, then he hangs his hands over my hips and tugs me against him like I'm not.

Now we still have a ways to go: how fast depends on how fast he decides that he can go through with it. That's what men are needed for: plunging in when a person with any sense would hold back.

Eunice once said that if a man's little head didn't rule his big one, there'd be so little intercourse the human race would die out.

Is this Ford boy seeing red yet? Almost.

I love the thought of his sex doubled in on itself inside his tight jeans. There's something sweet about it, too: it's like a blind animal pushing out of a burrow for a feel of the sun. And I love the bruise I get on my belly from dancing with a man with a hard on. The next day I can tell the length of his inseam from the mark he leaves on my skin.

We're going to dance some more tonight—this Ford is no quick draw. He's loving each move and not hurrying for more. He likes a break, too. We go off and talk to Eunice and I introduce him to Marie and Katherine. Katherine looks him over and I know she sees what I see. The way I feel tonight, I think I'd put my hands around her throat if she were to come near him.

I've never been jealous at Jolene's before. Oh, I've been mean and there's people I can't tolerate, but I let them know it so they'll stay away from me. That's the thing about Jolene's: you spend the night with a partner and in the morning you're both gone and next week you'll be with somebody different. There've been fights, but anybody who'd mess somebody up rather than mess with somebody doesn't get invited back. There's always plenty of men and women to go around. You can get what you want. If you want a man to love-talk your sex, in a dance and a drink or two you can have old Horace Smith—he can't keep it up, but he has an agile and curious tongue.

Ford and I dance some more, and talk with the girls again. He's much easier in their company than with the men. He's got a little of the clown in him and knows he can make us laugh.

Jolene gives us the bedroom under the eaves where we can't hear anyone. The breeze blows in one triangular window and out the other, making the cotton bedspread billow up like there's more people than just us fooling around in there.

Long lovemaking makes me think of a war with no enemy. I see my forefathers running single file through the arroyo on a hot night. They are naked and wet, and sore from running a hundred miles. You can see the

whites of their eyes. When the moonlight falls to the
bottom of the cliff you can see their faces. They have no
expression. The men groan with each breath. Every piece
of them is strung tight with wanting to run another
hundred miles.

When the clock in the hall strikes three I've lost
count of myself but Ford comes for the first time. He's
fighting it, and that's the best kind. I have to push him
over the edge and for a minute he looks like a man who
has forgotten how to fly. His arms and legs jerk. He
ducks his head like he's afraid to be caught making a
terrible face, then he raises it so I can see him. He looks
like a dog with porcupine quills in his mouth and eyes.

He crawls off me and kneels with his butt in the air
and his head on the bed between his hands. He rocks like
a baby, his sex swinging against his belly.

That isn't all, but that's the idea.

I think to myself as I lie here petting his hair, I could
almost take this one home; I could take him back down
the Crazy River.

There's a new family in Duck Creek. The woman is
white and she's married to a Pennsylvania Lenape. They
have a little girl, I hear.

One afternoon I see them moving into Crescencio
Garcia's old house. There are mattresses, no beds. The
husband and a white man are pulling the mattresses out
of the pickup when I walk past on my way home from
school. The white man is Ford.

I turn my face away to the dry stream bed and
Franny One Post House's brown autumn garden.

It's no use; the next morning Ford brings the little
girl to school.

I cannot be made to blush at Jolene's, but here in the
Duck Creek Reservation School something hot and
needling crawls over me.

Ford stares at me for a moment as if I should be
very familiar to him but he cannot quite place me. Then
he begins to smile shyly like a boy does when you ask
him questions — he does not know the answers, but he

loves your attention. When I do not smile back he stops himself but keeps staring.

He talks to the little girl, then lets go of her hand.

She comes up the center aisle between the desks with her hand held out and white paper between her fingers. She is a beautiful child: she has the features and dark skin of her father; her mother has given her hair like a mahogany helmet. She glides smoothly toward me, holding up the paper for her flag.

She stares at me boldly, even tipping her head back when I come closer to take the note. It gives her name, Willa Ann, and her age, eight.

I tell her my name and point to a seat. When I look up Ford is gone.

"Why are you here?" I'm standing in the doorway of my house. I've crossed my arms against my waist. I'm glad I haven't had time to take down my hair.

"I asked where you live. I came as soon as I saw the children walking home from school."

Ford stands in front of me. He had almost bounded up the path from the road. He hardly noticed my not smiling, my blocking the doorway. His voice was happy. Now, he begins to understand that he is trespassing.

He tries to explain why he is here. His eldest sister married this Lenape. The man is a legal assistant and met Ford's sister when he took a research job in Santa Fe for one of the Pueblo councils.

Ford tells me this as if he hopes I will like his story, despite its being about people and places I do not know nor ever care to know. He pushes his hat back and wipes his forehead, then wipes his hand back and forth on his leg.

I stare at him as if I don't recognize him. I know there is not a whisper of dislike or irritation on my face.

He keeps nodding and talking. I catch a word here and there. It seems he might be staying in Duck Creek for some time, or he might be going the next day. I do not attend. I watch my trees along the road shiver their pale leaves.

He has to go. I think he waves.

I stand in my doorway long enough for the shadows of the trees to cover my feet. I stand long enough that when I go inside my clock surprises me.

I do not like my cup when I take it down for my coffee. I do not love my old stove or my clay pots. I do not want my bath. The blankets on my bed are not enough to cover me. I wish I could peel the rugs off my floor and lay them one upon the other over me. I want to cut off my hair. I will never go up the Crazy River again.

I lie on my bed until the middle of the night. Then I bathe and brush out my hair because there is nothing else to do and that is what I always do. I take my iron and smooth the blouse I washed yesterday. I polish my shoes.

At dawn I drink coffee from my cup and decide it is not such a bad cup. I walk to school.

"You have something I'm looking for," Ford says.

He has come through my open door and now stands in the middle of my kitchen.

"Can I have a coffee?" he asks.

I pour a cup and give it to him as if he is an uncle I do not know very well.

"Can I sit down?" he asks.

I could nod my head but I only point to a chair.

"You have what I'm looking for."

I turn my face to him politely.

"You are my spirit bird," he says.

"Don't talk like that to me," I tell him.

"Like what?" He is truly puzzled.

"Like poetry by primitive people. It makes you sound stupid and ingratiating."

He is surprised. "I thought I could say whatever I need to say to you."

"Oh, yes. I can tolerate almost anything."

"I don't mean it that way."

"Leave me alone. Don't talk to me."

He leans back in his chair and crosses his arms over his chest. "If this was Jolene's I could talk to you."

"It's not."

"But if it was, we would talk and dance and then go upstairs and make love."

"Not after this."

"Why not? I wanted to see you again. Seeing you here was like a miracle."

"It's not. I live here."

"I didn't know that. I wanted to talk to you again. I wanted to see you."

"I don't want to see you."

He comes to me that night. It's cold and very dark. The only way to tell the sky from the earth is to see where the stars stop.

I am sitting in my bedroom, on my windowsill, with my back to the night. Ford comes up from the road. The window is low enough that he can lean against me. His chest is hot against my back; his head bows on my shoulder. He does not touch me with his hands.

I think these things: I can give in tonight and he will love me. Later he will abuse me. In time I will need his abuse, but he will tire of giving it and leave me.

Or I can fight him, and our lovemaking will be exquisitely painful. Tomorrow when he comes I will cling to him and beg him to stay longer. Soon he will come less and less often. We will always fight before we make love. The ending will drag on for months, both of us too tired to stop.

I say his name. I tell him that we will not make love tonight, but that if he would like to stay for a while just as he is outside my window, he is welcome. During the day he may come visit me and talk with me, if I am not occupied with other things. I do not want sex with him for a time, I don't know how long. He will know when I'm ready. In the meantime he is free to come and he is free to go away.

Ford is silent for a while then he says, "What about Jolene's? Could we go to Jolene's?"

No, I tell him. I'm not going to Jolene's for a time. I don't know how long.

"Oh," he says, and then: "May I kiss you hello and goodbye? Can I give you a hug?"

I'm amazed he wants to know more. "You may kiss me on the cheek," I say. "You may not embrace me."

He kisses me on the cheek when he leaves.

The next night he stands outside my window and howls like a wolf. He is drunk. I stand deep in my bedroom waiting for him to go away.

He shouts at me: "I hate the smell of your skin. I hate your hair. I hate the smell of your sex. If my mother knew I'd stuck my prick into the dirt between your legs she would spit on me."

I close the shutters. I go to each window and close the shutters.

I hear him wailing. He wants me to let him in. He will die if he cannot see me. After a time he goes away.

But he does not leave Duck Creek. He comes every evening to see his sister and his niece and then he comes to visit me.

One evening he brings wine and I grill lamb for him over an open fire. We sit outside and drink and eat and play poker until it's too dark to see the cards. He asks to stay the night and I say no. He tries to hold me before he goes and I say no.

He gets a job in Santa Tomas.

One night I answer the door and it is his niece come to see me. She has a note that says Ford telephoned and cannot come until tomorrow.

I ask Willa Ann if she would like a soda.

She sits at my table. She's wearing a long, deep purple dress. She bows her head to sip from the glass without lifting it off the tabletop. With her hair solid around her face she is a dark, hooded presence, but when she looks up all I see are her child's eyes.

"I can't come to school Monday," she says. "I'm going to live in Santo Tomas with Mommy. I get to stay with Daddy Saturdays but there's no school on Saturday so I can't see you."

"Would you like to come visit me here?" I ask her.

"Yes, I think that would be good sometimes."

I know what she means.

When Ford comes the next day I don't say anything about his sister and her husband and the child, but he does. He talks about the situation for a long time and then I join in.

After we eat he tells me he likes his job in Santo Tomas. He has an apartment there and he says that he would like me to see it. He says he would like to get some chairs first but after that I could come visit him. I say, we'll see.

EUGENE KRAFT

THE YEAR THE DEVIL CAME

The Kansa, who also called themselves the Ordinary People, did not notice when Kansas became a state in 1861, nor did they notice other momentous or non-momentous years. They sang songs of the Great Rain Year, the Year of the Flying Brown Eaters, the Year of the Windiest Winter. The Great Rain Year and the Year of the Windiest Winter came next to each other, which was normal, for the Ordinary People know God and the Devil are close together. In fact, many of their doctors say God and the Devil are the same and are called What Happened. The songs of God and the Devil ride together over the flat land. They ride there still, clearly, lasting longer even than the Ordinary People; listen, in the middle of a hot summer day, looking at the heat waves above the waving wheat. It was altogether ordinary, then, that the Year of the Birth of the Most Normal One should also be the Year the Devil Came.

And the Whitmores also came early in the spring of 1893, from a part of the country that was hilly and green and had fences of stone. It does not matter what part of the country it was, because they came to Kansas, which turned people into something new, since there is nothing to look at. The Whitmores failed in the green, hilly

country with its fences of stone and had come to succeed. They seemed to feel destined or different as the
train and then the wagon climbed higher and higher to
the table next to the sky. It was a table tilted downward,
with the Great Plains rising to the west. The Whitmores
kept going until they were at the very top, where everything was flat below and there was nothing above. Then
they stopped.

There was absolutely nothing to look at. The land
was totally flat; there was nothing else to say about it.
The sky covered them like a dome; they were so close to
it they might almost have touched it, and yet they were
very far away from it. But they did not notice these
things because they had come to succeed, and the land
and sky must be matched to the determination in their
minds.

The Whitmores' first nine months on the land were
so terrible it was not even a time—it became a dream impossible to think about, impossible later even to recall.
They were seventy miles west of Fort Hays, which was
the limit, as far as they could go. Before they got to their
land, Whitmore decided to get one hundred acres of
wheat, corn, and oats under cultivation that year. In a
few months the figure had shrunk to fifty. When winter
came they recognized that a more realistic goal would be
to stay alive.

They stayed alive, believing that to be a realistic
goal. They had not had enough time to build a sod
house, only enough to dig away at the one small sloping
hill that marked their land and to stick a tin chimney
through the top of it. Whitmore, Genevieve, and the two
boys lived in a dugout the size of one small room. They
had rabbit, badger, and buffalo to eat.

In Fort Hays there had not been enough plows,
enough harness, enough horses, or enough homesteaders.
Whitmore decided there was no point in risking further
death by going for supplies. Besides, he had no money.

One thing that came with the blizzards was mud;
another was horse manure in front of the dugout. Before
the winter storms came, it had been a foot deep, because

there was no other place to tie the horses. Genevieve's skirt was caked with filth up to her knees. The mud was almost as bad in the dugout itself, though, and the blankets they slept in were as hard as canvas. The boys' fingernails became so caked with dried mud they could not pare them. There was no lye soap and the creek was frozen over. Soon they ceased to wash their faces. They lay all day and all night, while the blizzards raged, with nothing to do, nothing to say, nothing to think. In early December they ran out of kerosene, a month later out of candles. They had no potatoes, no cornmeal, no coffee. They had no whiskey.

At first they took care of their eliminative needs by going out singly onto the prairie. As the weather got worse they paid no attention to these refinements and soon their own wastes mingled with those of the horses in front of the dugout.

But the one characteristic which separated the Whitmores from other families was their absolute unity. When the family climbed down off the train in St. Louis, people noticed it. The four stood in a circle and talked only to each other on the railway platform. Their attitude may have implied less hostility or hatred than simple lack of interest. But something had happened to them back in that green, gardenlike country — they may have come less of their own volition than by compulsion. They came to Kansas guilty. And they all looked very much alike, much more so than most families. The males dressed identically, in hats with round crowns to them, collarless gray shirts, dark coats, and dark trousers. Genevieve had the sharpest nose of the four, but under her dirty black bonnet she looked only at her men. And they all looked at St. Louis, at Kansas City, at the hills and plains slowly moving outside the train window not as things in themselves, but only for information, signals.

At night in the dugout there was absolutely no privacy. But there was none in the daytime either. And when the blizzards came, it was always night. Whitmore had not had time to build a window in the front of the dugout; the snow came too quickly.

Under such circumstances, human beings become animals, dark and dirty beasts. At the end of the March, Genevieve found she was pregnant.

They might be rich, Whitmore figured, rich already, he had a homestead deed to eight hundred acres, which he had registered to himself under his three Christian names he could claim were three imaginary brothers if the law came this far (the law never came this far). But he quickly learned that though you may be actually rich, you can still starve. So when April came, he told his wife and the boys, "Build a house. Make it straight and strong and make the walls thick. I'll plow and plant." The boys and Genevieve had never even thought about building a house. But *he* had never thought of breaking Kansas soil.

The baby came in September, one of the boys holding Genevieve's legs, one holding her arms. (Whitmore knew birthing was women's work.) And shortly after the baby came, the Grasshopper Plague came. At first they thought it was a thunderstorm, a bad one, and they ran for the dugout. Then the grasshoppers started falling. In an hour the corn and maize were completely gone. Later they found some of the trees down by the river had their branches broken off by piles of grasshoppers sitting on them. Genevieve sat in the dugout, shaking, not from the disaster, but from the feel of the wet, slimy insects on her skin. None of them looked at Whitmore.

They had a little wheat. But what if the Plague came again next year?

The baby made happy, gurgling sounds.

But on a trip to Fort Hays later that week (the Whitmores had decided to stay, because they had come as far as they could), Whitmore heard of some Russians down by the Osage River who had a different kind of wheat, Turkey Red, they called it, and also winter wheat. He rode down to the Osage and managed to borrow a wagon.

And the next winter was worse than the preceding one — later the family learned it was the worst winter in the history of the state. The Whitmores felt free, though, because something seemed to be conspiring against them. At such a time, they seemed to know all you have to do is stay alive. That itself is winning.

And on a clear December day in Fort Hays, they learned about a new kind of wire: "barbed wire." It would keep everything off their land that was not theirs and keep everything on that was. Later, years later, the Whitmores marked the coming of the barbed wire as the best thing that ever happened to them. They did not know why they strung some up. To keep their three cows near the dugout? Something else could so easily destroy the animals. But they liked the look and idea of the wire.

As he dug the holes for the fence posts, .Whitmore worked murderously. He felt he would not be surprised to see blood rise from the post holes he made in the earth. And he slammed the posts into the holes as though driving a thick spear into his enemy's chest.

Great exertion was needed to stretch the wire. As they tightened it over the buffalo grass, all three Whitmore men were thinking, "Now it's mine. Now this corner is *mine*. Now. *This part is. Mine.*"

That night, by the light of the dim lamp, Whitmore grew a little expansive. "From the beginning of the world," he said loudly, "to now, nobody's touched this land. It's been no use to anybody. From Adam to Moses to. . . ." his large gesture swept toward the baby, "but we're goin' to *put it to use*."

They decided to call the baby Aaron Lee, because Moses was Whitmore's first name.

"Hey!" Whitmore would shout, his face close to the infant's, "Who're you workin' fer anyway? After you come we get nothin' but trouble. First the grasshoppers. Then the bad winter. You workin' fer us or agin' us?"

Oddly, the baby was not frightened by his father's roars or his harsh laughter, and since it did not draw back or cry at these sounds, the Whitmores began to wonder if it was deaf or blind. But its sight turned out to be normal; it was fascinated by the fire and the firelight on Whitmore's pocket watch. And its sense of hearing seemed abnormally acute. Even in its first year it loved the sound of the wind and lifted its arms when the strong plains winds blew. But since its head was so large, its arms and legs shorter than normal, Whitmore gradually avoided looking at the child.

At first Genevieve worried a little about leaving the baby hour after hour while she worked with the men, but there was no alternative. However, Aaron Lee never seemed to mind. They never unlatched the door at the end of the day without hearing his singing and crowing. The two boys played with him all evening until, suddenly exhausted, he fell asleep and never woke until morning. Genevieve worked all evening, glancing over her shoulder at her three children. She didn't smile — it hurts a determined woman to smile — but at such times she seemed to be reaching out her arms and drawing gold to her breast. She might need it later.

Whitmore never smiled either — he never had. He always spoke to the baby harshly, but with numerous and ironic intent. "What, we've been out workin' all day and you just lay there. Think you're the Prince or something?" "Hey, you little Devil," he would say, "Plant any timber today?" "You little Devil, you're completely worthless," he would say, pushing his face down to the baby's. "Can't even plant a garden, like a woman." He never once touched the baby. Enough food and shelter after a Kansas winter drove people mad, but the baby got them through; it made everything a little comical.

In the next years the Whitmores gained even more; then still more. Kansas was working for them.

The baby grew a little — he didn't grow quickly they noticed — and his large eyes became even larger. He didn't talk either, and it was about time for him to begin doing so. One day Whitmore drove to Fort Hays with one of the boys (they were gone three days) and when they came back they had 160 acres more of land, registered under the name of Aaron Lee Whitmore. If the authorities came this far (no authorities ever came this far) Whitmore could say that Aaron Lee was his brother who had run off to Texas and left the land deed in title to him.

The baby made high, singing noises when his father said to him, "Well, Little Devil, you got a quarter of a section to your name!"

When they came back to the house at sunset, covered with sweat covered with dust covered with sweat, they could hear the baby singing and chirruping on the ground by the door. "Aralee! Aralee!" the boys would shout, and the baby would begin singing even louder. In the gray and brown landscape he seemed to feel a great affinity for color, and since sunflowers furnished the only strong color, he would crawl toward them, pull down the high stems and draw the blossoms to him. Wherever the baby was, there were sunflowers. When he had pulled many of them down, he liked to make a large, loose pile and roll in the blooms. Genevieve had never noticed the sunflowers (her hands were so chapped she covered them with pig's lard; she didn't notice sunflowers), but now she tore off some of the blooms and put them in a tin can in the house. They drew the Whitmores' eyes like the sun does, after a long series of cloudy days. The baby was outside when she did this. When he crawled inside the dusty house, covered with dust himself, he saw the shining sunflowers and began yelping happily and crawled into his mother's lap.

"What, ye little Devil!" Whitmore shouted. "Like flowers, do ye? Ye a woman or a man? What are ye, anyway?"

"Hey! What are ye?" the boys' shout echoed their father's.

The boys laughed and picked up the baby from Genevieve's lap.

By hiring some of what he called "vermin" in Fort Hays, farmers who had failed, ones who had not had sense enough to plant winter or Turkey Red wheat, Whitmore was able to sell buffalo bones and horns on the land surrounding his spread (it was a spread now) for several hundred dollars. He told the vermin he would not pay them until they had sold three hundred dollars of buffalo bones and horns. So the men shot buffalo for several days. The acres surrounding Whitmore's were littered with the stinking garbage of dead buffalo.

But the baby did not talk. It was their one failure. He was still comical and as agile as a rat, but that didn't make him normal. Once, at the day's end, they found him perched on the roof of the house, right above the door like a statue on a church, crowing and singing. Or he might have been the figurehead on a ship, a ship sailing through the waves of grass and the light, dry air. The baby had torn sunflower blossoms off and tied them around his neck and stuck them in his hair. The Whitmores stood and laughed at him.

That year was a bad one for the Kansa, and, as Whitmore said, they were too much like animals to plan for the future. So he drove to their territory and brought back a wagonload of them. In two months—it was howling a blizzard when the Kansa stretched the last strand—his entire spread was surrounded by shining nettles of wire. Whitmore then told the Indians to kill everything inside his fences, except the cattle. They seemed reluctant to do this, but after he told them he would give them no wheat or corn if they did not, they shot the animals.

"Whee! Whee!" chanted the baby in a high voice.

The Whitmores had a granary now, standing beside the barn. We're ahead of everybody within a hundred miles of Fort Hays, Whitmore thought.

But Aralee had begun to irritate him. The rest of the family disregarded the baby, though. The boys talked about the horse they would buy themselves on their next trip to town, Genevieve thought about a stove. If we can do so much in just three short years, how much more can we do in six years?

But all of them gradually realized that the baby could not walk or talk at all. There seemed to be something wrong with its head, which was much too large. Because it only crawled, Genevieve had sewn a sort of skirt for it, and this made it look even odder. Also, with so much crawling, its feet and legs became twisted. It looked so

odd Genevieve had difficulty forcing herself to bathe it,
and eventually it went for months without a bath. It
looked like a fish; its feet were like fins. It crawled
through the dust as though it were crawling on the
bottom on the river.

They didn't bother to cut its hair, either; the long
blond curls made it resemble a girl (if it resembled anything). Now, every day when the others were out working their sixteen-hour day, the baby crawled down to
the creek just outside Whitmore's land, where there was
a grove of cottonwoods. When they used to come in for
supper, the boys would hear it singing in various high
tones and would always call to it. Now they no longer
did so. They were afraid somebody might visit them and
see it.

"It's bad luck havin' it around here," one of the boys
growled one night.

No one answered him.

The Whitmores gained even more in the next two
years. Whitmore never talked; he just listened. But he
always seemed to know when one of the neighbors was
pulling up stakes and selling off cheap, or when one of
them needed something badly and he could ask twice the
price of what he was selling. The barbed wire encircled
even more land.

Once, on a Sunday, one of the boys found it with
about a dozen Indians, down by the creek. The boy had
a moment of terror, until he remembered the Kansa traveled west at this time, for their hunting, and they were
not warriors. Though he was still frightened, none of the
Indians paid any attention to him. They were sitting on
the ground, watching Aralee, who was singing in his
usual way. The baby had climbed onto a low branch and
was laughing and chirruping. When his brother made a
movement to take Aralee away, a dozen very quiet eyes
turned to him. Later, when Whitmore came down, the
Indians had gone and the baby was playing among dust
and sunflowers.

As the family gained more, the individual members
began to look different from one another; the family lost

its extraordinary conformity. The boys began to exhibit different personalities, the elder to become interested in property, like his father, the younger to spend his free time hunting. Genevieve ceased to wear only black. Whitmore went to the barber in Fort Hays and had his hair cut and his beard trimmed.

In the first years the family had spoken with its eyes. Now it spoke with its mouth. The words "prices," "money," and "saleable" came fluently to their lips, and gradually they began to forget the baby for long periods of time. It seemed to eat and sleep regularly, but that did not make it a success. It was as cheerful as ever, though; because it showed no sign of knowledge of the others' attitude, the others felt no guilt. It seemed to know that they did not want it to be seen around the house, so it spent each day down by the cottonwoods. The only sign of depression on the baby's part occurred on winter days when there was no sun, and no sunflowers, of course. It uttered no sounds of distress, but it stayed all day behind the house, its eyes wide. Genevieve never bathed it now.

"An animal," one of the boys said.

"Dirty as a hog," the other said.

They themselves began to stay much cleaner than they had been. In the evenings, when Whitmore was in the house, the baby stayed in its corner, as far as possible from its father's chair. Whitmore never talked to the child now. He didn't know what to do with it. Once he said, "Can't even kill it, like a chicken."

It was a reminder of their earlier failures.

They had a hired man now, who got drunk most summer evenings. He had a banjo and would go down by the river and sing and play. He knew only four or five songs, songs everybody knew, which he played over and over:

> *And here is the tale of Sweet Betsy from Pike;*
> *She crossed the wild country with her lover, Ike.*

When evening came the baby always crawled down to the trees and waited for the banjo. It sang in its usual

high-pitched tones, until the hired man arrived. Then it
was silent.

> *With one spavined horse and an old lame hound dog;*
> *An old Shangai rooster and one spotted hog.*

Everybody knew the song. One of the amusements
at church picnics and quilting bees was to make up new
verses to it:

> *And that was the year that they broke up the clods;*
> *They killed off the game and they banished the gods.*
> *The endin' of love, the beginnin' of hate:*
> *The year that the Devil came into the state.*

The baby was gone for days now; the Whitmores
may or may not have been aware of the fact. They could
not bear the sight of him, he smelled so bad and looked
so odd. They began calling him "the idiot." Several times
more they discovered the peaceful Kansa down by the
creek, listening to him. Sometimes only one or two of
the Indians were there, listening to his singing.

Finally they did not see him for a long time. "Well,
go on out and see where it is!" Whitmore exploded, one
evening. The boy was not by the river and did not seem
to be anywhere else. No one said anything. A few weeks
later, one night, Whitmore said, "We'll say it drowned in
the river."

A long time after, all four of the family were sitting on
the porch of their white house. It was Sunday afternoon.
A large group of Kansa, heading west, came up to the
edge of the farm and paused by the glittering wire, looking at the Whitmores, as they always did. The Indians
had a few horses, but only one of them was riding. The
others were using the horses to drag packs covered with
buffalo hides.

The one riding was a dwarf with a large head, large
blue eyes, and long, sun-colored hair which came down
further than his shoulders. Because his legs were so short
and stunted, two men walked beside his horse, balancing
him with ropes tied around his waist. Just in front of the

dwarf's horse walked an old man with many feathers in his bonnet. But the dwarf was a much more brilliant sight than the chief. He sat on a red blanket and had bright red and blue clothes. There were yellow feathers and animals tails sewn onto the cloth on his shoulders. His bridle was decorated with bright feathers, and he wore many necklaces of beads and bright stones. There were some sort of yellow flowers twined in his hair.

The Indians looked at the Whitmores for a long time, without saying anything. They then slowly moved on toward the Higher Plains.

"Normal One," said Chief Two-Horses, "Why is there water on your face?"

"Why do you ask a foolish question, Chief Two-Horses?" asked Normal One. "I am sad."

"Do you know those people?" asked the Chief.

"Yes," said Normal One. "They are my father and my mother and my brothers."

"Then I understand."

"No. It is not for that. But that they are so strange."

"They *seemed* very strange," said Chief Two-Horses. "Now. Why do they have that shining, pronged wire on the land? It is the ugliest thing I ever saw."

"Yes. It is horrible. It is straight from the Devil," said Normal One.

"They are human beings, those people," he continued, "but they are very sick. Or too strange to understand."

"But that horrible wire," said the Chief. "Why do they have it? It keeps everything out. Now. What is the reason?"

"I am not from the Devil or from hell. So I do not know."

"This is amazing," said the Chief. "We name you Most Normal One, Great Middle-of-the-Road, Great Average One, because you know so much. But you do not know this."

"No."

The group went on for a long time. The Kansa looked at the horizon and at the sky.

"Anyway," said Chief Two-Horses, "No one, however normal, knows everything."

CHRIS SPAIN

LET THE BABIES KEEP THEIR HEARTS

I hunker in the alfalfa, in the shade of my split-axle dump truck, in a daydream that's all tropical downpours. I'm chewing at a stalk of volunteer barley, working up spit enough so I won't choke myself to death on the dust Harold kicks up every time he swings by. It's bone dry out here, and if it weren't for center pivots this crappy land would be dead. I can't believe the idiot farmer who's having us take a third cutting off the pitiful stuff. It's like taking part in a massacre. No way it'll make it through winter.

Harold is making one last sweep with his excuse for a hay swather, an old nameless thing he's dragging with a yellow John Deere, and it comes to me that nothing looks stupider than a yellow John Deere. When he shuts down I gun my truck under the unloading chute of his hopper. Harold's wearing a pair of goggles and a red bandanna and looks like a lost tank commander. He takes off the goggles and looks at me, his face twisted up the way it gets when he's been thinking.

"I don't understand how they can kill babies and take the hearts out of them just so's they can save a baboon," is what Harold finally says.

It takes me about two beats to figure this out. Harold's been reading *Newsweek* again, and as per usual he's got the story all ass-backwards.

"It's probably not just any baboon," I say, thinking Jesus will kill me for this one. "It's probably a space baboon or a special smart one they're saving."

"But killing babies," says Harold. "I mean whose babies are they?"

"Sure they're not regular babies," I say. "They must be brain dead already, or sick, or maybe they aren't even American."

I leave Harold worrying about his heart-robbed babies and hook it for the mill. It's my last run of the day and I'm feeling a little ragged. Great Western operates seven days a week, twenty-four hours a day, and we drivers work twelve-hour shifts. Every two weeks we switch from days to nights or vice-versa, and put in an eighteen hour swing. Tomorrow I'm swinging from days to nights. There must be something illegal about it; I keep going to sleep at the wheel and ending up on cornfields and irrigation ditches. The mill only shuts down when it rains, and it's been blue skies since the day we started cutting. Spend the best part of my brains wishing for a monsoon.

I wheel into the mill yard, back the truck up to the dumping bin, leave the dumping to Mike, who works my opposite shift and shares my truck, and head for the truck barn to punch out. The truck barn has two work bays, a wall full of tools, a workbench, a coffeepot, a time clock, our time cards, and a "Number of Days Without an Accident" sign which is in double digits for the first time this summer.

Gus is at the workbench, making coffee, but he's forgotten to put the pot underneath the filter and the coffee is streaming down on the hot plate, hissing and steaming, and spilling to the floor.

"Shit, shit, shit," says Gus, running one way and then the other, grabbing for something to catch the coffee with. This is not atypical Great Western driver behavior.

"Good thing you aren't an airline pilot," I say.

The only way to stay alive around this place is to inhale speed, legal or otherwise, and right now Gus looks to be operating about thirty feet off the ground. My own hands started shaking the Fourth of July.

"Shit, shit, shit," says Gus, burning himself as he sticks an oil drip pan underneath the streaming coffee.

I punch out and head for Fort Collins, taking Highway 14 so I won't have to pass the sheep feedlots. Fourteen is not the fastest way but there's nothing in the world that smells worse to me than sheep shit. I'd rather eat a cow shit sandwich than step in sheep shit with my work boots on.

Take the back door through town, vault the railroad tracks, and pass the gherkin factory. A guy once fell into the vats and they didn't find him for ten years. They looked all over for him and finally decided he'd left his wife, run off with another woman. Nobody imagined he was getting pickled for life.

I stop at Avogadro's Number for a #4 Gobbley-Gook, which is what happens to a turkey if he walks through a kitchen combine and gets lettuce and mayo tossed on him. I used to eat here when I went to college one time. I lived on the third floor of a high rise dormitory and we called ourselves the Pukes. We even had a Puke cheer. This one dumb shit Ag major went to a party on the tenth floor and tilted his beer back too far and fell out the window. That's about all I remember.

I down my sandwich and head west toward Rist Canyon. Sue Ellen, my sometimes girlfriend, and Melinda own a little horse-riding ranch ten miles up and they rent me their used-to-be potato barn for fifty dollars a month. That includes sharing the bathroom and the kitchen in the main house. I'm still not sure who's getting the better end of the deal. The Rist is a little canyon I would've called a gulch. Following the curves in the road I move in and out of shadows, and with my window open I feel that the darker air is already cold. This summer's been so dry and after the melt was gone the creek just altogether disappeared. All that's left are these lonely-looking round stones.

The girls have stereo speakers strung out to the barn and Willie yelling up the canyon. Couple of tough guys these girls. They're in the corral with Bo and Blackie, circled around a fire. Bo is Melinda's black lab, and Blackie is an albino Shetland pony. They're about halfway through a case of Buckhorns, which tells you something about the slimness of the horse-riding business.

"Well if it ain't old Manual Labor," says Sue Ellen.

Sue Ellen is blonde as California, has boy-shoulders, and has shit-kickers on the end of her Baja California legs. I give her a kiss.

"Hey," says Melinda.

"Don't say that word," I say.

I sit in the dirt and lean back against the corral wood.

"Man alive," I say. "This is a hurting pup you're looking at."

"You ought to quit that job," says Melinda. "You're working yourself to death."

I call her Muy Linda in my heart. She's a barrel racer, and calf roper, a mountain climber of El Capitan forwards and backwards, and she's got the most beautiful scarred kneecaps you've ever seen. I don't know, maybe it's my own kneecaps as a boy that I'm after, but when she wears those knee-ragged jeans, and I see those white scars, God Jesus. I shouldn't be thinking like this.

She throws me a Buckhorn.

"Drink," she says.

The sun crashes into the Mummy range and Melinda grabs a rotten ponderosa pine fence post and throws it on the fire. The wind is blowing from the Divide so we sit together on the west side of the corral to keep the smoke out of our faces. We finish the Buckhorns and Melinda digs for some Mad Dog.

"No sir," I say. "This kid's driving a swing shift tomorrow."

"Manual, Manual," says Sue Ellen. "Tomorrow's tomorrow."

That Mad Dog gets us elevated. We crank the music and start dancing like wild horses. I dance with Bo, and Sue Ellen tries to ride Blackie. Melinda is flamed-up and when the radio comes out with a grinding beat she starts shaking her hips and circling the fire.

"Do us a rain dance," I say.

Melinda tears her shirt off so fast that a button pops to the dust. Bo and I stop to watch. She holds her arms way out from her body and moves them back and forth like a Tahiti woman, her leg and arm bone shadows doing a broken puppet dance on the corral railings. Her bra is black and it barely holds her in as she shimmies and kicks up dirt. Sue Ellen stomps beer cans and I Yahoo, but when Melinda takes her bra off I say to myself, Pedro, you better sit down. She has this tiny waist that her jeans barely grab on to, and you can see her bottom three sets of ribs perfectly. Above that it's just acres of Annapurnas, Kilimanjaros, and K-2's which she shakes for me and Sue Ellen and Bo and Blackie and all the stars in the sky.

"If that don't make it rain," I say. "It ain't raining."

"Why didn't y'all join me?" says Melinda, getting cold pretty quick and getting her shirt back on.

" 'Cause I don't got nothing like you do," says Sue Ellen.

She's right about that. I'm a witness. Her chest looks like it's been gone over three times with a tandem field plane.

"I don't have nothing either," I say.

We make pillows out of feed sacks and say we're going to watch for shooting stars. It takes about thirty seconds for a big monster one to go plowing past.

"Make a wish, make a wish," says Melinda.

"I'm wishing for a gully washer," I say. "I'm wishing for one telephone call to God, I'll say, Jack, time to drowned the world again. Forty days and forty nights and then some."

"I'm wishing for a Marlboro man," says Melinda. "Some guy to come by so I can tie him up and talk French to him."

God Jesus.

"I wish I had tits like Melinda," says Sue Ellen. "But we got to wait for another star 'cause if you say your wish out loud it doesn't count."

When I wake up the fire is cold. Melinda comes around but Sue Ellen is dead to the world.

"Who's going to carry her?" I ask.

"She's your girlfriend."

Sue Ellen won't let go of her feed-sack pillow. I put her over my shoulder.

"Help, my back," I say. "This girl's all choice."

Melinda holds open the doors. I hear Sue Ellen's head smack against something on the way through the kitchen and then I drop her on her bed, feed sack and all. When I turn around Melinda already has her shirt off again.

I feel like I'm thinking with some kind of extinct dinosaur brain. Don't sleep with the help? That's not it. Don't sleep with the landlord? That might be it. Don't sleep with your sometimes girlfriend's best girlfriend? That's it. She drops her pants and I see those kneecaps.

"I'm going to bed," says Melinda. "You think it's too cold, you can stay the night in the house."

If I think it's too cold?

When my Timex Triathlon watch alarm goes wa, wa, wa, I think maybe somebody's let a kicking mule loose inside of my head. It keeps on wa, wa-ing and I think that that's what I get for living up a canyon with screaming mountain women. On about the last three wa, wa, wa's I put together that I'm not in my potato barn, that I'm not in my bed, and that I'm not in Sue Ellen's bed either. Oh shit. I open my eyes. This doesn't look familiar. This is a most unfamiliar landscape. Then I realize I'm face to kneecaps with the most beautiful kneecaps in the world. Oh shit. Oh shit. I don't even want to right myself to get the big picture but I do. Oh shit, oh shit, oh shit. Melinda's naked but for her boots.

I cover the evidence with a blanket, lift the blanket for one last look, God Jesus, dive into my jeans which are green and stiff with alfalfa juice, and bang into about four walls stumbling for the bathroom. When I turn the light on I wish I hadn't. I see Sue Ellen's black stockings strung over the shower curtain like dead king snakes, I see her panties and bras hanging on the drying line like shot and skinned animals, and then I see me.

I wash myself from the armpits up, on the way through the kitchen grab a packet of Instant Breakfast, and when I stumble outside I nearly brown in my green pants.

"Yikes," I say.

Standing right at the back door, blowing big puffs of steam from each nostril, is Blackie looking like a midget horse-ghost.

"Here I slave my guts out for the likes of you," I say. "And for thanks you scare the shit out of me?"

It's nine thousand degrees below zero and my hair nearly freezes in the fifty feet between the house and my truck. I jump the truck into reverse and I'm doing about five miles an hour when I ka-whamo the shit out of something. Shit, shit, shit.

I get out to look. It's still too dark to see. It's Sue Ellen's Toyota. I feel with my hand along the side of the Toyota to know what's happened. Just behind the front wheel well I've pushed in the body metal a good six inches. For about one trillionth of a second I consider telling her, but then my better judgment kicks in. No reason to ruin her day before the sun is up. No reason to end my life either.

At the bottom of the Rist, out of the canyon shadow, the road rises hard to the left where I once dumped my bike when I was in high school. This girl I was in love with was on the back. She burned the shit out of her leg on the muffler. It was springtime. Got caught in some sand left over from winter. Every time I see her she brings up her opinion that I ruined her

chances for Miss Colorado, Miss America, and beyond. I
left some skin on this corner myself.

One look at the sky tells me Melinda's rain dance
didn't do any good. Not my wishing either. I turn south
and swing past Horsetooth to check the water. I heard
on the radio-news that the level's the lowest it's been
since they built the dam. The long narrow gleam coming
off the reservoir hurts my head. Some guy was once
water-skiing and he skied right through a ball of rattlesnakes. He was dead before he got wet.

I pull into the mill yard, park, and carefully put my one
foot in front of the other one over to the truck barn,
heading for the coffee.

"You chasing parked cars?" asks Mike.

I'm concentrating on making my hands pour a cup
of coffee. I shake the battalion-sized bottle of aspirin
over the mug until I count enough splashes that I think
it might help.

"How about the new *Newsweek?*" asks Mike.

Beginning of summer I got a subscription to *Newsweek* to celebrate getting my job. I keep them stashed
under the driver's seat so I'll have something to read if
the mower breaks or if the mill shuts in. Mike didn't
associate with me for all of June just 'cause I was reading
Newsweek. Then he started reading it himself.

I try to answer him, tell him to go away already or
something, but it turns out that my mouth isn't working
yet. I've still got half a dry Instant Breakfast stuck in my
throat.

"I read that last one four times," says Mike.

I look at the mug I'm drinking out of. It says on it,
Kiss me, I'm confused. Un-huh.

Feeling like I'm in some pretty thick ground fog, I
check the air in the tires and put a couple quarts of oil in
the engine. It's lousy death-for-sure equipment they got
us driving, so I do everything I can in the way of pre-
ventative maintenance. Gus comes staggering in looking
for his truck too. There's three of us driving trucks on
each shift to keep a steady flow of hay arriving at the

mill. Working my shift driving trucks are Gus and Chet, and goombay Harold is out in the field on the tractor. Harold's only been with us a month. He hired on after some other tractor-driving Harold stuck his hand in the mower's chopping box without disconnecting the PTO. When the stone he was trying to unstick came unstuck, the blades started turning again. I'm sure glad I wasn't there to see that mess.

When I get to the field Harold is already waiting with a load. He climbs up in the cab to get out of the chill and I pour him a cup of coffee.

"Gosh I hope not," says Harold.

"Gosh I hope not what?" I ask.

"Gosh I hope they aren't taking the hearts out of just any old baby."

This, I figure out, is more of yesterday's conversation.

"Don't you ever talk to anybody at home?" I ask.

Operating close to brain-dead across the morning, I try to hyperventilate myself to stay conscious and out of the bar ditches. I keep getting last night flashbacks that land on my brain like bricks. I try to chase 'em from my head before I see anything bad, but it's ugly. There's me kissing and declaring eternal love to a pair of kneecaps; there's me saying, Let's play mountain climbing, you're Mount Everest, and my lips are Sir Edmund Percival Hillary and his faithful Sherpa Tenzing; there's me saying, Sherpa Tenzing, help me, help me, oxygen, I think I got a case of high altitude sickness; there's me saying, Oh, no, Sir Edmund, it appears we have ascended the wrong massif, look at that other one, it's taller, we got to do it all over; there's me again saying, Sure, when Melinda asks if she should get her lariat so we can really rodeo. There's her saying, One guy used to take down the bull by biting him on the lip. There's a demonstration of that. It gets worse. Be lucky not to come out of this a steer.

*   *   *

When I'm making what seems like about my twenty millionth run, I see another bird-shit yellow truck coming the other way. Whenever Gus and I pass each other on the road we play a game of halfhearted chicken to wake ourselves. At four telephone poles we cross into each other's lane, and at two telephone poles we cross back. This time I switch lanes no problem and so does Gus. Then I cross back. Now we're closing at about one hundred twenty-five and Gus is not moving back. At one telephone pole his truck starts crabbing for the other side but it looks highly unlikely to me that it will make it. Gus's bugged out eyes are getting closer and closer and I'm wishing for a seat belt. With a six-foot drop running both sides of the road I bury my brakes and get ready for dead. This will solve a lot of problems. The last thing I see before I close my eyes is my own scared-shitless reflection in Gus's windshield, and then our mirrors tick.

At the mill I go shaky-legged looking for Joe Bill, our occasional foreman. I find him cleaning out the gravel screens. Joe Bill pretty much put the ug in ugly. He's got tobacco-stained baby teeth, he's round as a barrel, and on his feet he has these little itty-bitty Nacona boots that don't look like they could give him any kind of balance.

"Say," I say. "You wouldn't happen to know if this Gus is trying to kill himself, would you?"

"Why?" says Joe Bill.

"That pud-knocker just about head-oned me," I say.

"Every one of you idiots deserves to get killed dead," says Joe Bill.

Gus comes wheeling back into the yard and parks alongside the truck barn. I take a long mean look at him but he looks too sick to be mad at. He's all white in the face and looking like he wants to puke. I wait for him to get out of his truck but he doesn't so I walk over.

"You not feeling too good?" I ask.

"We almost nearly got killed," says Gus.

"Telling me, you dumb bastard," I say.

Gus gets out of his truck and wobbles toward his front tire. He used to be a pretty good basketball player until he got thrown off the team for drinking. He's got no touch for the ball anymore and all he has left are these mile-long arms and legs that get in the way of everything he does, like walking.

"I was taking a load of pellets to the feed store," says Gus. "I never done that with a load of pellets. I had nine tons on the bed and she wouldn't come back."

I start feeling a little queasy myself when I get what Gus is talking about. A load of fresh alfalfa only weighs a couple of tons, and seven more tons makes a whole lot of steering difference.

"Guess we better not do that anymore," I say.

"No me, un-uh, not me," says Gus, and then he wobbles off toward the toilet, probably to clean out his shorts.

The mill backed up while they cleaned the gravel screens so we're doing the sitting and waiting routine. We have Big Gulp Dr. Peppers for lunch and then Chet takes the Bobcat out in the mill yard and starts popping wheelies. He raises the scoop halfway and takes off in reverse and then jams it into forward. The machine momentarily looks like it's back-flipping, then it charges for about twenty feet before the front whomps down. Gus has revived himself and is throwing clods at Chet and the clods smack against the wire protection screen and spatter.

"It's Front-end Loader Man," shouts Chet. "He's invincible."

I pick up a clod and heave it, and as it leaves my hand Chet spins the cat around and I know he's in trouble. That clod goes right between the screens and straight for his face like a homing missile. Chet has the control levers locked and is laying down donuts in the gravel and bleeding pretty good by the time Gus and I get to him. We chase around trying to get him to stop. Finally I hit the kill switch and the motor sputters out.

Chet looks at me funny from beneath his N-Serve farmers' cap.

"I think I might of broke your nose, Chet," I say.

Nothing's getting through to Chet and he's happy to just stay sitting. Then I see Joe Bill come out of the office and I wish I wasn't where I am.

"Chet broke his nose," I say.

"You fighting?" asks Joe Bill.

"He got hit with a dirt clod."

"Who did it?"

"Didn't mean to," I say. "You want me to take him to the hospital?"

Joe Bill gets old Chet out of the Bobcat and leads him across the yard like a lost dog.

"Sorry, Chet," I say.

"You two morons get back to driving," says Joe Bill.

We watch them leave.

"Don't worry," Gus says. "Joe Bill's just pissed 'cause he'll have to change the 'Number of Days Without an Accident' sign back to zero."

The monster long afternoon stretches out in front of me on a shimmering two lane of asphalt that seems to go on and on out into the middle of some death valley where it disappears into heat waves. I just keep telling myself that we're putting the bread on the table, that we're an essential cog in the great American food factory. That's only a good argument when you're too wired to remember that people don't eat alfalfa pellets, and cows don't eat alfalfa pellets; it's horses we're risking our lives for, Blackie and her friends. I try not to think about it when my feet are anywhere near the ground.

For what feels like about a year there aren't any shadows, the sun so bright that it beats right through everything, including the roof of the truck, banging on my head. My whole body sticks to the black plastic seat. I get a crick in my neck from looking over my shoulder for a dented Toyota assassin vehicle that I keep imagining is following me. Finally the light stretches out longer, and then I'm chasing a big truck shadow when

I'm going east to the field, and frying my eyes out when I'm going west to the mill. And then the sun goes down and I say, Thank-you-Lord because that means there's only four hours to go before this day's done.

Late summer air cools off fast, dropping into gullies and depressions in the land. In the field I park on hilltops of warmth. When I'm waiting to dump a load at the mill I stand next to the dryer. It's a big cylinder about ten feet across and has something like a Saturn Five rocket engine strapped on one end. The flames go shooting through the cylinder where the wet hay is and dry it out. The inside of the cylinder is fluted so that the hay moves away from the flames and finally is dumped out dry at the other end. Then it gets crushed into powder and compacted into pellets. Anyway, that's how I understand it.

A red moon starts climbing out of the plains and I try to remember if red moons have anything to do with storms and sailors taking warning. Then I remember that there aren't any sailors for about two thousand miles. One thing for sure, it ain't raining.

When I get back to the field, Harold's rig is just an unmoving black lump in the alfalfa. It jolts me because I always worry about him running over himself. This new Harold is the only hay cutter I've ever met who stops for rabbits. He gets off his tractor to move the baby ones out of the way. Getting off a tractor in the middle of the night is a sure way to kill yourself. It's too easy to bump something and start the tractor chasing you. Turn you into a farm version of an Avogadro's Number. Make a GobbleyGeek out of Harold. I drive out to see what's happened. Harold's lounging in his chair.

"What's the matter?" I ask.

"Sheared all my bolts," says Harold. "And I'm all run out of spares."

I radio Joe Bill that we need shear-bolts, then shut down the engine, and it's quiet in the alfalfa patch.

"I'm going to start a campaign to stop that baby killing," says Harold.

"It's not Christian," Harold says.

"What's going to be your slogan?" I ask.

"What?" asks Harold.

"Your saying," I say. "You gotta have a good saying or nobody'll be interested."

"Oh," says Harold, and he twists up his face to think.

I'm about to drop off.

"Let the babies keep their hearts," Harold finally says.

"That's good," I say. "You make the posters, I'll stand on street corners with you."

"If it ever rains," I say.

"Or maybe in October," I say.

This mill-hand named Randy finally shows up with the shear-bolts and I print my forehead on the steering wheel while Harold circles the field to fill his hopper. I take that load and two others, and then by my calculations I'm making my last run, which is a good thing, because on the way back to the mill I come awake twice when I'm carving up the double yellows.

It's eleven forty-five and I dump the hay and park my truck. Gus has outfoxed the coffee maker and he's standing next to Joe Bill's office door, sipping from a mug. I drag myself over to the truck barn to punch out, but before I can get there Gus starts hollering.

"Fire, we got a fire," yells Gus.

This really is almost too much already. I consider walking straight to my pickup, climbing in it, and never looking back. Only thing stopping me is that I don't know where I'd go. Smoke's already spewing through the cracks in the mill barn roof. Joe Bill comes galloping out of his office and knocks Gus flat. Then the two of them take off across the yard for the mill barn, Joe Bill looking like a bowling ball with legs, and Gus two feet taller and only legs.

This pellet mill is real prone to catching fire if you dry the hay too much. It catches in the dryer and the conveyors carry the burning through the whole building. I wander over at a safe pace. When I peek inside I see Gus flat out on his back and wondering where he's at. He's run smack into a piece of angle iron that supports one of the pellet bins. Joe Bill is cursing the fire and Gus for smacking his head. The "Number of Days Without an Accident" sign hasn't even gotten back up to half a day.

I drag Gus out of the mill and dump him on the cement pad and look at his head. He's got a square imprint between his eyes where he caught the angle iron, but there's no blood so I'm not too worried.

Back inside the mill it's a haze of pellet dust and smoke. Joe Bill has a mask over his face and a fire extinguisher in each hand and looks like a stepped-on John Wayne. He's pointing the extinguisher at the swirls of smoke and blasting away. When he breaks open the pellet press the smoke comes rolling across the floor like waves in the ocean.

"Call the fire department," yells Joe Bill.

I chug to the office but I can't find the fire department number. Then I get temporarily smarter and call the operator and she connects me.

"We got a fire at Great Western," I say.

"What's on fire?"

"Everything," I say.

Joe Bill's just inside the mill barn door, cradling an empty extinguisher. When I hear the fire engine I go drag Gus farther out of the way so he won't get run over. The firemen tear-ass into the mill and spray water all over everything and in about fifteen minutes they got it wiped out.

Gus looks at me like he might know me, but he's not sure.

"My head's noisy," says Gus.

" 'Cause you tried to knock down the mill barn with it," I say.

"Good news is it's after twelve," I say.

Joe Bill comes walking out of the mill barn. He's covered in alfalfa ashes.

"How about this idiot?" asks Joe Bill.

"He's got a headache," I say.

"You better drop him off on your way home," says Joe Bill.

"And both you better get your sleep, we're gonna have plenty catching-up cutting to do by morning," Joe Bill says.

I drag old Gus by the arm, but it's an open debate as to who should be dragging who.

Mike's sitting in his Camaro. I get Gus in the pickup and walk over to Mike.

"Say," I say to him. "You been letting Harold look at the *Newsweeks*?"

"Couple times," says Mike.

"You better cut that out," I say.

I pull up to Gus's trailer and honk. Gus's girlfriend comes out.

"You might want to help Gus inside," I say.

"You all right, Gus?" she asks.

"Who?" says Gus.

I take the fast road to town. Going by the sheep feedlots I hold my breath until I see two moons in the sky. I pass the gherkin factory, get visions of that poor guy glugging green-faced on the bottom of a pickle vat all those years. There's no traffic and soon I'm winding up the canyon. Sue Ellen is probably waiting up to kick my butt for the body work I did on her car, or the body work I did on Melinda, or Melinda did on me, or either or. I think I may just let her beat me to death. The mica chips in the stones on the canyon walls catch my high beams and look like millions of little stop signs. I don't stop I just keep driving, keep yelling, keep praying for rain.

LAURA HENDRIE

WHAT LASTS

Our mailman, Mr. Salazar, likes our new mailbox. He's lived out here all his life and he found my mother the last time she got lost in the corn, and he told Pop a high mailbox is a damn good idea because otherwise, come July, no one will be able to find anybody. That's how deep the corn grows around our place and how far out in the middle of it we are. It goes on forever and it's all corn and sky and about one car a day. You can stand out in the middle of a hot day and forget your own name. You can forget which silo is yours or what direction you came from or how long you've been gone. Corn, corn, corn. Maybe in town, where there are houses and clocks and dates to remember, forgetting where you are is a sign of something, like Aunt Maple said, but out here forgetting doesn't mean squat. Forgetting is easy. If you never lived out in the middle of it like we do, you can't know.

That's why Pop built the mailbox. Our other mailboxes were the regular kind, like Aunt Maple has in town. Three of them ended up shot to death and lying in the ditch with their jaws kicked in, and the fourth one I found out in the corn up at the north end, squashed so flat and full of bullet holes I wasn't even sure whose it was, it looked so different. But not this one. This one's got an iron leg six feet tall planted in concrete and it's big as a steamer trunk. Quarter-inch steel Pop and I

painted pitch black, LOPERS: RT 286, it says, arc-
welded, drilled, and riveted, right out there on the highway next to our front gate, pointing out who we are and
where we live. It's got a jaw as big as a serving dish and
silver flag on top as long as Pop's arm. Mr. Salazar criss-
crosses the whole county to deliver mail and he says
there's nothing like our mailbox anywhere except here.
It's so tall he has to get out of his car to toss mail in, and
I have to stand on the top rail of our front gate to fish it
out. But nobody's going to run this one over, and
nobody's going to miss it either. If you ever got lost, like
my mother did last time, even if you headed east where
there are miles to go, miles before you find anything but
corn, still there will be the mailbox when you're ready to
come home. Aunt Maple and Dr. Seymour and the
others in town, they can talk what they want about
Pop's new ideas. They'll drive past our place and, just
like my mother when she goes on her walks, they'll
know it a mile off.

It's early afternoon and Pop and I are finishing with
George Washington, our prize hog, when she comes out
on the porch. She's got her hair pulled back with
barrettes, she's holding her pocketbook, and she's wearing Pop's muck boots again. I drop the hog pole on the
steps and slip back down into the root cellar, calling into
the dark. Pop's on a kitchen chair in the back, his head
sinking over a carton of seasonings in his lap, his feet
tucked pigeon-toed under the chair, the flashlight still in
his hand. Nowadays he is always tired. I pull his hair and
shout Pop! and he staggers to his feet, dropping the carton. Edie, he calls and thunders up the steps out into the
yard, hog knives dangling like teeth from his belt. I put
the spices back in the box and the box back on the shelf,
and he is already beside her, I can hear him out there in
the dusty heat, telling her about falling asleep while
looking for hog salt, poking fun at himself. "Oh, Ray,"
she says, and I hear her laugh too. My mother has a nice
clean laugh. Through the shaft of light from the door I
can see the edge of the smokehouse roof and the gray

smoke of George Washington curling around it and all the rest of the sky that hangs over our fields, waiting to take it in.

"That's some mailbox, isn't it?" Pop is saying when I come out. His voice is still heavy with sleep. He is cupping her elbow in one hand and fumbling to pull up his suspenders. "You could see it from here to Chama," he says. He finishes with his suspenders and slides his hand down her arm to her wrist before letting go. "Couldn't you, Edie?"

"My goodness," gasps my mother, laughing again for us. "You certainly can." She opens her pocketbook and begins to hunt through it, pawing loose change from one side to the other. "Does anybody here know what time it is?"

Pop pretends not to hear. His eyes are on the mailbox, his face tight with satisfaction. I take her arm. She is so skinny nowadays that her wrist feels like a little piece of corn shuck wrapped around bone. "Look," I say, pointing to the cracked face of her watch. "Ten to five."

"Ten to five," says my mother. "Oh my."

"You remember how I used to get us lost in the woods when we were first married, Ed?" says Pop. "We didn't have a landmark to look for in those days, did we. I remember one time we were out till dawn." He turns to me. "Her sister Maple was ready to shoot me when I brought her back."

"You were awful," says my mother suddenly. "You told me we were heading east and we headed straight for the reservoir. You told Maple we had a flat."

"A flat," says Pop in delight. "I did say we had a flat. I did. How in the heck did you remember that, Ed?"

My mother stops, looking young and flushed. She puts her hand on her chest like she is catching her breath. "Well," she says. "I don't know. I don't know at all now."

"But you remember the reservoir?" says Pop pressing at her. "Tesuque reservoir? You remember the flat?"

"Oh god," she says, waving him off to open her pocketbook again. "Who could forget?"

Pop turns to the view, his whole face lighter. "Ed," he says. "You're getting better now. Every day a little better. I'm sure of it."

"Of course it is," says my mother. But she's not listening. I hold up her wrist to show her her watch again. Pop's hand comes down between us.

"Not now, Ruth," he says. "If she wants to go for a walk, she goes for a walk."

My mother covers her mouth and looks at Pop. "Is Maple coming back today or is it tomorrow? I have to make dinner now, don't I? Isn't it time?"

"Actually," says Pop, checking his watch, "it's almost one. Three minutes to one to be exact. And besides, Ruth and I are making dinner. Barbeque tonight, via George Washington. Fat back ribs, just the way you like them. We've been working all day on him. We have it all under control."

My mother looks frightened. "But what if Maple comes," she says. "What if she doesn't like barbeques?"

"Aunt Maple won't come," I say. "Pop told her not to. She's not allowed. Neither is Dr. Seymour. Remember?"

"Aaa—" Pop breathes in and slaps his chest. "If I were you, Ed, I'd take a walk. Relax. Get some of this clean, healthy air in your lungs."

My mother stands there. She looks at Pop and then closes her mouth and looks at me.

"She doesn't have to go for a walk," I say, "does she?"

Pop talks at me with his eyes and then he looks away.

"But Pop," I say. "She's got on the muck boots. Where's she going to go with muck boots?"

"That's enough," he barks.

My mother flattens her dress against her legs to look, and the way she does it, the thing that stops behind her eyes when she sees her feet makes my stomach skip. "Oh no," she says. She pushes the strap of her pocketbook up to the crook of her elbow and puts her hand over her mouth. When she bends for a closer look, the points of her spine rise up sharp enough to tear through her dress. I want to touch her, but Pop is there, watching.

"Ruth," he says. "Why don't you go marinate the meat for us."

"They're all wrong," says my mother. "Aren't they." She straightens up and stares at Pop. "They're too black, Ray," she says. "They're much too black. My slippers are better than these."

"Okay, slippers." His voice is getting tighter. "Don't go for a walk then. You put the boots on, take them off. You can do that, can't you?"

"Of course I can do that," says my mother, her voice rising. "But these are much too black. These aren't right at all."

"No," roars Pop. "They're wrong. You're right. They're totally wrong. Go." He turns and slams open the screen door. "Slippers are a damn good idea."

My mother rolls her eyes and then looks over at me and moves her mouth, trying to remember. "It's ten to five," I say.

My mother sighs with relief. She turns to Pop. "So there," she says, and goes back inside, clomping across the kitchen floor back to her bedroom.

I look at Pop but he will not look.

"She was going to leave," I whisper. "I saw the way she came out the door. She had her pocketbook and those boots, just like before—"

Pop leans into my face. "Who do you think you are," he hisses. "Some kind of mind reader? I should knock you straight into next week." But instead, he lifts back and waves his arms. "Maybe she wanted to wear muck boots for a change. Maybe her feet are cold. Maybe she thought it would rain. God almighty," he says, turning to me, "what business is it of yours what she thinks?"

"It's not my business," I say, edging away. "You were asleep."

"And that gives you the right to tell her she's wrong?"

"You do."

"Yeah?" he says and then he roars, "Well, I'm not thirteen years old neither."

My mother is coming back, the big black boots shuffling across the linoleum. Pop gives me a last look and pulls away. Sometimes he is like a rifle about to fire, his face nearly purple with it. He puts his hands on his hips to stop it and stares out at the view.

My mother is behind the screen door with a grocery bag in her arms, pushing against the hinged side. "Here," I say, stepping back. "This way."

"Well," she says when I open the door. "So there you are."

"I'm hungry." I step around her. "Anybody want lunch?" But by the time I get back, it's too late. She is already out to the edge of the corn. Pop is watching from the porch, his hands hanging at his sides now like things that do not belong to him. "No," he says hoarsely when I try to slip past. "She's going for a walk." He clears his throat and calls out to her.

"No more getting lost then," he says, licking the edge of his mouth. "How bout it, Ed?"

But my mother does not answer. She walks quickly, in spite of the boots, leaning forward over the bag like the wind is blowing, like she is late for something, like she has heard someone calling for her out in the corn.

Three hours later, I'm on the porch, mixing potato salad and listening to the blackbirds call good night. Pop is wolfing down half a jelly sandwich and keeping his eyes on the distance. The sky is beginning to cool at the edges, but there's no movement in the dark green wall of corn around the house, nothing but heat ghosts rising from the fields. No problem, says Pop, she'll be hungry soon, she'll smell dinner cooking, but when the grill is ready, instead of sending me to the kitchen for the ribs, he sends me up in the silo for a bird's-eye.

From the top window I watch Pop walking around the yard, calling, his shadow a black crowbar following his feet. Over in the side yard, the coals in the barbeque look like a little piece of sunset fell out of the sky. For every direction the corn is still. Route 286 is empty. I wiggle onto the sill and pull my half of the jelly sandwich out of my shirt. I take a bite and then put it down and pick at a spot on my shorts. It could be that Aunt Maple has come back and picked her up on the road. Maybe she had clothes in the bag she was carrying. Maybe they're not coming back. There are lots worse things that could happen. What if the ladder broke and I had to stay up here all night? What if I fell, scratching my nails against the metal siding all the way to the bottom? The echo would turn me deaf for life. What if they all died? But when I look between my feet and see how dark it's gotten down below all of a sudden, so that even Pop has disappeared now, I get a shiver so bad my teeth knock. I scat down and run home, feeling my way through the corn.

The way he's slamming around the house, turning on lights, calling, calling, I know it's for real this time. Aunt Maple and Dr. Seymour have scared him. "Get out of the way dammit," when I bump into his heels. Attic, pantry, closets, mud room. She's taken her slippers, she's taken her air force parka. I start calling too. Over the black corn the moon is coming now, round as an orange. Pop walks to the barn without bending his legs. Tool shed, stalls, smokehouse, the station wagon, even George Washington's butcher pen. Pop stops me in the hayloft. "Now wait a minute," he says. He sits on a bale and holds my shoulder. Under the bare bulb light, his face glitters pale under straw dust and sweat. "There's no need to lose our heads. What we need is perspective." Pop believes in perspective. He looks at me. "Lighten up, partner. Edie probably just wanted a little peace and quiet." He gets up to restack the bales and sits again, making me sit, too, resting a hand on my knee. "Now then," he says, wiping his face. "Now we put on our thinking caps."

His eyes go away, like he's forgotten everything, even me. When I can't stand it any longer, I get up and head-butt him. His belly gives like a pillow. "What," he says. "You think I'm giving up? No faith, that's your

problem. I know her. She's got on that fancy dress of
hers, she's not going to try crossing the fence this time.
What we do is go to the south end and work our way
around from opposite directions until we meet at the
mailbo—" He and I look at each other, shocked, and
then I'm on the ladder. "Slow down," he shouts, "you'll
break your goddamn neck," but as I run out across the
yard lit up like a stage in the moonlight, and break into
the dark corn, I can hear stalks already snapping behind
me and, in a stride, he's pushed me out of the way and
gone on ahead. "Edie! Edie!" The moon shines on his
bald spot. I follow with my hands up, stumbling blind
over the rows.

She's at the foot of the mailbox, sitting on the cinder
blocks with the parka on. When we come busting
through the corn, she stands up, scared by our noise.
She's holding something in both hands and the moon
shining on Route 286 behind her is so bright I can see
her legs through her dress, two pale sticks coming out
from the bulk of her parka and disappearing into the big
black muck boots.

"Is the phone for me?" she says.

"Wait—" Pop is sweaty and wheezing for breath. He
holds up one hand and leans over to catch his wind.
"Shit, Edie," he says. "I haven't run—like that—since I
was—in the army. You must be—trying to kill me." He
leans back to say something else, but when he sees what
she is holding, he stops dead.

"Mom," I say. "What are you doing with George
Washington's ribs?"

I don't mean it to be funny, but Pop is laughing. He
bunches up his shoulders and points at the pan of ribs
and then at me and then he rocks forward, slapping his
legs. When he rears back the gold filling in the back of
his mouth glints at the moon. He's got tears on his
cheeks, he's shaking and helpless with it, holding his
sides and bowing over. "Oh," he says. "Oh. Oh."

My mother looks thin and shivery as paper. She
looks down at that plate of barbeque as if she doesn't

know what it's doing there in her hand, and she hands it
to me.

"Pop," I say. "Come on. It's not funny."

"Didn't the phone ring?" she says. "I thought I heard
the phone."

My voice feels like something crawling out of itself,
crawling over Pop's laughter and off into the corn. "The
phone?" I say. "We don't have a phone anymore. Pop
threw it away. We don't have one anymore." I turn to
Pop and stamp my foot. He has his back to us, he's
shaking his head at the moon with his hands on his hips.
"Pop," I cry. "You've got to stop. You've got to quit it
now."

"Ray," she says, and the way she says it, so sharp and
clear all of a sudden, makes Pop freeze. "This is so ridiculous," she says. "I think something is wrong with me."

"Wrong with you?" says Pop, turning. His voice is
soft and furry. "Wrong with you?"

"Well yes," she says sharply. "Of course there is."

"Edie," Pop sighs and wipes his face, so hard his eyes
roll to white. "You found the mailbox, didn't you?"

"But I've been looking for hours and I can't find a
single other familiar thing," she says. Her voice is rising
on itself. "I can't even find my house. What is all this
corn?"

Pop stares at her a moment and then turns to me.
"Go home," he says. "Get."

But I don't. "Mom," I say. "Mom, it's ten to five."

My mother isn't listening. There is something inside
her that is not her anymore, it has been there for a long
time but now I can see it pushing both her eyes out. It is
breathing through her mouth, pushing her aside to listen
through her ears, and nothing Pop and I have done can
stop it. My mother points at the mailbox, her finger as
pale and thin as corn stubbles. "This is not my mailbox,"
she says. "This is not my mailbox."

"Oh Edie," says Pop. He takes a step closer and she
raises her hand to strike. "No," he says. "Edie, it's me.
It's your husband." He reaches for her slowly. She is
staring out at the world like something with its foot

caught in a trap. He unpins the barrette that is dangling
by her cheek and refastens it to the top of her head.
"Sometimes everybody's crazy," he says to her. "Sometimes nobody's right anymore."

I haven't said anything, I haven't breathed, but he
turns and looks fiercely at me then like I have. "You
don't believe me?" he says. "You don't think I'm right?"
With one hand, he picks up the pan of George Washington ribs. "Then watch," he says, and throws them, pan
and all, into the corn.

My mother is crying, holding the furry hood of the
air force parka against her cheeks. Pop puts his arm
around her and she leans into him as if blown by wind
and I watch them go down the driveway, fading into the
dark toward the house in the corn. They are one shadow
with two arms and four legs and then they are nothing
at all.

The quiet out on Route 286 shines off in either direction, bright as a rope of silver. After a while, I step up
on the gate and pull down the jaw of the mailbox. It
drops like the mouth of a furnace. There is nothing inside but the dark and a bullet hole in the very back, a
sting of moon shining through.

I push off from the gate and wedge inside. I wiggle
in to my waist until my shoulders are pinned. Behind
me, where I can't see, I feel a little breeze brush the back
of my legs.

Maybe I'll get stuck trying to get out and Pop won't
come. Maybe someone driving along Route 286 for a
pot shot won't notice my legs sticking out. In the dark
my breath comes from behind like someone else. Lots of
things could happen. Worse things than this.

I find the spent bullet and pick it up with my teeth. I
roll it around on my tongue and I swallow it, bitter and
real.

But the mailbox will last. Maybe Pop won't and
neither will my mother, but the mailbox will. It will last
with or without us. It will last forever. And when I
square my eye to the pinhole, I see our old house at the
end of time, with everyone gone and all the windows

and doors blown out and the corn growing wild and up
to the windows, twisting and tangling and reaching
inside.

T. M. McNALLY

PARIS, THE EASY WAY

I first learned the importance of air at the Casper Community Pool during my brother's thirteenth birthday party—a big one because now he had finished the eighth grade and was learning to kiss his girlfriend, also our neighbor, Sally Sconzalla. Like my brother, I had a crush on Sally, but what she could do for my brother I was still too underdeveloped to appreciate. I merely liked the way she combed her hair, which was yellow and loose, and I liked the sound of her voice.

At the Casper Community Pool she and my brother were diving from the springboard when I decided to join them. Never before had I been in water so deep. I swam my short, choppy strokes, stopping every five feet to hang onto the wall. I must have been thinking about something. Maybe I thought I was near the wall. Maybe I thought the water was shallow. Either way, I took in half the pool, the air washed out of my lungs, and my body caught on—this was not the proper way to float. I couldn't hear anything but the water, and my voice in the water, but I'm sure it was Sally who saw me. I was lifted out with one arm by a big, tan lifeguard. And later, when Sally wrapped me in her towel and told me I would be all right, this is what I learned. I learned that when our lungs are filled with something they shouldn't be, no one, not even the person we decide to love most in the world will ever hear us. This was back in Wyoming, during the summer of 1965, where we were all still growing up under a sky the size of history and equally dull.

As a kid watching "Star Trek," I used to wait for something new to happen: an unfamiliar spaceship, a forceful encounter, things suddenly appearing as soon as the ship's viewscreen was turned on. Now I'm wondering who cleaned the viewscreen, the big windshield they drove behind. I think even space must have debris the way the West has dust.

The windshield wipers on my truck have smeared the dust into mud, and thirty, maybe forty miles ahead, somewhere over Trinidad, lightning rips open the sky — long brilliant seams opening for just a moment the possibilities beyond our own atmosphere. Lightning, gravity, love — I've never properly understood any of it.

I went to college. During the '81 recession, when I couldn't get a job, I did the circuit well enough to break even. For two years I was an overpaid stable manager in Sedona. In my old office, which was really a tack room full of broken down saddles and loose stirrups, hangs a recent photograph of Sally. She is sitting on a beach in Monaco, her top off, her face angled toward the sea, and on the back she has written, "You'd really love it here."

I decided to leave the Boyton Canyon Resort the day after I received Sally's picture, the day Old Man McClenahan showed up early for his ride. His face had been detailed by the sun, by age and the weather, and I watched the lines shift in his face while he grew angry with me because I hadn't yet grained his mare, Cleo.

"It's climbing," he said, pointing at the sun. "It's climbing. Where's my Cleo!"

I fed his horse, offered him coffee while we waited. Mrs. McClenahan wouldn't be by to pick him up until noon for lunch and his nap. After his ride, after he'd

finished brushing Cleo down, he would ask me to
inspect a hoof, trim a frog. Later he'd wander around
behind me and talk with the guests or help Gomez with
his English. It was hard to dislike either, the old horse or
the old man.

But that morning as we sat in the tack room, drinking coffee and enjoying the morning, the lingering smells
of hay and shit and grain dust, the old man grew serious.

"Hey, Good Buddy," he said.

"Hey," I said.

"When you gonna leave?"

"Leave where, Mac?"

"Leave," he said, nodding toward the door. "When
you gonna leave? You know."

"No," I said. "I don't know."

"Cleo, her lungs are about to bust."

"They're fine," I said. "Just a little used up."

"Used up? They're all used up with the heaves. No.
Maybe," he said, shaking his head. He began to laugh
and looked at the picture of Sally over my desk. "Not
like her," he said, laughing. "Not like her, Good Buddy."

The old man left for his ride, Gomez showed up
hungover and late, and I took out a pair of tourists: a
husband and wife team from Phoenix, newly married by
the looks. They made jokes and giggled while I told
them about all the cowboys Rooster had crippled back in
his prime. The man kept a sharp lookout for rattlesnakes
and occasional mountain lions, and I thought about the
old man and his mare, Cleo, combing the countryside
next to highway 89A looking for something vaguely
familiar and safe. The old man had kids, he said, only he
didn't know where they were, which is why I suppose
he told me.

After the incident at the Casper Community Pool, it was
decided I would learn to swim as well as I did my chores
or homework. My father would drive me into Casper
for weekly lessons to an indoor pool, where I would
wear black nylon suits and take instruction from people
not much older than my brother or Sally. Once, after a

lesson, while waiting in a public hallway for my dad, I watched him pull up to the curb. I had been waiting with the others and I left them to meet my dad halfway across the snow and ice. The cold made my hair freeze. My dad waved, slipped, and fell. He fell about as gracefully as a horse—scrambling, all legs and panic, trying to pretend that either this hadn't happened or that he did this all the time. I could hear the kids laughing through the still open door. He waved again, this time to the kids behind me; he patted at his hip as if feeling for injury.

In the truck he breathed heavily and gripped the steering wheel. "Whew," he said, trying to laugh. "Your old man's not as limber as he used to be."

And I think what I felt then was my embarrassment shift to worry, to a slight tremor of mortality. Hearing my dad call himself old meant he would only get older and, eventually, leave me to myself while I was still young. In the water, after nearly drowning, I had been frightened, but I was not frightened by death. The fear was too inarticulate to be specific.

"Dad," I said, "you're not an old man!"

And really he wasn't. He was the same age I am now, but when we feel as if we're getting old, there's not much that's going to change that feeling. My father is now fifty-two. He raises some of the finest Morgans in Wyoming and he raises his grandson, Robert, much in the same way he raised me. Only now he really isn't as limber as he used to be. I suppose in truth no one really is.

Why didn't I marry Sally Sconzalla? I suppose because my brother already had. My brother was like one of those ensigns or corpsman who open up every episode of "Star Trek." The nameless one we've never seen before. The one who beams down with the landing party and gets lost or vaporized by misunderstanding aliens. My brother enlisted in 1970, was beamed down into Cambodia, and disappeared without a trace.

As for the old man, he combed the hillside with his mare while I told the tourists stories. When I returned

the tourists to the barn, Gomez took their money and
told them to have a nice day. I stood at the corral and
watched them leave, walking nervously between the
loose horses while I admired the man's wife. I watched
one horse prepare to kick another. I watched the old man
rub down Cleo and lead her into a paddock. Later that
afternoon, a large group of realtors from Tucson was
scheduled for a ride and cookout: Gomez would meet us
at the sight with hamburgers and beer, and later he
would take out his guitar to sing love songs from
Ethiopia. In the office, he sat in my chair, his feet
propped on my desk, leafing through a book entitled
Paris, The Easy Way.

"Bonjour," he said. "Comment ça va?"

"Fine," I said. I poured coffee and asked about the
status of a horse with fistulous withers, so bad the pus
still ran after six weeks—a lingering, festering sore
caused by an ill-fitting saddle.

"She sure is pretty," Gomez said, rising from the chair
and pointing at the picture of Sally. "Pretty like my
sister, you know. Bonita. Tres Belle, Ohh la la."

I drank my coffee, brown and badly burnt, and
studied the picture while Gomez loaded up an injection
of Combiotic and brought out the hydrogen peroxide.

"I gonna play darts now," he said, referring to the
syringe. "And you gonna feel sad for a while. But you
get over it. Ciao."

A month ago, Gomez had been Italian. He left while
I sat and considered the photograph of Sally. I considered the slow curve of her flank. In the photograph she
has a neck like an antelope, and I thought about my
father's hayloft where she told me what to do without
ever telling me, as if between us someone had strung a
fine wire, a telegraph of instruction. Later, she left
Wyoming to teach at a Catholic school in Los Angeles,
and my brother never came home, which is something I
think we each always knew even when we didn't know
it. Maybe he was gone too long for any of us to remember clearly. Who knows what we really used to know?

* * *

One thing I know is this: if confined, a horse under a sky with lightning is a dangerous thing. It wants only to run because the lightning is too inexplicable, too close to the bone to be considered safe from even a distance. A horse reacts to lightning the way a stud will a mare, and the coupling of horses is not a simple enterprise.

Right now the weather grows temporarily safe. The sky blisters with ions, waiting for rain, and the air is so clear it looks like glass—it's that transparent. The Colorado border smells like rain, like creosote and dust, and I know Sebastian, my own horse in the trailer behind me, is no longer frightened because I, too, am no longer frightened.

We can only know what we once didn't know. At my brother's wedding, I was the best man because his best friend had already been shipped to Asia, and our father thought it would be nice this way. Sally was dressed like an angel, I stood behind my brother, and at the proper time I held out the ring he'd spent six months saving for. It was a pretty, gold ring. A wedding ring, he'd explained, and chock-full of meaning.

We stood up against the fence and watched my father work a yearling; my brother, just in from town, took the ring out of his box to show me. The dust from the corral floated all around us, but it never touched the ring. The ring was still too new for dust. "Do you see how it's round?" he said. "That's the meaningful part. The finger is the man and the ring is the woman, and once you're married the two go at it forever, and as long as you wear your ring, you can never go at it with someone else or the whole deal gets all shot to hell."

I found the old man face down in the paddock with a fly on his neck. The horses had circled away from him and he lay in the orange dirt alone. I rolled him over and searched for a pulse. I beat on his chest. I cleared his airway and removed a loose denture. I began to breathe. I beat again on his chest, losing count, searching for his heart because I wasn't sure where it was. I felt his ribs crack beneath my hands and feared having to breathe into him again — my mouth on his, his lips rough and smelling of garlic and decay and later the whiff of his gut rising up through the throat while I kept breathing into his lungs. I felt them rise while mine collapsed. After a while, I realized he was supposed to be dead, and so I left him in the paddock under the sun with the horses still frightened by the suddenness and smell of death.

By nature, a horse has only three gaits; the others are learned. After work each day Gomez and I would go to the Oak Creek Tavern, order a pitcher and shoot pool. Last summer, though, the local network in Chicago began showing reruns of "Star Trek" — the same reruns I had watched in college, the same episodes I had watched as a kid in Wyoming. So instead of playing 8-ball, I began to reacquaint myself with plots and character traits: who was logical, who was emotional, who was both, which was really all of us. The tavern had a satellite hookup, and watching all these episodes reminded me of the sixties and how hopeful and naive we were all becoming while I was still completely un-aware of the world which had created it — Ford Mustang, Simon and Garfunkel, the race for the moon.

    I once lived with a woman in Santa Fe. I ran a barn for Lazarus Arabians, where I was instructed by the part-time owners of syndicated studs on the proper music for mares about to foal (Mozart, piped through the stalls with air-conditioning), where I learned to keep my mouth shut and watch people make wise investments. At home it was worse. The woman would paint bad imita-tions of Georgia O'Keeffe and read D. H. Lawrence, nonstop, reading aloud always the passages which had to do with men and horses and lust until, finally, she asked me to marry her. It was the first time I'd ever been asked, and the next day I gave my notice.

I gave Gomez the blender, my contribution to the barn since I was going to argue with the owner of the Boyton

Canyon Resort that, illegal or not, Gomez most deserved the blender. Make him the boss, I would say; the tourists will like the color. They would like the color the way they liked the rocks of Sedona, the red, angry cliffs shaped by the wind into the names of things like Coffee Pot, like Cathedral and Bell.

We sat in the tack room and drank margaritas; Paul Harvey was over, and I advised Gomez to get rid of the horse with bad withers, and to get rid of Cleo, too; sell her quick and send the money to Mrs. McClenahan. "Do it right," I said, "and she'll send you a bottle."

"Oui," said Gomez, looking almost lost. "But what about her?" He pointed to the picture of Sally on the wall. Right up there by Will Rogers and a bilingual notice to employees, she really was a fine addition to the wall. It seemed to me she'd do more good on the wall in Boyton Canyon than she would anywhere else.

"I had to kill a horse once," I said. "It ran through a fence and nearly cut off its leg. It wasn't worth the vet bills. The leg would never heal, so I shot it in the head just like the movies. I shot it in the head with a Remington I had to borrow. But the bad part wasn't killing it. The bad part was figuring out what to do next. How do you move a dead horse?"

"Slowly," said Gomez, nodding.

"I put a chain around its neck and drug it out of the corral with a Jeep. I called the foundry, the guy couldn't pick it up for two days. I covered the horse with a ground cloth and put wagon wheels against it—decorations, you know, to please the guests. Four days later it was still there, rising like a balloon—this dead horse covered with wagon wheels and plastic and flies. But what I remember most was wrapping the chain around its neck and pulling it out of the mud with the Jeep. The chain left marks in the neck. When the guy finally showed up, he had to pull her on a flatbed with a winch."

When my brother finished basic training, he came home on leave. His hair was short, he wore green clothes, and he spent most of his time with Sally in the big room our

father had fixed up just for them. A week later we drove
him to the airport where he would catch a plane to
Alaska and then pick up a transport going somewhere
else. We stood at the gate, my father and Sally and me,
and said goodbye. My brother had something special to
say to everyone, and he told me to take care of the
family, to watch over Dad and the ranch. "We got problems U.T.A.," he said. "But we got you. Take care of
Sally," he said. And then he whispered something in
Sally's ear, kissed her on the mouth, and walked away up
the runway. On the way home, my father pulled over
the truck to let me drive, and Sally turned on the radio.

I attended McClenahan's funeral, of course. It was
Catholic, long and overcrowded. I saw lawyers and doctors and people who had flown to Sedona from New
York and Boston and Chicago in private airplanes. A
memorial service was held outdoors beneath the shadow
of Bell Rock, a large and brightly colored geological
oddity, a source of crystals, of immeasurable energy,
swollen with meaning and mystery for the new age.
      Mrs. McClenahan was a handsome woman. She
stood among these people I would never know and
listened to them say nice things about her husband.
      "Mac was very fond of you," she said to me.
      "I'm sorry," I said.
      "He said you always took good care of Cleo. You
reminded him of our boys."
      But the boys were not present. I had learned one of
them was dead, the other in a foreign country. I told
Mrs. McClenahan not to worry about Cleo, and she
looked at me sadly, as if there were no reason why she
ever should. Later that afternoon the body was shipped
on a private plane to a cemetery in Illinois.

I think being in space must be like being in water: there
is no air. The rain is hard now. It washes over the shell
of the truck like a river; it films the windows and the
wipers beat at the rain like oars. Denver is still a long
way north. I feel the tires skim over flat spots on the

road where water stands, and I adjust my speed accordingly.

After I found the old man, after I'd cracked his ribs and breathed into his lungs, I went to the barn and had a drink. I called the ambulance, said they didn't need to rush. I called Mrs. McClenahan.

She arrived before the paramedics. She drove her big car straight past the barn and up to the paddock. Her hair, streaked with gray, glimmered in the light; her face was pale as a woman's breast.

And I watched her go to her husband. She knelt on her heels, cocked in the dirt, and reached for his hand which must have felt unexpectedly cool. The sun was hot, the hand cool, and by the time the paramedics had arrived, she knew where she wanted him sent. I brought her into the barn, the tack room, where she sat very quietly in my chair while I poured her a shot of whiskey. She held the cup in her hands and stared at the coffee stains on the cheap porcelain as if trying to identify the shapes.

"Once," she said. "Once before, I thought he was dead. I had to make sure."

"He had a nice ride," I said.

"Yes," she said, nodding, "I'm sure he did."

I watched her watch her drink. The rings on her hands pinched her fingers, grown swollen with age, and I watched the rings pinch her fingers thinking someday the rings are going to slip loose because that's what life does. It eats away at us until we're empty.

Space may very well be the final frontier, but in what direction should we travel? Right now I'm going home, traveling north, which on a map is not as far away as it seems—a few days' drive up I-25. It's as easy as sending a half-naked picture of yourself through the mail. And while I think about everyone I've ever known and probably damaged, one way or another, this is what I think about most: I think about the old man I couldn't save, the old man lying quietly inside his sealed box, unable to

go anywhere but in, inside himself to the core of what
he once was. He lies in a grave somewhere in Illinois and
he keeps going inside himself, because now when it matters most he can't get out. He can't get out, so he goes
in. He goes in, deep inside himself, so deep until he
finally discovers that maybe the space around the living
is more important than any of us ever thought. Because
maybe after a while there really is no place left for us to
go.

ELIZABETH TALLENT

HONEY

Solidity, sober commitment, a roof over each dark Dominguez head—those are the things Mercedes desires for her children, desires with the erratic detachment from them illuminating this, her sixty-third year. She did not bring seven children from Nicaragua in order for them to choose the doomed American existence of nerves rubbed raw by divorce, of quarrels, mutual contempt, and lawyers' costly ministrations, but their lives unravel in spite of her, coming undone even as she grows older, more secretly watchful, and increasingly pained in her estimation of what they are wasting. In the wavy mirror with which the airline has grudgingly outfitted its ladies', Mercedes could be sixty-eight, her pinned hair harshly white, or fifty-five, her pupils as pitch-black as when her husband, long dead, found his tiny horseshoe-mustached reflection there. Mercedes observes her eyes lovingly in the mirror and discovers she can no longer summon up his face.

She was his life, he said, his heart, his dove, tendernesses that, thus recollected, sting faintly as they pass through on their way back to the cool black vault that holds her marriage, her children's childhoods, and their life in Nicaragua. For an instant, under unlocked Nicaraguan palms, a child rides her shoulders, rubbing a leaf over Mercedes's forehead; another child swings crying from her husband's hand, two more race barefoot

down the darkening dirt road before them. The friction
of these details against Mercedes's composure is urgent;
far worse is the shock of her gross, consummate infidelity in having forgotten her husband's face. Her heart
thuds alertly, fearfully trying to take the measure of
this event. This is the first form grief takes with her —
a sudden despair in standing still — and because the dim
stainless-steel wedge of a bathroom could not be more
confining, she turns stiffly around and around until diz-
ziness seats her politely on the closed lid of the toy toilet.
Someone knocks and goes away. The ache, which
belongs to her heart, abruptly descends to her stomach.
Mercedes kneels to vomit. The pilot, a voice from far
away, announces they are beginning the initial descent
into Albuquerque, New Mexico, where the temperature
on the ground is ninety-nine degrees. Mercedes scarcely
has the will to wash, to repin her disheveled hair, to
neaten her clothes, before finding her seat between two
salesmen. On earth, she is met by someone ponderously
tall, absurdly red-haired, breathing wine into her face as
he bends to her, as he tastes her pitiless old cheekbone
with a son-in-law's kiss.

This son-in-law, burdened by her bags, blind to her
mood, finds the chip of emerald that is his old BMW in
the glittering midsummer parking lot. Mercedes feels
herself begin to fear it, the desert. In the car's backseat,
sheltered from the sun by the almost subsonic purr of air
conditioning, is a boy, chin on his knees, eyes closed,
Sony Walkman riding his ears. The boy has achieved the
other-worldly privacy of a fetus, and is not about to
acknowledge their arrival. Stranger still, the son-in-law
offers no apology for his son's rudeness. Mercedes
remembers him distinctly as a nice boy, too tall for his
age, touched with the guilty displeasure in himself of
adolescence, an elusive, embarrassed presence at his
father's wedding to her daughter. Swinging out into
swift late-afternoon traffic, the son-in-law runs through
deferential Spanish phrases. He inquires whether she
recalls his son from the wedding. She admits that she
does, wondering just how much he is taking in over the

mosquito-sized voices in his ears. Yes: he had handed his father the ring, while Mercedes from her vantage point studied him sharply, believing him to be the chief obstacle to her daughter's happiness. Mercedes's son-in-law wonders whether her flight was comfortable, hopes that she is not overtired, and assures her that her daughter will be insanely happy now that she is here at last.

Mercedes prefers to keep her distance from her children, her two sons and five daughters. In the domino theory of daughters, each, submissively tipping into domesticity, sets the next in motion. Only troublesome Caro resisted. Rumors of her love life filtered across the U.S.A. to the tiny, drab, harmonious Brooklyn garret where Mercedes sews for her living, though none of her children like it that she lives alone. Anything could happen to her, they threaten. Seven children have taken turns at badgering or sweet-talking her out of Brooklyn. Her own vigilance, which made her more or less adroit in protecting small, straying children, is intensely irritating to Mercedes, now that it has been instilled in those very children. What Mercedes likes is settling each morning to her old Singer before her domain of roofs, of spires, of bare trees and tire swings. Summer is best, when the wind balms the nape of her neck, exposed by the pinned-up wiry wreck of her old hair, her cat sleeps on the windowsill, and the Brooklyn light falls lovingly on the cloth.

A lunar mountain range glides by on the right, steep points of bare stone, crevasses shadowed in powerful deathly blue. Her son-in-law wonders in English whether she is feeling the altitude. "It might make you sleepy," he says. The mountain range is replaced by a vast dun horizon in which there is no hope at all. "Why did you come, Kev, if you're not going to talk?" Hart asks. No answer, only the popping and sizzling of miniaturized rock and roll.

In the strange, rambling house, Mercedes follows the boy. Like his father, he is an American giant, burdened by her bags, constrained by her frailty. Already she is tired of making tall people uncomfortable. He runs through an explanation she can't follow, either because she's exhausted or because in his embarrassed adolescent way he talks too fast. Swinging around at a doorway, he says, "Sorry," and offers with transparently faked, kind-to-a-stranger patience, "I was only saying Caro's sleeping. She's never out of bed in the afternoon anymore."

Determined to convince him she's understood perfectly, Mercedes fixes her face into a trance of shrewd attentiveness, but the expression fails to convince him, because her elderly foreignness slides between them like a glass door.

Her beautiful daughter must have been eating like a pig for months. Her deep-set Dominguez eyelids have fattened, her small jaw is soft, and her belly is the moon. "Oh, Mama," Caro says, pushing up in bed. "You know what I want? I want you to braid my terrible hair." They touch cheeks; they kiss; this time it is a mother-and-daughter kiss, tolerance on one side, charming pleading on the other. Caro has always wanted something from her mother; what she wants varies, but invariably she never quite gets it. Mercedes confronts her mass of hair, warm because Caro's been sleeping on it. It is Mercedes's own hair of thirty years before. Mercedes says, "A brush," is handed one, and notices, as she begins with a particularly cruel snarl, that her daughter's left ear, once triply pierced and adorned with opals and gold, has been let heal smoothly, and is naked, and therefore touchingly childlike again.

"I went to the doctor this morning, Mama."

"You did? So?"

"Nothing, *nada,* no dilation, no softening of the cervix. No sign that I'm going into labor. Time is so long now, Mama. A day is ten years."

At her wedding, Caro acquired not only her older husband but that husband's son, complex relations with the husband's WASPy ex-wife, and this house set remotely in Rio Grande gorge. At first it was the house—a straggle of light-starved adobe rooms, very old—that puzzled Mercedes most. Dirt walls, water

bugs, and neighbors with goats—they had those in
Nicaragua. How to keep the grandchild from falling into
the river that breathes a reedy dankness right into the
house when a window's left up? Caro has no idea how
children are.

"She said—"

"Who said?"

"Mama, the *doctor* said we might try making love.
Sometimes sex gets labor going."

How children are: they scald their hands, and puffs
of blister as translucently unreal as jellyfish fill their
palms. They get stung, and howl. They stain themselves
with food, muck, blood, dust. In their bowel movements
appear lost buttons and pale snail shells. Rashes flourish
on their thin arms and disappear overnight. Storms of
coughing begin at moonrise.

"But, Mama, it's been months since we made love.
Months."

In swift, habitual rhythm, Mercedes braids.

"I have to tell you what's wrong with Kevin, too."
Caro glances over her shoulder to stop her mother's
hands. Caro says, "A girl he liked killed herself five
months ago. She swallowed a bottle of her mother's pre-
scription sleeping pills."

Mercedes touches forehead, heart, shoulder, shoulder. "Her poor mother," Mercedes says. "Her poor
father."

"Her father wasn't there."

"And why not?"

"Mama, that's irrelevant. They were divorced a long
time ago. Kevin didn't love this girl."

"He says that?"

"He says he loves her. He's a child. How would he
know? It's just too bad that he happened to go out with
her more than he'd ever been out with anyone before,
but it's not as if she were his girlfriend, really, and he
didn't even tell Hart or me anything about her until the
funeral. Since then he's gone to pieces. No one can say
anything to him now." Caro sighs. "Hart and I try, but
no one can reason with him. It will take time, we say,

and he shrugs as if he hates us. He seems so far away from all our little concerns. I love him, you know. I keep trying to draw him back in."

"And?"

"Nothing works. Nothing. He's making his father crazy." Caro yawns. "And, Mama, I'm selfish enough to wish they weren't all I was thinking about right now. The baby has only this little leftover piece of my attention. Look." She tosses *Your Baby and Child* at the closet, jammed with Hart's shirts and the lighthearted thrift-shop dresses the unpregnant Caro fancied. "I wanted to start there," Caro says. There is a crib in the corner, but it isn't made up. The exposed mattress ticking bothers Mercedes, as does the decal of a dancing bear, one of its paws torn off. "I thought I'd get the nesting instinct," Caro says, "and instead I'm the Blob." Mercedes counts dirty teacups on the dresser. She had expected Caro's house to be cleaner, and finds herself disapproving. The disapproval is a mother's, nimbly inserting itself into a welter of other, more reasonable emotions, where it will be hard to weed out.

"Lie down. Put your head in my lap," Mercedes instructs. A pregnant daughter calls on her mother for solidity, reassurance, proof that her fears are thin as air, and will vanish at the first maternal reproof. Caro sleeps. Mercedes has her work cut out for her. This room, then the rest of the house. What is needed here is not only Mercedes's brand of astringent housekeeping but a make-shift serenity. A harmony sufficient for a baby to be born into. The old sensation of being hemmed in by need sweeps over Mercedes. Today she has come three thousand miles. She arches her tired back, and doubles an elastic band around the end of Caro's braid, a spit of hair like that which tips a paintbrush. On the messy bed in the sad room, Mercedes begins to shake her head, slowly at first, anxiously, tiredly, then stops. Stops to wonder what she thinks she is doing here, and how she found the strength to stay away so long.

* * *

This old woman with the quaintly strained English, her dry cheeks collapsed inward below cheekbones so big and smooth they are bulbous, her too-large eyes hyper-critically aglitter, causes Hart to feel himself a lurching monster in his own house. He rests his Frankenstein forehead in his huge white-male hands and appeals for help, for something to save him from this plate of black beans, rice, and *huevos,* two doilies of fried egg slopped from the spatula onto his plate as his wife's huge ninth-month belly bumps the back of his chair. *Consider your cholesterol level,* Phil Donahue says, far back in Hart's brain. *Have you been drinking already this morning, and can anyone in this audience tell?* The old woman wields her flat-ware with dainty persistence. Black beans and rice mean home to her, and home has always been Nicaragua.

Breakfast, for Kevin, is a cup of loganberry yogurt. He is so silent Caro does not argue with him about eggs. He can stand his father, stepmother, and Mrs. Dominguez only as long as it takes to consume three hundred calories. He is six feet tall.

Kevin's mother, Hannah, is away now, gone to Europe with her boyfriend Florian, a doctor who has his own house on a canal in Amsterdam. A modest house, but filled with aqueous shimmer, with goosedown duvets, mirrors, antiques, and a bathroom with bidet, heaven for Hannah, whose home has no bathroom at all. She has been poor ever since the divorce, maliciously, flauntingly penniless, with a poverty she can throw in Hart's face. She sold their big suburban place after the divorce to buy, near El Rito, a ruin needing everything: floors sanded down, roof insulation laid in, windows double-glazed against the northern New Mexico winters. In short, a fortune vanished there. The house was a black hole, but Hannah will never divorce it, and Kevin, cutting kindling, lugging a chainsaw out through biting wind to the woodpile, latching the outhouse door against the vast nights, grew up fast. In that house, alone with Hannah, he had responsibilities, and they did him no harm.

Of course Kevin led another, parallel life, as children
of dissolved marriages do. Hart went through a series of
viewless condos and cheap apartments. Into each of
these, one after the other, Kevin helped him move. Hart
would boil up two of those frozen dinners that came in
pouches, then tip the steaming water, with its pale plas-
ticky smell, into cups for instant coffee. He was troubled
by insomnia, the worst of his life, and he fell in love
every other month, and was bewildered when an
ex-lover came knocking on his door, or ranted at him
over the phone. Living long weekends with Hart, Kevin
learned roughly a thousand times more about him than
Hart ever knew about his own father. Moreover, Kevin
seemed infatuated with an existence in which he could be
the ordering force. He slid Roach Motels behind the
grimy stoves, he dyed the water in the toilets azure. He
scoured the sinks, he read letters left lying around, he
knew and forgave everything, at least until the unexpected happened: his father and his mother began going
out together. Parties, galleries. Oh, they were careful
with each other, and very, very careful to be sure that
Kev's hopes were not aroused. Hart came in so very,
very softly from those dates that, one night, he over-
heard, "You love each other, you love each other,"
recited by Kevin, belly down in his soiled sleeping bag,
the door of his room half open. But Hart and Hannah
failed again in slow motion, because some time in the
middle of this, Hart met Caro.

Kevin swigs coffee. "Not so fast," Hart says, surprised to find himself talking in Phil Donahue's paternal
tone, and is countered by his son's silence, the slender,
nervous gliding of bolts into place.

Kevin met Molly at a party on their lawn alongside
the river last spring, when the Rio Grande had a glassy
green, rising smoothness from snowmelt, and the guests
were all pleasantly sweated up from working on the
fence on the slope. Among the hammering, nailing
grownups was a girl. A mare's tail of fine dark hair clung
to her baby-oiled back, and when she turned to stare at
somebody over her shoulder, a line of new tenpenny

nails glittered in her clenched mouth. Hart has thought back to it again and again, that girl with the indifferently beautiful back turning to reveal her sea-urchin mouth.

She was looking at Kevin for the first time. At Kevin whose dark head is bent tediously over yogurt. Hart asks, "Have you gone through that Blue Book yet?"

"What?"

"You were supposed to check those used-car prices, so that when we went looking you'd know what was a fair offer. You said you'd take an active part in this."

"Hart." Caro intervenes so softly it stops him. Too late.

"I will. I'm going to." But Kevin's tone is defensive, and Hart guesses he can be no help to anyone on anything yet, but it would be a good thing if he had a car. They're so isolated, out here in the gorge. They're about to disappear into baby world, leaving Kevin behind, on his own. On his slender own.

"I expect you to do what you tell me you'll do," Hart says.

Kevin swears softly, rattling Mrs. Dominguez, who draws herself up, frigid Catholicism in a housedress.

Hart, who has never had much room for anyone else's disapproval of Kevin, jumps into decisiveness. "We'll go this afternoon anyway, all right? Want to, Kev?"

"Not today," Caro says. "Not now." "Now" rhymes with "miaow," it's so plaintive.

Is it doing Caro any good, having her mother here? At night, Caro seizes Hart's shoulder or tugs at his hair; grinding his molars together to stifle his yawn, eyes slitted, he rolls over, he asks her tenderly, "What?" and she tells him. She dreamed she was about to give birth in a strange, dirty swimming pool. She was going into labor in the stall of a public restroom, graffiti spangling its walls, Fuck You and Fuck Me and the telephone numbers. Or the baby was born and she'd lost it. This last dream was particularly vulnerable to transmutation. She'd lost the baby in Safeway, she'd lost the baby in the hospital, or she'd left the baby sleeping on the lawn and it rolled into the river. After any of these nightmares, she is slow to be consoled. A backrub, a cup of tea, another quilt added to her heap, and she cries in his arms before sealing herself back into sleep, leaving him awake to prowl the house, studying the black, child-eating river through the living room's plate glass.

"I won't know where to find you," Caro says, "if you're wandering all over Santa Fe."

"Your mother is here," Hart says. The old woman gleams his way, dispatching her coffee. Caro travels light-footedly to the pot. Odd, for all her bulk, that she is still so prettily swift in anticipating her mama's wish. Mercedes pats the arm that pours the coffee, and Hart sees what he sometimes doubts: that they are, they clearly are, mother and daughter.

"Maybe you should go." Reversing herself, Caro grows cheerful. "Maybe your being gone will bring it on. A watched pot."

"I'll call in the middle of the afternoon," Hart promises.

The daughter bends for a hairpin and deftly drives it into the old woman's knot of white horsehair without again acknowledging her husband's existence.

One after the other, the cars they search out are junk. Blasted Chevys, battered Volkswagen beetles well into their second or third mechanical reincarnations. All morning and well into afternoon, the only car Kevin likes is a brutalized MG with a bumper sticker reading, "Hug a Vet." The vet is Monroe, idly tossing Oreos to his rottweiller while he explains that though he has led a long and happy life with the car he could be persuaded to part with it now for seven hundred and fifty dollars. "What a crock," Hart says, over cheesecake at Denny's. Kevin argues hard. He's mechanical, and anyway he has a friend who works on foreign cars and owns all the wrenches. The MG is cool.

"No," Hart says, but the MG appeals to him as a car for Kevin. It's pleasingly seedy interior, so small a girl (what girl? When will Kevin risk another girl?) would have to ride knee to knee with the driver, its quality of scraped daredeviltry so great for a first car. So infinitely desirable. "It'll cost a fortune in parts."

"I can take care of it. I will." Kevin's fingers alight on his breastbone—a vow, an unconscious one. Wow, Hart thinks, happy at this eagerness, which could not be more genuine. For once, possibly for the first time, Kevin has forgotten Molly Dubov.

"You'd have to."

"So, let me show you."

"So, let me think about it."

"I had an offer this morning," Monroe says when they swing by for a parting look. "It might still come through. I can't guarantee you this car will still be here when you get around to making up your minds."

"Let's go for it," Kevin pleads.

"That's not the way to make a major purchase, honey, under pressure," Hart says, and the magic of covetousness dies from his son's face. Hart has slipped and called Kevin "honey" in front of this earringed vet with his mean dog careening around his bare yard and his afternoon's beer cans lined up on the MG's hood, and something of the car's promise, the small-scale imported machismo it holds out to Kevin, dims.

Therefore, and probably predictably, Hart grows anxious to have the car. A subtle current of remorse, Hart's toward Kevin, runs just underneath the surface of the transaction, which Monroe senses and would exploit, if he did not feel sorry for Kevin.

Kevin twists the key and the MG startles into rattle-trap authority. This is the honeyed moment, the thrill Hart has sabotaged for his son: Kevin's pleasure is partly, mostly faked, and rings false. Hart says, "I'll follow you," and does, taking from his glove compartment a Spice Islands jar that once held—he sniffs—nutmeg. He drinks Johnnie Walker Black and tries to remember what newborns are like. They can't hold up their heads, he thinks, and when they mew, you wrap them tightly in a blanket so that only their faces show, making little Taos Indians of them. He thinks he remembers Kevin that way. How could that girl bear to kill herself? The MG's

canvas roof is up. From behind, it appears enviably snug.
It is evidence of Kevin's tense, imperfect bliss that he did
not at once wrench the roof down for this first drive.
Black exhaust gorges from the MG's tailpipe on a long
curve, and the father's heart goes *guilty, guilty, guilty,* all
the way home.

Caro comes up the slope, her belly leading, her flip-
flops clapping. The MG is exposed in all its failings. Its
dented fender, its dappling of rust. Its broken headlight,
crackled white quartz in chrome. Caro's disbelief, hidden
by her sunglasses, finds a gesture: the flat of a hand set
in the deep saddle of her back, her back arching more
deeply, her belly jutting more extravagantly, tightening
her swollen jumper. "How much?"

"Seven hundred and fifty. What do you think?"

"Do I think we have seven hundred and fifty?"

"Would I have bought the car otherwise?"

"You don't agree you're sometimes impulsive?"

"No matter what it cost, you would have implied,
'Too much,' Caro, wouldn't you? Anyway, it's too late
now. It's done."

"He'll take it back."

"You don't know this guy."

"He'll take it back," she repeats. "The stupid, senseless
greedy who sold it to you, you'll make him take it,
you'll tell him it's not what you want after all. It's not
safe. It's already been wrecked once, hasn't it?"

"Don't," Kevin says.

"Kevin is a good reliable driver. You have to —"

"How can you yell?" Kevin says. "She's pregnant.
How can you stand there and yell at her? If she hates the
car, I don't like it either. I don't want it. I could see you
thinking it would do me good."

Caro turns dazzling dark sunglass lenses his way.
"Would it?" she asks. "Help?"

"Right. Would it help for me to have a car you hate?
Right."

"If I stopped hating it?"

"If you stopped hating it, you'd be lying."

"If it was something you wanted, I wouldn't hate it.
I'd stop."

"Because you think it would make me better."

"Because nothing else seems—"

"You think a *car* could do that? Right."

"Kev," his father warns.

"It's not going to be a car," Kevin says.

"I can see that," Hart says. "Then what?"

"It's not going to be you," Kevin says. "Not a swine
like you." He looks at Caro. "And it's not you. I don't
know you."

She says, "You know me," two suns flitting across
her sunglasses as she swings her chin up toward him.

"Kevin, you stop," Hart says.

"You love my father who left my mother when she
did fucking nothing to deserve it. You don't know how
good she is. I don't have any idea why you married
someone like him. I don't have any idea why you're having this baby."

Caro says, "Ow," her expression a delicate mix:
alarm, satisfaction, wistfulness, fear. "It doesn't hurt," she
says, marveling downward so that her sunglasses slide to
the end of her long, upturned nose. "It feels like a little
ribbon rippling around, like a drawstring getting drawn
in."

"It's my fault," Kevin says.

"So what?" Caro says. "This is a fine time."

"You think everything in the world is your fault,"
Hart says to Kevin, and to Caro, "You're supposed to
walk."

"To walk? Walk where?"

"Down the road. To encourage the contractions.
Come on."

"Come too, Kev? Keep me company?"

He won't. He shakes his head. "I don't want to be
here."

Hart takes her elbow. "Another little pain's coming
girdling around," she says. "Ow. It's nice. Ow. If my
mother wasn't here, nothing would have been done in

time, would it? The baby's bed would never have been made. Do you think she's cooking dinner?"

"Walk," Hart tells her.

Kevin runs down the slope. The screen door's single bark rides up the hot air toward them, and Caro asks, "Why did he run?"

"To boil water," Hart says.

They walk down the dirt road, Caro swatting early mosquitoes from her bare arms, her gait duck-footed and majestic. "Nothing else," she says, and ten minutes later adds, "I'm sorry. It's not happening." She's still wearing her sunglasses, but her mouth, when she turns her face up, is stricken.

"Hey, so we go eat Mercedes's dinner," Hart says. "It's not the end of the world."

"Don't you want this baby?" Caro asks. And clop-clops away from him through hard sunlight, full of hurt. She would run if she could.

"We won't let you go on too long after your due date, no," Dr. Mendez says.

Caro asks, sounding anxious, "You don't induce labor, do you?"

"When the baby is two weeks late, the placenta is aging, and may no longer be supporting the baby well, and, yes, we sometimes do induce labor. First we'd run some tests to determine whether the baby is under stress — "

"Then Pitocin," Hart says.

"Then Pitocin, possibly, yes," the doctor says. She smiles from Caro to Hart, who is visibly anxious too, and asks, "Did you try my suggestion?"

They both glance guiltily away.

Hannah has a Dutch boyfriend, Florian, with a head of curly hair and a libertine's merry eyes. He has, in addition, a quality of possessing great personal freedom in his relations with women. He is simply very clever with women; he knows how to catch them up immediately into conversation, a kind of conversation that another

man would find repellent, almost viciously competitive—
Florian presenting himself and his virtues—but often
enough women respond to this approach delightedly, in-
dulgently, coquettishly. Sexually. Women love Florian.
He wandered into a bookstore in Santa Fe and captured
Hannah, who had been slouching against a wall under a
bad but beautifully framed print, abstractly rubbing
strands of her own hair between thumb and forefinger,
estimating their loss of silkiness, the onslaught of her
own middle age, the probability that she would never
have another child, her positively oppressive sense that
she should at last read *The Mill on the Floss,* she should
devote herself to that fat paperback for a hundred nights
under her electric blanket although *Great Expectations*
looks like more fun. Spendthrift that she was, she could
afford both, and just as she was about to throw herself
into the arms of the Victorians there was cool Florian,
his sexually forthright city as far from dampened
England as it was possible to get in Europe, his eyes
wondering just who *she* was, evaluating and elevating
her, because there had been in Hannah's recent life such a
dearth of male attention of any kind, shape, or form—
except for that of her son and her ex-husband, of course;
how could they count?—that finding herself read as a
sexual creature caused her to unslouch herself, shake her
fair head, and let her eyes focus on this interested foreign
face. Here was Florian, full of promise. He'd come for
her. Both knew it. It wasn't long before they disappeared
together.

Now, whatever has happened between the divorced
husband and wife, and almost everything has, she has
never before left Hart behind. Hart knows about Florian
because Hannah has always confided in him. Her confid-
ing in him is a symptom of the fact that from the world
of men who approached her, Hannah had chosen Hart
for herself, and remained assiduously true to her choice
well after they were divorced, suffering rather lightly the
inevitable desertion of one fleeting boyfriend, a carpenter
she had taken on more passively than passionately. Or so
it seemed to her ex-husband. Since the carpenter, who

left last year, the one and only man Hannah has slept with is Hart. Their lovemaking was an act so baldly needy and spontaneous, so short, unadorned, and potentially devastating, that Hart can't bring himself to weigh its meaning. Oddly, it appeared to mean more to him than to Hannah. What right has Hannah to flaunt her new equilibrium in his face? She was once sure she could not live without him. No longer. She doesn't even like him, she told him in bed. She doesn't like the way he lives his life — an amazing, cold, unexpected remark. It hurt and stirred him. In bed with her he had felt the change begin, a subtle thing and small, dwarfed by the bitterness in her voice when she repeated, "I don't like you. I don't like the things you do." The change, pitted from the first against skepticism harsh as Hannah's, had nonetheless begun there, in Hannah's bed, under Hannah's quilts, with Hannah's electric heater purring away at the sole of the single lovely, high-arched foot she aimed at it, with roughly the same degree of unselfconsciously sensual practicality with which she had, five minutes before, shoved her pelvis upward to receive him more deeply. More satisfactorily. She had managed that for herself, though she no longer loved him.

Worse, as he soon came to realize, she was ashamed of having slept with him. As she came and went, dropping off or retrieving their son, Hart kept getting whiffs of her shame. Caro, five months pregnant, had begun to show. Hannah's shame smelled like a child's dirty hair, a sodden diaper, a cast about to come off a broken arm — some soiled, infinitely intimate thing.

This was the situation Florian stole her from. Hart, who can't blame her for going, can't forgive Hannah, either, for causing him to feel as if he has just, freshly, lost her; as if it were not he who had brought about their divorce, but her whimsical infatuation with Florian that tore apart some old, honest, married love.

When really Hart's only honest, relatively sane love is for Caro. Until she got pregnant she was, in bed, rich felicity, his great good luck. Pregnancy made her queer and touchy; her tongue flew through astounding

recriminations, even as her body receded from him to
the pearly white, indifferent shore of late pregnancy.
The fetus defeated its father, or at least its father's desire.
It was, in Hart's experience, an unprecedented thing
for desire to do—simply to leave him as easily as it
had come—but once it was gone, he settled himself in to
play expectant husband. He could believe himself
happy among the squatting and blowing couples of
their natural-childbirth class. He could time a pretend-
contraction with the best of them, and never avert his
eyes from the film when the baby's head, surfacing like
the glossily dark pit of a halved avocado, crowned in the
huge vagina.

He pads barefoot into the cold kitchen. Mercedes has
tidied it until it reflects the status of—of Heaven, he sup-
poses, or possibly of her Brooklyn garret, sanctified by
widowhood. He throws open the refrigerator door. His
scrotum contracts in brilliant arctic air, his heart aches,
and he smells old bologna. He makes himself a huge,
comforting feast of a sandwich, like a cartoon husband
comically unaware of his place in the world—his humili-
atingly small, dark niche gazed into by huge, decisive
women as they pass. Well, hello, telephone. The
receiver's poison-control-center sticker, skull and cross-
bones, glows in the dark. Hart remembers the way that,
in Hannah's warm bed, he felt the brisk angel's wing of
his future pass over his heart. What had he wanted, how
had he judged his chances, at that instant, her heater
purring, the points of her collarbone flaring in her flat-
tish, freckled chest when she threw her head back into
the pillow, when she came? There is the telephone. Her
number is on a slip of paper held with a magnet to their
refrigerator. Like it or not, here it is, his new life: his ex-
wife's number on the refrigerator among the coupons for
Pampers, the Polaroids of friends' kids, the pre-divorce,
pre-distrust picture of Kevin, then smaller, slighter, and
more radiant, crowned by a soccer ball, crowing with
triumph, sun pouring down on him, on the green field
he spent his eleventh summer on. Caro's eternal

unfinished shopping list that reads *skim milk, chicken breasts, toilet paper.* As far as he knows never a day passes when his household does not need chicken breasts. Caro is ready for this baby. Is he? He examines himself with an intensity that eats away at a great rust of habitual, second-nature self-deceit and finds that, no, astonishingly, no, assuredly, *no,* he's not ready for this baby. He wades through the muck of this *no,* this terrifying black *no* nothing in him rises up to refute, to the telephone, and taps out the digits that will fly his voice toward a satellite, ricochet it off spacy cold metal to Europe, to that decaying old sea city where she is. *She answers on the second ring.* His surprise is slight, given the event.

But then again, so is hers. "You don't sound good," she says. "Let me sit up so I can think. There. I'm sitting." Then she recollects the terms they parted on. "What do you want? Is it Kev?"

"Nothing's wrong with Kev. This is me."

She's silent. "Hannah," he says.

"Yes. I said *yes,* here I am, you found me. I'm hanging up."

"No, Hannah, no, it's this baby. I don't want this baby. I'm not ready."

She laughs.

"Hannah, don't laugh. I don't want it."

"Then you *are* in trouble," she says with a lilt, her voice not as unkind as her words.

"Don't tell me that."

"Don't tell you that? When anyone can see it? I'm going now."

"Hannah. Say you won't go until I'm all right."

"I can't do that," she says.

"*Please.*"

Hart turns, hearing a sound. Behind him in the darkened kitchen, gazing at him with pitiless, timeless recognition, is his mother-in-law. His mother-in-law has just heard him beg, despairingly, in the dark kitchen, "*Please.*"

He swipes a dishtowel from the counter and hangs it in front of his genitals. He says very clearly, "I'm not a bad man. Not as bad as you think."

Hannah says distantly, into his ear, "Try A.A., Hart."

Mercedes says nothing at all.

He fidgets the dishtowel until his genitals are completely sheltered. How long does she mean to stand there? He says, "I can change."

Hannah says distantly, into his ear, "Goodbye."

Mercedes says nothing at all.

It leaves him nothing to go on, no clue about what will happen, the silence in which Mercedes sweeps from the kitchen.

In the small bathroom, in a dimness that seems to her unnatural—no lights outside the window; sounds, but no lights—Mercedes undresses down to the nitroglycerin patch she donned two hours ago against proof of her son-in-law's infidelity. It had been, for Mercedes, a scene of great violence, the big man with the dishtowel hanging before him; the woman, whoever she was, who is so shameless as to fool with the husband of a hugely pregnant woman, to quarrel with him over the telephone in his own home in the middle of the night. In the middle of the night when such things should have been long ago settled, and the husband and wife in bed together.

Of course, Mercedes reflects, her own husband sometimes went prowling from their bed at just such a hour. Of course he went catting around, dishonoring their life together and all she was. His infidelity, great secret that it was, still pains Mercedes, two decades later and thousands of miles away, as she is an old woman meticulously flossing her long, elegant yellow teeth. He was unfaithful, and it was love between him and Mercedes. Though he was unfaithful, it was love and it remained love. Once or twice when he'd left the bed, she'd been no less pregnant than her light-footed, besotted daughter is now. The difference between Caro and Mercedes is that she, Mercedes, will never see her husband's face again. No one exists to come back to bed. In her garret there are pictures, of course, but none of them precisely the face she wants. The long, gallant salt-and-pepper mustache, the wide wings of the aggressive nose, the cobble of chin, the bright lover's eyes, had not photographed well. They are not who she needs. They are inexact as memory never was. Seizing the nitroglycerin patch by its corner, Mercedes peels it away. It leaves a small chemically scorched rectangle, pink as sunburn, over her heart.

He said, "I'm not a bad man," and though that was a baffling thing for him to assert under the circumstances, there is something in it Mercedes can't dismiss. When he said, "I can change," it was, and she knows it was, the truth, and so they will go on together, her daughter and this palely alien American, and their life together will baffle Mercedes, surely, whatever else she learns about it, just the way her life would baffle them — or for that matter, any of her children — if she ever choose to tell them anything about it. But really it was none of their business, how you lived. It was their business that you took care of them, that you were there to nurse them through fevers and catch them before they fell into the river, but what, apart from love like that, did they need? The truth is that she is almost done with them.

In her robe she stares down the hallway to the opening window, and finds Kevin climbing clumsily in. To Mercedes's surprise, he is naked except for drenched cutoff jeans. This must be her night for coming across hugely tall, nearly naked Anglos. He is as astonished to see her as she is to see him. He could not have expected from her such a torrent of hair, or such self-possession.

"I'm sorry," he says, crouching over the window. "You heard something, and were frightened."

"Do I look frightened? Is this the way you come into the house?"

"I am sorry," he says, and then, as if she were not standing there, he rakes his hand down his side, his long boyish bare rib cage, and Mercedes, coming closer, sees the rising dappling of hundreds of mosquito bites. He goes for them feverishly with bitten fingernails, so harsh with himself she can hear the scratching. She says,

"You'll bleed." "I can't help it." "Stop that," she com-
mands, but his is the impotent impatience of someone
whose skin is *itching,* and despite his evident wish to
appear polite to her, he can't stop. She reaches forward
and seizes his wrist, which has a compact, knit-together
solidity that feels adult and male, as does his reluctance
to yield to her, but she is a general of little emergencies.
"My room," she directs, and once there daubs his spots
with oil of camphor from a neat brown bottle as he sits
on the edge of her bed, leaning forward, his huge elbows
on his big knees, his entire attitude a fusion of miserable
courtesy and real relief. Through the tonic vapor of camphor she smells cold water drying from a child's skin.
"You were in the river," she accuses his back.

Embarrassment freezes him.

"I could never have gone into a river," she tells his
back. At his nape, his hair is drying in a curl. "No matter what I felt, I could never have gone into a river."

"It's our river," he says, and shudders when she
touches his back again.

"You mean you're used to it."

"The way you're used to the subway, and the gangs."

"I do not court death," she says.

"Because to you, it's a sin."

"To you, it's not?" she asks, her voice going provoca-
tively rueful. "And your father, and my daughter who
loves you now, and the little brother or sister who is
coming? You go into the water thinking of what they'll
feel?"

His resentment is intact again. It lies in the milli-
metric tensing of his cold white back, and in the texture
of his skin, which shifts in that instant from a grateful to
a guarded passivity, so that she stops her doctoring and
waits until he says, "I do think of them."

"You don't think of them enough, then. Imagine a
vast hurt."

She gives him a moment to imagine it.

"Imagine them feeling it."

She gives him another moment.

"You would cause them such pain."

The expanse of his bare back, with its fine muscles, its rather daintily set shoulder blades and the long channel, deeply indented, of the spine, waits on her.

She says, "You can't do that to them."

She says, "It's simply a thing you can't do."

She says, tipping the bottle into cotton, fitting cotton to a welt, "You're through with this now?"

He says, "I just want to stop feeling what I feel."

She takes a deep breath. She inhales hugely, as against some formidable physical task. She apologizes to her dead husband's beautiful forgotten face for the calm with which she is about to tell this truth. She says, "You will."

When Hart rolls over, he is as quiet as can be, but it's no use. He dislodges Caro from sleep. Her curly long hair lies in a mess on the pillow. When she turns toward him, he tries to take his bearings from her expression. "I had a good dream," she says. "I was riding my mother's shoulders down this dirt road, and it was going dark, and I was rubbing a leaf across her forehead, I don't know why."

"Why was that a good dream?"

"I had some idea the leaf was magic. That it could keep us all safe."

"You know what I wish?" Hart says. "I wish that damn girl had listened for her mother's key in the lock before she started swallowing."

"No one could have expected there to be a traffic jam that evening," Caro says.

He tries to settle into a position that is both companionable and will still allow for the possibility of sleep, but she sits up tailor-fashion and begins caressing her belly.

"Anything?" Hart says.

"Not a thing."

"You and your body," he says. "Don't you think you're as stubborn as your mother? Let me ask you something."

"Ask."

"What is it? Why hasn't she ever liked me?"

"She likes you." He looks at her, arching his eyebrows morosely. "My mother," she says. "My mother is a mystery. All the time when we were children, living together in the tiniest house" — she fixes him with a dark, judicious, almost accusing gaze — "in intimacy you can't even begin to imagine, each of us knowing every single thing about all the others, we still knew she was a mystery. I don't think you can change her mind about you, Hart. But it doesn't matter to me, what she thinks."

What will happen now? Hart wonders, resting his knuckles on her defiant belly, pretending to knock, saying softly, "Come out, come out, and I'll be good to you," and she laughs and falls carefully onto her side in the rumpled sheets, the quilt sliding silently from the bed, she bringing her knees up and giving him a quarter-profile glance, and he locks a long arm around her, above her belly, under her breasts, and enters her from behind, and their pleasure in each other is so acute they forget it is meant to bring on pain.

DAVID KRANES

THE MAN WHO MIGHT HAVE BEEN MY FATHER

Whenen I was in the fifth grade at Walt Whitman Elementary in Brooklyn, my mother, who worked at a place called Rodeo nights and tried out for plays during the day, pulled me out of school and said we were going on a trip. I was less than excited. It was October, just after the Olympics, and it seemed all my mother could talk about was Florence Joyner. She said: boys should be excited about Florence Joyner too. Okay—if you say so.

My mother had been writing to a man in Idaho. A lot of days, I'd get the mail before she'd be there, and there'd be one of his letters. They came in fat little white envelopes, which, most of the time, looked dirty. In one corner, they'd say: B. Mitchell, with a box number and then: Sunbeam Springs, Idaho. When I asked, she always said, "He's a man," (which I'd figured), or, sometimes, "Honey: we just write." I asked if they'd ever met; she said, "Not really." She said it was crazy: one time, she'd been making a phone call to New Jersey and wasn't watching and dialed the wrong code and got this B. Mitchell, "Buddy" (right!) way off in Idaho. And they had talked. And she, I guess, had said enough so that, the next week, *he'd* called *her.* And that had started it, their speaking and writing back and forth for almost three years. And so it was B. Mitchell who she had taken me out of Walt Whitman for (which didn't thrill me). She had gotten a cheap car too, and we were going to be driving out in it to some place called Sunbeam Springs in Idaho to see him.

I had never had a father. Which was fine. My mother said he'd been "an indiscretion." She said, "theater people sometimes *do* things." Right. My mother was good, though. She was unusual. And pretty. And she could always surprise a person, which I liked, with a different voice or song or something. We would walk everywhere, and I would look and she would be, usually, the most interesting, wherever we went. She said her monologues to me. The ones she did when she auditioned. She said them to me all over. Sometimes, at home, going to bed; sometimes in the park by the bridge; sometimes, if it wasn't too crowded, in the subway. She said *Antigone,* and she said Beatrice from Shakespeare. She said Nina, from *The Sea Gull;* she said someone called the Princess and another called Julia and a woman called Marjorie from a play called *Extremities.* Her voice would go all over . . . everywhere, up and down. She'd laugh; I'd laugh. She'd cry and she'd get me sometimes (though I never told her).

"How long does it take to get to Idaho?" I asked. I was thinking about all the soccer games in the park I'd be missing.

"I'm not sure," she said.

"Did B. Mitchell *ask* you?" I said.

"More or less," she said. "B. Mitchell opened it up."

I nodded.

"I have to say . . ." and she did a funny thing, lifting her eyes, " . . . he certainly opened the possibility up. And I earned a little money this summer. From that commercial. So why not spent it . . . right?"

"I guess so," I said.

"And I'm not getting any younger, either—am I?" she said; then she said, like it was only half a question, "So . . ."

I had never really been with her in a car. It was a Honda. And where the paint was still on, it was blue. It was actually *two* colors: some places blue, some places brownish. And it had silver tape on one of the back windows where jerks, I'm sure, had tried to break in. She'd parked it a block from our apartment on Bergen Street, and I got to pack some clothes and books and a sketch pad in a Safeway's bag. And she put some clothes into a suitcase for herself and some cold pizza and some fruit and some sandwiches in another bag, and we headed off.

It was night. The car smelled like a stuffed chair and made, I suppose, the usual car noises but also a noise sort of like grating carrots. "This may be touch and go," my mother said as we crossed the bridge. I thought: *we're not even going to get to Pennsylvania.*

There was no radio in the car; it had been ripped out, and there was just its hole, but we'd brought the Quasar, and it played our tapes. My mother had a hundred plays on tape, but she didn't play those the first night. She played Anne Murray and Reba McEntire. And then Willie Nelson. "It's where we're going, honey," she said. "It's where we're going. I like the music."

I fell asleep. But before I fell asleep I remember the lights of New York behind, across the bridge, getting yellower and yellower and more and more like I was seeing them through a spider web. Meanwhile Reba McEntire was singing, "The Sweetest Gift." I remember my mother, with her arm around me, her hand patting my head: how she started singing: *It was a halo . . . sent down from Heaven.* "Oh, Sweet Jesus," I remember she stopped in her singing along and said—except it was to herself and I could tell that she probably thought I was asleep already—"Oh, Sweet Jesus . . . what am I getting into?"

When I woke up, it was still dark, and my mother was still driving. Now humming. My head was on her lap, the rest of my body out along the seat. "What time is it?" I asked. Her face was looking small, floating and white. She gave me a pat but kept looking ahead. "It's late," she said. "It's definitely late." She laughed.

"Are we stopping?" I asked.

"I don't know," she said.

I didn't understand.

"I suppose sometime," she said. "I suppose sometime we'll stop." She laughed again: "I mean, I guess we'll have to."

"Where are we?" I asked.

"Ohio!" she said, as if it were in one of her monologues, "Ohio!" as if the word *Ohio* were funny.

"How old is B. Mitchell?" I asked.

"His name is Buddy," she said.

"I know," I said.

"Buddy Mitchell!" She said his name the way she'd said Ohio! It was the way *I* would have said it. "Buddy Mitchell, of Sunbeam Springs, Idaho!" And she pulled a face.

"So, okay . . . how *old* is he?"

"Oh . . . thirtyish," she said and then smiled: "Or . . . thirty something."

"Thirty-one?" I asked.

"Thirty-two, thirty-three . . . thirty-eight . . . nine . . . forty. Somewhere there." She was twenty-nine. I was twelve. "I asked him once," she said. "'Are you on the downside of 45?' . . . and he said, 'Yes' . . . Would you like to stop?" she asked me.

"I guess," I said. "Where would we do that?"

"I'll find a motel," she said.

The motel was called the Piker Motel, and it had a red and green sign that would have seemed small in Brooklyn but seemed huge, actually, where it was—I guess, still in Ohio—because there were no other lights and only trees and the motel itself anywhere near. It was okay. The room and television were bigger than our apartment and television on Bergen Street—except it was three in the morning and there weren't, really, any programs on.

"Good night, honey," my mother said. She reached across from her bed to mine.

"Are you going to marry B. Mitchell?" I asked.

She didn't say anything.

"Mom?" I said.

"Idaho's a long way," she said.

"So, then . . . would I have a father?" I asked. It seemed weird, the whole idea: some guy, sitting in our kitchenette, asking me to eat more of my artichoke or something.

My mother did something then, when I asked that question about would I have a father. She did something with her breath . . . sucked it a funny way. Then breathed out. Then sucked it again. I waited. "Stranger things have happened," she said. And then we fell off to sleep. I think, actually, she may have said it a second time. It was a habit of hers: saying anything twice: "Stranger things have happened."

I got put in charge of the map. It was okay. I had this friend in Brooklyn, Pincy, who collected atlases, and he would have *loved* it, and it was probably better than my *doodling* all the time on my sketch pad. We were on I-80, except it was also I-90. It was early in the morning, and we were going past towns in the state of Indiana with names like Nevada Mills and Hudson Lake. And then it was noon, and it was like New Jersey, except not because it was still Indiana, a place called Gary. And then it was Chicago—on a lake and in Illinois. And then, in the afternoon, after we stopped at a place called Taco Burger and had something which made my mother laugh, called *huevos McMuffin,* it was just I-90 and the towns we rode past and then past some more were called things like Elgin and Winnebago and Woodbine.

The Judds were playing; my mother really liked "The Sweetest Gift." But there was also George Strait and Marty Robbins and Emmy Lou Harris. And then, when we changed again, this time into Wisconsin, hundreds of towns, all with Indian names—Tomah and Onalaska and Winona—and my mother started doing monologues. Reba McEntire was doing "My Mind Is

On You," and the town of White Creek was just out the window and it was getting dark, and my mother suddenly rolled down her window and yelled out, "I am what became of your child!" and then told me it was from a play called *Night Mother.* It was pretty amazing.

But also . . . the car wasn't sounding very good. It was making little spits and big rattles. At first my mother said, "Don't listen. Just read the map." But then they began coming more and sounding louder. So by St. Charles, in Minnesota, my mother had pulled into a Chevron, where a man with *Carl* on his suit said he'd "give it a shot." I wasn't too confident. It was seven at night, so we got a room at the Whitewater Motel . . . which had a big, yellow rubber raft on the roof, over our room.

It was nice; it was okay. My mother called and told the man, Carl, at the Chevron, where we were, and we went out for pizza . . . which was okay, except not as good as the pizza at Ray's on Sixth Avenue. It was okay, though, I suppose for Minnesota pizza. We brought it back to our room and watched "Moonlighting." My mother seemed nervous. She kept looking at the phone and getting up and going into the bathroom and running the water and coming back and standing and watching the screen and going to the motel window and pulling the curtains back and looking out.

"Does B. Mitchell . . ." I started to say something, but stopped. My mother looked at me. I started in again: "Does B. Mitchell know we're coming?" I asked.

"He does," she said. Then repeated it. Then looked back, out, toward the street.

"Have you called him?" I said.

"Have I called him when?" she said and I could see her biting her lip.

"Have you called him on our trip?"

"Not yet," she said.

"Should you?" I asked.

She looked like she was mad at first then like she couldn't figure my question. "Sometime," she said finally. "Of course. Sometime. Eventually."

"Do you think Carl will be able to fix our car?" I said.

"Honey . . ." Sometimes she would tell me not to push something. That was a favorite expression: *Honey, don't push it.* " . . . not so many questions . . . okay? Please, tonight," she said. So I said *sure* and went back to "Hawk" on television.

I don't think my mother slept very well. I almost think I heard her crying. I lay in bed . . . with light the color of some Chinese restaurant fish tank water sneaking through the curtains, and I tried to picture in my mind what it was that B. Mitchell might possibly look like. He was sort of short at first. Then he was sort of tall. Then he had a checked shirt on. Red and black. No tie. He looked pretty serious. Except, sometimes, he would smile. He also had on a pair of boots. With long laces. And his hair wasn't all that combed. And then he had a beard . . . but then the beard went away . . . except just a little . . . because he probably needed to shave. And then he had one of those vests on. Like the sleeping bags. When we'd gone out on the streets, in St. Charles, for pizza, there'd been a lot of guys with those vests: *down* my mother told me. And his face was lumpy . . . but okay; what I mean is: with edges . . . like a rock; it was all right. And his eyes were dark. And he had, like, really big, bushy eyebrows. Then I fell asleep.

The next day Carl told us "bad news." It was going to cost a lot to fix up what was wrong. "If you can give me another day, though, with the rascal . . . then I think I can do 'er," he said. Then smiled. He had what my mother guessed was zucchini on his teeth. "I've done a kind of baling wire job in the meantime," he said. "Just in case."

"That will have to do," my mother said.

"It might hold," he said. "It might not."

My mother thanked Carl and paid him, and when we started the car up, it sounded better.

It wasn't a good day, though. We were still in Minnesota, and it was raining. It was *really* raining, and the windshield wipers didn't work all that well. My mother had to lean forward and put her face almost *against* the windshield to drive. She started crying around Uexter. "Honey—don't mind me," she said. "I just need to cry a little. It's like the rain—I just need to . . . *do* this for a while and get it out of my system." I felt badly.

We had to drive pretty slowly. Near another town, called Blue Earth, the car started to go *thump-thump-thump-thump.*

We had a flat tire. She pulled over. She just sat for a while, with the engine running, moving her tongue around on the inside of her teeth, doing back-and-forth things with her jaw. "Okay," she said finally: "Okay . . . I can do this. It's a flat tire: why is it seeming like a problem? I just jack the car. I wrench the lugs. I lift one tire off, put the other one on, tighten the nuts again . . . we're on our way. This is not a problem. Are you feeling strong?" she asked me.

I said yes.

"Are you feeling like my right-hand man?"

I said yes again. What was she asking?

It was really raining.

We got out. She opened the trunk. She bent forward and then just stared in. She stood up straight. She wrapped her arms around herself . . . like a person who's cold . . . which she may have been. "I don't believe this," she said. "This isn't true. People don't sell other people cars without jacks and tools." She took deep breaths. Her blond hair dripped down over her face like weeds. She stared some more into the open trunk and then shut it and said, "I'm sorry. Back into the car."

I followed her.

She put our dim lights on. We sat a long time before a man driving a pipe truck stopped and asked what the matter was. She told him what had happened. The truck driver started looking at me. "How far are you going?" he asked. My mother told him Idaho. He looked at me a couple more times. He was a really skinny guy in a blue moving suit. "Let me see if I can rouse anybody in Fairmont," he said, and then, to my mother: "You want to sit with me in my cab while I make the call?"

"Isn't that a winch on the front of your cab?" my mother said.

"You know what a winch is?" he asked her.

"Isn't that one?"

"Well—I believe it is!" he said. He looked angry. He looked at me again. He looked frustrated.

"And it looks like you've got a cable on it," my mother said.

"Well, so it does!" he said and looked even angrier.

"Do you have tools?"

"I might," he said.

My mother wouldn't let him help. The only thing: she just asked him to lift our car with his winch and cable and then let us use his tools. She and I changed our tire in his headlights . . . there in the rain, while he sat in his cab, not looking happy. I loved it! . . . sort of. I loved *something* about it. I'm not sure. It was sometime in the afternoon. The rain in all the trees sounded like paper bags rattling. I pushed the wrench with her and helped her lift the one tire off and the next tire on. My mother's hands got so red that I asked her if they were bleeding, but she said no. And then she leaned in, with the rain over both our faces, and gave me a kiss. When we finished and looked up, there was a deer . . . who'd come out of the woods and to the edge of the road on the other side. He didn't look wet at all. He knew we were there. "Oh . . . !" my mother said: "Oh, my God . . . isn't he beautiful!"

My mother gave the skinny truck driver twenty dollars when he lowered and disconnected us from the cable.

"Who do you think I am?" he said.

"I have no idea," my mother said.

"I didn't stop for the money," he told her.

My mother looked like she was going to say something, then didn't. He kept pinching his nose with his thumb and his next finger.

"Do you have any children?" my mother asked him.

Now *he* looked like he would almost say something. "My ex-wife has a boy and a girl," he said.

"Keep the twenty," my mother said. "A wrecker would have cost a lot more."

The trucker eyed the twenty. I wanted him to look like a nicer person. His hand was the color of motor oil. "You know the problem with today's women?" he asked.

My mother said she had no idea.

"They *do* everything," the trucker said.

"We're just trying to share the planet," my mother said.

"With what?" the trucker said.

"Well, right now, I'm not sure," my mother said.

"My point exactly," the trucker said, and he held up an index finger with a black nail.

"Maybe it would be better if we all got out of this rain," my mother said.

And we did.

My mother played a Whitney Houston tape for about the next hundred miles . . . through towns like Imogene and Sherburn and Spafford: I was still on the map . . . though I sensed that probably that night, wherever we were, in whatever motel, I'd get my pad out and sketch the trucker, and that I'd probably get all the little twists in his face pretty right.

It started raining less. Then less. Which was good, because it was dark now, and before we knew, it wasn't raining at all, and there were stars, even—way up through the windshield and an almost-full moon. My mother rolled down her window. It was cold. I said that: I said, "Mom, it's pretty cold," and she said: "Honey, I know . . . but just let me drive a while letting it in." And so that was fine.

She changed the Whitney Houston for our Marty Robbins and began to smile. "You must be hungry," she said.

I said I was.

"Next place," she said.

The next place was Magnolia, with a cafe called the Split Rock Ranch.

"I'm ordering a steak," my mother said. "We're in the West, so I'm ordering a steak. Maybe you'd like one."

"You never eat meat," I said to her.

"We're twenty miles from South Dakota," my mother said.

I didn't get it.

"Once I ate meat," she said: "I may do it again . . . I may do it again!" she repeated and laughed.

The steaks were good. Our waitress's name was Cornelia. She had red hair and cheeks like pancakes. We had pie and ice cream afterwards.

"I feel really good tonight," my mother said. "I feel really positive and glad we did this."

"It's fun," I said. I said it to make her feel good . . . still, it wasn't that much of a lie. "Have you called B. Mitchell?" I asked.

"Tonight, we sleep in South Dakota," she said. "Isn't that a great name for a state—South Dakota?"

We stayed in Brandon. "Big day tomorrow!" my mother said.

And it was. We went totally across South Dakota and into Livingston, Montana. In South Dakota, we kept going past places called national grasslands: Fort Pierre National Grasslands, Buffalo Gap National Grasslands. All they were were *grass*. But they were better than The Badlands . . . which was, like, all sand, all *rock*. Even in the rain, I think I liked Minnesota better. In Minnesota, you could see places where people lived, houses with porches.

But my mother was happy. She was singing with The Judds. She was singing with Emmy Lou Harris and with Willie Nelson and with George Strait and calling all these different monologues out the window: "They're from *Fool For Love*," she said. I remember one line—she kept saying it: ". . . she was tresspassing! She was crossing this forbidden zone but couldn't help herself!" She was really happy.

We spent that night in Livingston. "This is where we drop down," my mother said. "Tomorrow we drop down through Yellowstone Park and into Idaho, and I want to see it."

"Will we see the fire?" I asked.

"We probably will," she said.

"It won't still be burning, though . . . right?" I said.

"No, I think it's all out," she said. "I think it's all out there now. I think they put it out so they could focus on the Olympics." And she laughed.

Our motel was called The Red Dog, but he wasn't around—there was just an orange cat when we checked in. It was sort of like a barn, The Red Dog; it had boards on the wall. And camera pictures of different men catching trout. They were interesting pictures. The men looked really glad they'd caught the fish they were holding. I wondered if any of them had kids along. On their trips. I wondered if any of the kids had taken any of the pictures.

"Do you know what we'd have done . . . if I were rich and famous and a lady of leisure?" my mother asked.

I said I didn't know.

"If I were rich and famous and a lady of leisure," she said, "we'd be staying tonight at a place with a heated indoor pool. And at this very moment . . . I'd be doing the backstroke."

"What would I be doing?" I said.

"That's a good question," she said. "Maybe it's just as well that things are as they are."

We had Italian food at a place called Gambini's. My mother said it was a joke, the restaurant name, but the food tasted good. She had something called angel hair pasta that she said was perfect. And garlic bread. She kept asking for more garlic bread. "What have I got to lose, right?" she said to the waiter.

He said, "It cures everything."

"Then I'm in great shape," my mother said and stuffed another piece in her mouth.

We had wine too. They brought it in what they called a "carafe," and I had a whole glass. When my mother finished the carafe, someone brought another. Also, one of the things about Gambini's was the pool table, where, sometimes, people played . . . sometimes they didn't. So: when they weren't and there was just garlic bread and wine on our table, my mother said: "What do you say we shoot some pool?"

I was excited. I'd played a couple times at an arcade. My mother was pretty good. She'd get up on her tiptoes and lean way over and squint her eyes and say "watch this" and, most times, make a shot. She beat me, and we shook hands, and while we were shaking, this guy came up, wearing a dark green woolly shirt and one of those sleeping bag vests and cowboys boots and Levis. And he was smiling. He slapped a quarter onto the edge of the pool table. And my mother smiled. "What do you say?" he said. She said, "what the hell!" He said his name was Todd, and she introduced me and herself. "Do you mind, honey?" she asked.

I said (as if I didn't know), "about what?" She said *if she played one game of pool with Todd*.

I didn't like the idea, but I could see that she was in the mood, so I said fine.

They played. Todd was pretty good. He hit the cue ball hard, and it slammed into the other balls and moved them around. He and my mother talked. I didn't hear everything; I kind of walked around. They were talking theater and stuff. I knew names of a lot of plays, but they were talking about poems too, and books, and I didn't know those.

They played a second game. Todd's hair was curly and the same color as my mother's. My mother grabbed the carafe of wine and brought it near the pool table, and they both kept pouring glasses. My mother was laughing. Todd was kidding around. He used his pool cue and did a thing that I'm pretty sure was a monologue because my mother shrieked and said, "I can't believe it! I can't believe it! I'm in Montana . . . and people are doing *The Cherry Orchard!*"

"You're in Livingston," Todd said. "It's very different."

After they finished their second game, they put quarters in the jukebox and danced. Close. My mother looked like she might go to sleep and then maybe like she *was* asleep and Todd was carrying her. Being careful.

But then I saw that she *wasn't* . . . asleep . . . because she was moving her hands on the very top of Todd's back.

Then they finished, and Todd brought her over to where I was eating corn chips. "Thanks for the loan," he said. "I appreciate it."

"What loan?" I said.

"He means me," my mother said.

I said I knew that.

She stared at him. He looked over and smiled. He looked a lot like the men in the pictures with the trout.

"Thank you, Ma'am," he said to her.

"Thank *you,* Sir," she said.

"She's a hell of a pool player," Todd said.

Back at the Red Dog, I did a sketch of Todd. I got his hair really well . . . and his eyes and sarcastic smile: it was pretty good. While we were getting ready for bed, I asked my mother did she *like* Todd. She didn't say anything. She was by the mirror, brushing her teeth and just looking in and in. When I asked again, after we were in our beds, she just said: "You'd like a father . . . you'd like a father, wouldn't you?"

I said I didn't care; it didn't matter: I could have a father or *not* have a father — it was all the same.

She said, "You don't meant that."

I didn't know what to say next. So, I asked her again *did she like Todd?*

"I'm six years older," she said. Then, like she does, she said it again: "I'm six years older. I'm twenty-nine, honey. He's twenty-three. But he was certainly nice." Then we fell asleep. Except I woke up in the middle of the night, and she was out of bed, the thin curtain at the window wrapped around her, and just staring out. I don't know why . . . but I didn't move; I stayed still.

We cut down into Yellowstone Park along U.S. 89. The sky was like a lake. When we got near the park, I saw smoke. "It's still the fire!" I said, but my mother said she didn't think so because the smoke was white not black, and it was probably steam. "Geysers," she said. And it was. They were all over. And smaller things with colored moss and water that they called paint pots. We

saw elk and bison and deer and huge birds. We got out
of our car and walked down a hill to where the fire had
been and walked into it—the black trees, the black
grass—but not all of the grass and not all of the trees
were burnt: there was green. And flowers. "So they
were right," my mother said.

"Who was right?" I asked.

"The people who said *Don't do anything*," she said.

"What people?"

"The people who said *Don't interfere*." And she reached
her hands out and grabbed the trunk of a burned tree
and twisted them, the way you do sometimes on a bat,
and then took her hands with the black on them and
rubbed them all over her face so she looked like a coal
miner. "Next year, I'll be blooming again," she said:
"And even better! It's not a problem."

We got onto U.S. 20 and crossed into Idaho. It was
afternoon, and my mother was really quiet. I watched
her forehead, which still had black on it, and her eyes.
They were going through something. "Do you want me
to change the tape?" I said around Big Springs, and she
said, "What tape?" She started drumming her fingers on
the steering wheel. We were by a town on the Snake
River called Last Chance when she said, "Well, I guess
it's time," and pulled in by what was called a fly shop,
where there was a phone booth and got out and placed a
call.

"Were you calling B. Mitchell?" I asked when she got
back in and we were going again and passing a place
called Harriman Ranch.

"His name is Buddy," my mother said.

"Were you calling Buddy Mitchell?" I asked.

"Yes," she said.

"What did he say?"

"He said he was looking forward to . . ."

" . . . What?" I said.

"I don't know," she said.

"He just said that he was *looking forward to . . .* ?"

"*Getting acquainted*: something like that," she said. Her voice sounded irritated — and she knew it, because then she said, "Honey, I'm sorry."

I said, "Are you going to wash your face first?"

We went by Sugar City. And Rexburg. And Idaho Falls. There were rocks everywhere from volcanoes and, in one place, water that shot out of a cliff. I tried to get my mother to do monologues, but she wouldn't. We went to Arco and then Carey and then Bellevue. It got dark. We went to Hailey and Ketchum, and my mother finally said something. She said: "Can you believe all these condominiums?"

"Are we ahead or behind time?" I said.

She looked at her watch. "I guess a little ahead," and then she said: "Can you last one more hour?"

"For what?" I said.

"For supper."

I said sure.

We climbed up mountains, and they were pretty steep. "These are the Sawtooths," my mother said. "This is called Galena Summit."

"I know," I said. "I've got the map."

We headed down again. And it was a huge valley. Even though it was night, you could see. Because the moon was full. And the whole valley lit up blue with the tops of the Sawtooths white and you could see why they called them The Sawtooths.

"This is pretty amazing," my mother said.

"It is." I agreed. And it was.

When we got to Stanley, just before Sunbeam Springs, it was almost nine, and the one place open for food belonged to Elvis Presley's drummer. That's what the man where we filled up on gas said: "Then," he said, "not now. Now he's dead. Elvis . . . not the drummer."

I had a cheeseburger; my mother just had a beer: she said she wasn't hungry. The place, Jack's, was huge, with a bar but practically no tables to eat. Mostly, it had space, which my mother called a dance floor . . . which was probably true, since a man and woman were dancing. My mother watched them and sipped her beer. She only finished half. I've tasted better cheeseburgers, but the french fries were okay.

When we got back in the car, after Jack's, my mother just sat at first, not moving.

"Aren't we going?" I said.

"It's thirteen miles," she said. "Thirteen miles . . . we're there."

"To B. Mitchell's house?" I said.

"There's a cafe," she said. "He's waiting."

"Does he know *I'm* here?" I asked.

My mother didn't say.

"Mom?"

"He does," she said. "He knows your name," she said. "And that you're along . . . and that you're twelve."

The road to Sunbeam Springs went along the Salmon River. Coming around one bend, our headlights filled up with smoke. "Oh!" my mother said.

It was like the steam in Yellowstone. "Honey, they're *hot* springs," she said; "From the mountain!" She was smiling, and I was glad. "Look! They go down to the river!" She turned the car into a pull-off and jumped out. "Come on," she said, "look!"

There was white steam everywhere—and the same smell we'd had that morning in the park. "God, this is amazing!" she said. "This is . . . I mean, this is extraordinary; I can't believe this!"

Then she took my hand, and walked me down a path to where the hot spring water washed into the black river. People had put stones around and made pools. "I love this!" my mother yelled up into the sky: "I just want you to know, I love this!" And then she bent and dipped a hand into a pool. "Oh God," she said; "Oh, dear!" And then she got . . . what-she-calls-when-I-get-it *antsy*. She got antsy and began wriggling and saying: "I don't know . . . I don't know if I can resist this . . . it's asking a lot." And then she said, "Oh hell, come on; you live once!" and then: "Are you with me?"

I wasn't sure. I wasn't sure what she was up to. I said: "With *what*?"

She said, "with *me*" then smiled; "with *me* . . . with *me*. What do you say?"

I said all right.

She said, "Just follow." And she pulled off her sneaks. And then her skirt. "It's an adventure," she said.

"I guess," I said . . . though I still didn't know what it was she was planning.

It was pretty cold. The wind came down the ravine where the river was . . . the way it sometimes blew down streets in Brooklyn. But I took my sneaks off. Then my pants. My mother was completely naked now and stepping into one of the pools and making sounds like a bird. Pretty soon I was in a different pool, close beside her, and it felt weird—I have to say that—it felt weird at first, a little weird: I felt uncomfortable to be naked . . . outside . . . in a river with my mother.

"Spectacular!" she yelled out at the sky: "Spectacular!"

"Spectacular!" I yelled. It seemed the thing to do.

"Spectacular!" she yelled again, and then we yelled "Spectacular!" together. I felt better.

She was pretty. I have to say that. She was really pretty, and the moon was full, and the water felt just amazing—hot, then cold—perfect. And my mother's skin—I shouldn't have looked at it, probably, but I did; I couldn't stop—it was pink. All the black from the Yellowstone fire had been washed away from her face. "You know: if it's just this," she said. "If it's only this . . . it's okay."

We dressed. We didn't have towels, but the wind dried us. It was icy cold. But it didn't feel bad. It didn't feel bad at all; the steam was nice. Then we climbed back to the car and started up.

Two miles later, we saw the Sunbeam Springs Cafe. It was lit. And as we got close, I could see a man sitting by the window, wearing a red hunting cap, and I could hear my mother pull in her breath. She saw him too. He got bigger but not big. He was looking through the glass. He wasn't young. He had marks on his face. My mother drove past and didn't pull in. She drove about a half mile and didn't talk. I knew I should keep quiet too.

When she pulled over, the car still running, I waited for her; I knew she wouldn't want me asking before she said. She put her hands together and hit the tips of her fingers against her lips and started shaking her head.

"I can't do it," she said.

I knew what she meant, and I knew she meant it.

We sat there together a while longer. Then she reached for her door handle. "I'll just be a minute," she said; "I need to breathe . . . some of this air again. You stay here." And she opened her door and got out and walked in front of the car where I could see her in the lights, and she put her head back so it was faced way up into where the stars were. And the moon. And I could see her breathing—big breaths—then letting them out. Her breath was like what had gone up out of the hot springs.

When she came back, she said: "Will you be angry?" And I said, "No. But I have to go to the bathroom." And she said, "I'll pull over onto the blind side of the cafe . . . and you can go in."

And she did that. And I went in. And B. Mitchell still was sitting by the window and looking out. He had a black shirt on and a yellow tie. I think he'd sprayed his hair. He looked okay. Not bad. He didn't look as old as he had driving past, but—but he was a lot older than my mother. And his face was one of those faces: my mother says they're people who've had complexion problems when they were young. I asked the man behind the counter where the restroom was. B. Mitchell heard me and he turned and looked. The counterman pointed down a hall. Now B. Mitchell was pressing his face hard against the glass and had a hand up to one side to help him see into the night.

I peed. I came out. B. Mitchell was there again and looked at me. I looked back. He nodded. I nodded. He looked like a nice person. He looked like a person who might be fun and might take you on a fishing trip or on a hike or on a horse somewhere. But he wasn't young. He said evening. His voice came real deep and quiet . . . like a voice that I wouldn't've minded if it came through a door. Except it wouldn't. Because he was just a guy — I can still draw him with a bumpy face and a black shirt and a yellow tie, sitting in a cafe by the Salmon River, drinking coffee, waiting, staring through a window. He was just a man with stuff on his hair who might have been my father.

MARK LITWICKI

STOLEN CHILD

The baby was still there where Joe had set it just beside the water in the dark part of the bank. The two boys sat in the dirt up above the baby, watching it. It had dark hair and dark skin; it looked like an Indian baby. The eyes were clamped shut tight. Joe was glad for that. He didn't want to see the baby's eyes.

There were a lot of flies on the baby. Joe told Taterhead.

"It doesn't bother the baby," Taterhead said.

Joe stood up. "Well Christ, Tate, it bothers me," he said. "How can you be so fucking calm all the time."

Tate looked up at him, not smiling, not not smiling. "We can't do anything about it," he said. "All we can do is wait for those guys to come back."

Joe walked to the Volkswagen, which seemed to be sinking deeper into the sand every time he went back to it. He brought a white T-shirt to the baby and shooed the flies away with it. Then he put the shirt on top of the baby, tucking it in around the sides, so the flies wouldn't get in. He bit down hard on his tongue. He sure as hell didn't like touching dead babies.

Then suddenly, despite his sorrow and disgust, he felt himself want to laugh. He stifled it back the same as he had his puke earlier and he went back up to sit beside Taterhead again. Then Joe started to laugh again, and even though he tried not to, it came out. He covered his mouth with his hand. Taterhead was looking out across the river.

"It's like one of those jokes," Joe said.

Taterhead turned, and Joe laughed more, still trying not to.

"Like one of those dead baby jokes. And we're in the middle of it. We're part of the joke, Taterhead." Joe covered his mouth, but he couldn't make himself stop shaking from the stupid laughter.

Taterhead looked at him, not smiling, not angry. He spoke firmly:

"You shouldn't laugh at that baby."

And that broke the humor out of Joe and brought reality back to him and he felt nauseous again, his empty stomach twisting itself tighter around the thought of it. They both sat for a long time quiet, looking out across the water to the reservation side of the river, where the sharp hills rose up into the desert. Joe wanted to tell Taterhead that he was sorry for laughing at the baby, but it seemed like a stupid thing to say. And it wouldn't matter anyway. Taterhead wasn't mad; he was sorry too that Joe laughed.

A big white bird, blinding in the afternoon sun, flew along with its wings almost touching the water and landed on the other side of the river. It stood on long orange legs in the shallow water near the bank.

"Jesus," Joe said. "Look at that." He'd never seen a bird like that on the river. The bird struck a pose; head turned, wings tucked in tight.

Tate sat and looked at it the same way he'd looked at the baby, the same way he looked at anything: as though he'd been looking at such things all his life, and knew just what it meant and what it was worth. The bird stuck out its chest and stretched its wings.

"I love birds," Tate said.

With a powerful flash of white wings the bird lifted off again out of the river.

Taterhead turned to look at Joe, his eyes big in
wonder, the kind of look where if you didn't know
Taterhead you'd think he couldn't be serious.

"They can fly!" he said, as if it were some great dis-
covery.

Joe nodded, watching the white bird as it disappeared around a bend in the river. It could fly, sure as
shit.

A long time went by and no one came for the baby; no
one came to relieve the boys of their death watch. The
baby was still there under Joe's T-shirt and Joe and Tate
still sat above it, watching. Sometimes they stood up and
walked around, drank some warm water from the bottle,
took a piss. But they always came back to that same spot
under the tall cottonwoods on the cool bank of the river.
Out in the road the sun burned down with all its summer fire and the sand was so hot you could feel it burning through your shoes. The hills across the river
wavered in the rising heat of the afternoon.

Tate swam for a while in the river, but he didn't go
up to the jumping rock; he just swam in the shallows
there in front of their sad encampment. Joe didn't want
to swim anymore; he didn't like the way the river looked
now. It was different from the night before, when they
were drunk and stumbling, splashing in the dark; different from the morning, when they'd jumped half asleep
from the jumping rock to wake themselves up in the ice-
cold water. If he went in now, he knew, he'd only start
thinking again, thinking about how he saw it floating
along, turning slowly in the current, and how he
thought it was a piece of wood at first, or trash, and
then when it was closer and he could see the little arms
and legs and the tiny bluish clenched fists he thought it
was a kid's doll and he'd almost gone to pull it out by
one leg, maybe hold it up above his head and yell look
what I caught, but then, when he saw what it was really,
he'd picked it up in his arms that felt like they were
someone else's arms, carried it just like it were a real
baby, like his sister in Tucson taught him to carry her

baby, carried it across to where Taterhead stood not saying anything but knowing what it was, so little and cold
and hard in Joe's arms, and then he set it down on the
bank where it was now, where Joe sat watching it, covered up in his T-shirt that said Camp Geronimo on the
back.

Joe told the hippie guy what he had found and the
guy put his beer down and said "No way," but then they
went over to look and the girlfriend said "Oh my God."
So they went for help in their truck, to get someone. The
police or something. They told Joe and Tate to wait.
That was a long time ago.

Taterhead was back from swimming; he sat dripping
in his place on the bank. The water sank into the thirsty
sand as fast as it fell.

"You should swim," he said. "It feels good." He
shook his head and water flew everywhere. It felt good
on Joe's arm. "It must be about a hundred and twenty
out here."

"What if they don't come back?" Joe said. Both of the
boys had been wondering about that for a while. The
sun had crossed to the other side of the river.

Tate didn't answer, and Joe didn't ask the question
again.

"I'm hungry," Tate said.

"We don't any have food."

"I'm still hungry."

"I don't think those guys are coming back," Tate said
finally. The sun was hanging above the hills across the
valley now. "It's been plenty of time. They could've
gone all the way to town and back by now."

Suddenly it seemed ridiculous that they had waited
so long. It was only about half an hour out to the main
road, maybe forty-five minutes to the nearest phone.

By car.

Joe looked over to his car, sunk up to the axle in the
soft sand. The road was on lower ground than the
shaded bank of the river, so all he could see was the
green roof of the car. It looked like the thing had sunk

almost completely away. Amazing, Joe thought, how useless a car is when it won't move.

"Maybe they got scared," Tate said. "Maybe they got scared and didn't want to talk to the cops."

Joe nodded. "I think those people probably had some serious drugs."

"Maybe they were out here hiding from the police."

"Maybe. This would be a good place for it."

They sat in silence as the sun sank lower, shining through the spines on the saguaros that marched up the hills far across the river, outlining each cactus in gold. Staring at the moving water, Joe could still hear himself laughing, that stupid helpless giggle, as if the sound had traveled across the river and hit the rocks and then bounced back to remind him. Now he couldn't understand why he'd laughed, why he'd thought it was funny. It didn't feel funny, hadn't felt like laughter. He wished he could reach across and smash the rocks, smash that laughter before it could echo back to show him how he sounded, show how he really was. Taterhead didn't laugh. Joe closed his eyes on the river and the baby, tried to forget they were there, forget he'd tried to make it seem like a joke when it wasn't a joke. Still, it was like a joke, Joe told himself. There were some jokes like that, and people thought they were funny.

When Joe opened his eyes the sun was gone behind the hills. And the baby was still there, wrapped in Joe's Boy Scout T-shirt.

Everything was quiet. Two dragonflies played at the water's edge.

"Fuck it," Joe said. "Let's go swimming."

Taterhead watched as Joe stood and marched defiantly off in the direction of the jumping rock. He looked at the baby once, then got up to follow.

The river was deep by the rocks, and Tate and Joe dove and swam for a while, trying to forget about the baby. Joe didn't feel too good about being in the river, so he'd just dive in and let the current carry him around to the bushes at the side where he could climb out and jump again. He'd never really cared for diving before, but now it seemed like the most fun he'd ever had. He wanted to go to the big cliffs where people jumped, but they were miles upriver, past the forks. It was a good place to go not only to jump but because sometimes girls climbed up there and took off their suits and jumped naked, and the people down below would cheer. The sheriff's deputies tried to make them stop because every so often someone would dive and forget to pull up when they hit the water and they'd break their necks on the bottom. But mostly the people survived it and had a good time. The cliffs were high, maybe ten times higher than the rock he stood on now, and Joe had only dived from them once, but now he wanted to go back. The girls who dived were crazy, or just drunk. Maybe it was one of those girls whose baby was down on the bank. Joe imagined a naked Indian girl standing on top of the cliff, with the people cheering. And no baby. "Where's your baby?" Joe said aloud, startling himself. Taterhead was swimming; he didn't hear. Joe said it again, louder. "Where's your baby?" Damn Indian girl. Joe didn't want to think about it, didn't want to think about anything, but the thoughts came to him anyway. He spat into the river and jumped. He liked hitting the water, then pulling up sharp, arching back and feeling like the whole world had slammed on the brakes, like gravity had reversed itself and was trying to throw him up out of the water, feeling everything slow way down just before his head broke the surface. He liked hitting the water that way, but what he liked most was just before hitting: he was happiest in mid-air, in that tiny space of time between jumping and hitting, a moment so short he could only know it after it happened.

He climbed out by the bushes and went up beside Taterhead on the jumping rock. Joe was going to push him in for fun, but Tater looked serious and all at once it seemed like it was almost dark; the sky above the hills was deep red, and Joe suddenly felt guilty, like they had been caught shirking their responsibilities, ignoring their

purpose. Their only task had been to watch that baby,
and now what were they doing?

"We better go back," Tate said.

"Let's swim down," Joe said, and he jumped in and
Tate followed and they swam out and let the current
carry them around the bend, and when they got to the
place under the cottonwoods where they'd left the baby,
they discovered it was gone.

The only thing worse than having the baby there, Joe
quickly realized, was having it gone. They walked
cautiously in across the shallows, staring stupidly at the
place where the baby had been.

"Jesus Christ," Joe said.

Without moving they searched the shadows of the
trees and beyond them for some sign, but the light was
draining fast from the sky. Everything was gray and disappearing; the color was almost gone from the trees. Joe
felt a chill and ran to the car to get the towels off the
hood, where they'd been drying. When he looked back
he saw Tate's silhouette against the river, the water's surface sparkling with the last light in the sky. Tate was
standing with one foot on top of the other, the way he
did when he was embarrassed, or nervous. The silhouette
swayed uncertainly against the river, between the dark,
unmoving trees, but as Joe watched it suddenly seemed
like Tate was standing still and everything else began to
move; the whole world behind Tate and around him and
between him and Joe seemed to be tilting, rolling like a
black sea, getting darker and more foreboding, and Joe
grabbed the towels and walked fast through the trees and
back to his friend.

"We'd have heard if someone came to get it, wouldn't
we, Joe?" Taterhead asked.

"Seems like it. We'd have heard a car at least."

"Sometimes the cops ride horses around here." The
shirt was gone, too. There was nothing left on the bank
where the baby had been.

"How long ago did we leave it?"

"Maybe half an hour. An hour. I don't know."

"Jesus, Tate," Joe said. "What if *no one* took it?"

Tate could barely make out Joe's face in the dark. "Then it would still be here."

"What I mean is, maybe it was animals. Coyotes or something," Joe said. Two nights before they'd seen two coyotes run across the road and argued about what was the right way to pronounce the word. Taterhead didn't say the 'e', and he said the reason Joe said it the other way was because he was born back east. Joe used Taterhead's pronunciation now. He threw his head back and looked up in the dark trees. "Man," he said, "coyotes probably took it to fucking eat. Oh Jesus, Tate, how do we get ourselves into shit like this?"

"You think one of those skinny things could carry a baby?"

"Taterhead, I don't know. But how the hell else can you explain it?"

Taterhead put his hand on Joe's arm. "I can't explain it, Joe," he said. "That baby is gone."

They stood for several minutes looking down where the baby had been, until they couldn't even see the ground anymore. The only sound was the heavy rush of the river moving past.

"It's like the baby never was there," Tate said.

"Like it was all a dream."

"We wish it was," Tate said. "But it really happened."

Joe remembered the weight of the baby in his arms. "It happened," he said.

The road their car was stuck in led back to the forks, where there was a big sand flat where people would leave their cars when they went tubing on the river. The people would take two cars and leave one at the forks and then take the other up to Bush Highway bridge or somewhere farther up the river, then float back down to the forks. No one ever went farther downstream than that. It might be days before someone would come so far down that Joe and Tate could ask for a ride out to the road.

By morning the bottle would be empty, and they'd be drinking out of the river, like animals. The river water was no good to drink. So they decided to walk to the forks. Someone might come there in the morning. Tate guessed it was about five miles; Joe guessed more.

"Either way," Tate said.

They took the water bottle out of the car, and took Joe's daypack with the towels and a pint of rum that had somehow been neglected the night before.

"Goddamn," Joe said, looking at the bottle and thinking for the first time about the night before. "We were drunk last night." He put the bottle in the pack, under the towels.

"You couldn't even walk," Tate said.

"Neither could you."

Even in the dark, Joe could tell Taterhead was smiling.

"At least I could crawl," Taterhead said.

"That's something," Joe said.

"It's important," Taterhead said. "You should at least be able to crawl."

Joe laughed, and it was a good laugh this time; it felt like laughter. Tate laughed too.

They walked for a long time without talking much, and each time the road forked they took the left side, closer to the river. It was still hot, even in the dark, and they sweated as they walked and before long the water bottle was empty and their good spirits faded, and as the road stretched on they got more and more depressed about everything. For a while they tried to decide what might have become of the baby, but they couldn't agree — Joe wanted to think of an explanation and Tate said that there wasn't any, and no use trying to find one. So they didn't talk at all for a couple miles, just walked and stumbled and tried to stay on the road as it rose and dipped into ruts and patches of soft, dry sand still hot from the day's sun. Thorny paloverde branches swept into the road in places, catching their shirts and tearing at their faces. In the darkness Joe couldn't tell what he was

seeing and what he wasn't. Shapes seemed to move at the
edge of his sight, but when he turned there would be
nothing. He imagined a shadowy form, running close
and silently along the ground, a skinny old coyote with
glowing red eyes and a baby tight in his jaws, wrapped
in white. Then he'd turn to look and the image would be
gone, vanished behind a creosote bush, or just into the
deep night air. After a while a thin piece of the moon
rose up and then it was easier to stay on the road, but
the feeble light only made the shadows deeper. Joe didn't
tell Tate about the coyote; he took comfort in the
thought that Tate didn't see any such thing, and he didn't
want to learn otherwise.

Later that night, when the air had cooled some and
become heavy with the sweet perfume of the desert, they
saw the light of a fire burning far away.

The man poked at the coils with a long stick, lifting and
twisting them as the flames jumped from one shape to
the next and up into the dark. From across the open lot
the boys could see another man, standing back from the
fire, beside a white flatbed truck. This man pulled
another bale down from the truck and carried it to the
fire. The blaze reflected orange on the white truck. He
threw the bale in and the flames grew taller than the
men, throwing a shower of sparks into the dark sky. The
boys entered the circle of light and walked toward the
men, who knew they were coming but didn't turn to see.

"Good evening," Tate said.

It was wire they were burning, the men explained.
They were Mexicans. They could sell the copper, but
only if they burned the insulation off first. The man with
the stick kept moving the coils so they would burn completely. The insulation burned fast and hot and smelled
like a car wreck, like burnt rubber. On one bale the loop
that held it together broke and the coiled wire sprang
apart, unwinding itself, twisting and snarling in the
flames like it was alive, and spitting droplets of burning
plastic across the sand. The man with the stick laughed
and jumped back.

The boys told them about the baby.

The men didn't show much reaction. The one who stood away from the fire said, "That's a real good story, my friend."

"It's true," Joe said.

The man with the stick spoke with a strong accent. "If es true," he said, "then you shoulden tell to anyone."

They stood and watched the fire die down a little, and then the man threw another bale on. The man with the stick pulled the uncoiled wire out of the flames and put it off to cool beside the other blackened coils. White smoke rose from the wire.

The man with the stick told the other man something in Spanish. He replied, "Maybe. Pero no, they're just crazy. Son locos."

"What did he say?" Tate asked.

"My friend he says it's la Llorona that took your little baby," the man said.

"What's that?"

"Just a fairy tale," the man said. The boys were watching him, so he went on. "About a lady, who drowned her kids. She's la Llorona, always she's crying." He smiled weakly, like he was embarrassed. "It is just a story."

The man with the stick rejoined them. "La Llorona es looking for here babies," he said. He leaned on the stick, hands clasped in front of him, and looked wild-eyed from side to side. A gold tooth flashed in the fire-light. "Looking, looking," he said. "Where my babies? Where my babies?"

Joe stared off into the darkness beyond the fire. He was sorry they'd told the men about the baby. He turned to Tate, but Tate was looking past the fire too, listening.

The first man laughed sharply, and not looking at his theatrical friend, he said, "Tú eres más loco than these guys, hombre."

His friend did not laugh. He looked at Joe, serious, and then raised his eyebrows, shrugged. He looked at Tate. "Who knows?" he said. "Quién sabe? Who knows?"

Joe felt a nudge at his side. It was Tate. He had the bottle of rum. Joe took it. The new bale began to catch, and the Mexican went back to poke at it.

Joe stared at the bottle, watching the fire reflected in the clear alcohol. He shook the bottle gently, and the flames danced. One of the men began to hum a song that Joe recognized from the jukebox at Dawson's back in town. It was a sad song about a woman who always returned, only to leave again. Mexicans loved that song; at Dawson's they would put it on the jukebox again and again when they played pool, and when they got drunk enough they would sing it. Joe removed the cap and lifted the bottle to his mouth.

The syrup-sweet taste of the rum burning down Joe's throat and into his empty stomach brought back slow, vague memories. He recalled with rising nausea the night before, so drunk he could hardly move, nine-tenths unconscious in the cool dirt of the river bank, and Tate swaying above him beside the hippie man who never came back, saying wake up, wake up, you're missing the party. And Joe remembered then with disbelief that he hadn't even had time that morning to have a hangover: he was still drunk when he woke up and by noon he'd forgotten having been drunk at all. He remembered the events of the day like a dream, like a story someone had told him, or pictures in a book. It didn't seem like it could have happened.

He thought it was a doll. He was going to pick it up by the leg, hold it up above his head. But it was a baby.

It was a joke; it was like a joke.

Joe took another drink and gave the rum to Tate. Tate drank, gave the bottle to the Mexican with the stick, who passed it to his friend. The friend drank and told the story of la Llorona again, and this time she lived under a bridge in Brownsville, Texas, where he was born. His oldest brother was killed in a bar there, and then the whole family moved to Phoenix. When he finished the story he took a long drink, and handed the rum sadly back to Joe.

The bottle went around a few times and then it was empty, and then the Mexicans brought out a bottle of Mexican brandy and they all drank from that, and they stood around the burning wire and talked. They told other stories and laughed quietly, and when the second bottle was gone the Mexicans found another in the truck. As the night grew cooler they moved closer to the fire. They talked for a long time, until the last bale of wire was left smoking in the sand to cool, but they did not talk about the baby again.

ROBERT SHAPARD

MOTEL

That night a pickup without its lights on cut across the dirt divider onto the highway in front of us. I had no chance to brake and swerved off the shoulder at sixty miles an hour, snapping down through the brush with no seat belts and Gayle Ann sliding hard against me. We bounced onto and off of an access road, missed a pole, and smashed into the back of a motel.

We were in my son's car, his first, a 1952 Buick he was restoring. He was visiting his grandmother. The motel was cinder block and the Buick went right through it, with a tremendous crump, then an avalanche of thuds and clunks that seemed to go on forever. Finally there was just dust and quiet.

I couldn't breathe. I couldn't move, but inside I was fighting upwards like a diver for air. In the dark the glowing red bips in the instrument panel seemed magical, floating. The windshield was smashed like a dark net full of glitters. Then my breath started coming in squeaks. Gayle Ann was crying. Charlie, please, she said. She was afraid I was dead.

I was fine. I just couldn't breathe. I was never happier in my life because all that mattered to me was that Gayle Ann was alive. My ribs were bruised, Gayle Ann's elbow was bruised, we had cuts, jammed fingers, bumps, but none of that bothered us. We were indestructible.

I got back against the door and cracked it open enough to squeeze out with Gayle Ann behind me. Up by the highway and beyond the motel there was nothing but scrub and moonlight, an August night, late but still hot. We were trembling, shaken but exalted because we were in love and alive, not touching because we were afraid of hurting one another.

The back of the motel was a dark wall, a black pit with a Buick buried in it. I got close and called, "Is anybody in there?" If anybody was in there, some man or a woman or a baby, they could all be dead. There was nothing but black silence.

"What about the bourbon?" Gayle Ann said.

We had a bottle from the party in Austin. I had a feeling we were going to get nailed for this. The guy in the pickup was probably drunk. That was the irony. This late at night he could weave all over the highway all the way back to his ranch and sleep it off and never get caught. He would never even remember it.

I went around to the front of the motel. The big sign was off, just the one floodlight shining in front of an empty gravel lot. A neon vacancy sign was glowing pink in the office window. A car was parked up there.

Along the line of rooms on the other side it was dark but just then a light came on in one of them, so I knocked and a guy opened the door. Dust boiled out of the doorway around us. He was gray and baggy-eyed but not old, some of the gray was dust. He had a big sagging belly and only undershorts on.

"Is anyone hurt?" I said.

He wanted to say something but had a coughing fit with dust shaking out of his head. I went in. The room was a mess. The front of the car was in it with the hood sprung and flattened with blocks and rubble. The dresser was splintered against the end of the bed. The head of the bed was snapped in two. There was a piece of cinder block on one of the pillows. It was just lying there like a small pink head. No arms, no legs. Nobody else in the room.

I got down by the wheel well. The light from the table lamp shone under the car in dusty shafts and outside through the gaps. I was coughing, too. I shouted, "Gayle Ann!"

Her foot and ankle appeared below a piece of chrome and turquoise metal, which was the lower part of the car door. "What?" She sounded frightened. I thought objectively for the first time what a terrible thing if she had been killed. She had two children. If I were dead it would be terrible, too, but my son was sixteen and could almost take care of himself.

I told her to try and start the car.

"Charlie?" Her ankle was gone but her voice was closer. Her hand planted itself on the ground in a puff of dust. Then came the fall of her hair, and an eye. "Should we do this?" she said. "What if the engine catches on fire?"

I said, "Just do it."

So she did. The engine turned over with a terrible banging, like somebody trying to axe his way out of a tin washtub. I told her to stop.

The grayish man was sitting on the bed. "I was asleep," he said. His voice was hoarse but at least he could talk now. We introduced ourselves—his name was Russ—and I asked him where we were.

"Texas," he said.

I said, "I know that. I mean what's the next town?"

He was hacking again. "Cotulla," he said.

I said I had told my wife the day before that I was going to Amarillo.

"Amarillo," Russ said. "That's about four hundred miles north of here."

I knew that, I said. I asked him if there was a telephone, and Russ said he was sure there was one in the room. We found a television not too badly smashed behind the dresser but not the telephone. We heard radio static somewhere outside, and voices. There was a loud knocking and we turned. It was Gayle Ann, horrified, in the doorway of the motel room. "My God," she said.

As far as I was concerned, nothing could ever be wrong with the world as long as Gayle Ann was smiling. The world wasn't right at the moment but at least there was a kind of relief in the way she was agog.

She had the bourbon and I sent her down to the Coke and ice machines that Russ said were by the office, then I helped Russ find his clothes. He was a local rancher. He didn't have a suitcase.

There were empty beer cans by the bed. Butts in the ashtray, with lipstick on them. So there had been a woman in the room. He said at nine o'clock every night the owner switched off the motel lights and passed out. If you were a friend and needed a room, you just went behind the desk and got a key.

I said, "Russ, the truck cut across the highway, right out of the dark, in front of us."

He found some plastic cups in the bathroom and dislodged a dinette chair from the wall by the bed. The voices were from the car radio on the other side of the wall—Gayle Ann hadn't switched the ignition key back all the way. Russ said nobody could blame us for having a drink after coming close to death. That was true. Also, if the highway patrol showed up and wanted to give us a balloon test, it would only prove we had drinks after the wreck, not before. When Gayle Ann got back we made drinks. We were all amazed at being alive.

Russ said he was asleep when the car smashed into the room. He was dreaming. He was in an ancient Mexican temple and could smell the stone. He knew about human sacrifice and was worried, but there wasn't anybody there. There were flowers and moonlight on the stones, a sphinx, a small one alive, like a panther with yellow eyes, watching. Creepy. Gayle Ann said it reminded her of a perfume ad in a slick magazine. Russ said it reminded him of an old girlfriend. He went on. In the dream he had opened his shaving kit and under his deodorant and toothbrush was a bluish-red, quivering, beating human heart.

I said, "Is this a cord? There's something under here that looks like a telephone cord."

Gayle Ann said, "Who are you going to call?"

"There's nothing in Cotulla," Russ said. "The gas pump doesn't open until seven in the morning."

Gayle Ann was flagging. She was in her jeans and sat on the bed with her legs crossed, Indian style. I said we could use some lime for the bourbon and Coke. She said we were going to need more than that. We were both beginning to hurt some.

"I'll hire a wrecker," I said. Gayle Ann's husband wasn't due back until Monday. That wasn't what worried me. "We'll tow the car home."

"Two hundred miles?" She looked doubtful.

"My insurance will pay for it." What worried me was that my son wasn't going to understand. I had taught him how to drive, coached his softball team, kissed him good-night and tucked him in when he was little, and took him camping. So what. He was going to hate this. It was a wonderful hulk of a car which is why I took it to the party—Gayle Ann thought it was wonderful.

"We sleep in, then get all this taken care of by lunchtime," I said. "Then we rent another car and by tomorrow afternoon we'll be strolling around the zocalo under the alamos. Just like we planned. Dinner and drinks at the Cadillac Bar." I sat on the bed and leaned back on my elbow next to Gayle Ann.

"We're only half an hour from the border," I said. "We've got plenty of time."

Gayle Ann had courage. She went over my scalp, checking for cuts. "You're just like a big old hound dog," she said. Then she said, "Charlie, I love you so much." Russ grinned and ducked his head and looked away. She had never had an affair before.

I said, "Don't worry, we'll get through this."

But we didn't get through it. In the morning the boy would only tow the car as far as his own garage. There weren't any rental cars. The motel owner was an older woman who trembled writing both of our home addresses and the names of both our insurance agents. Later, drinking coffee and something stronger, she asked if we were staying another night. I sent Gayle Ann back at two the next afternoon on the bus that stopped across from the John Deere lot and the Cotulla Cafe, so she could get home before her husband did, but she didn't make it.

Things didn't go well for me either. I lost several friends and my boy in the divorce.

Gayle Ann fought for custody of her son although her husband had already agreed to let the daughter, who was twelve, stay with her. For a month it was best not to see each other.

Then other things happened. We didn't know then that we would never see each other again.

But that night we wondered about Russ's dream. Gayle Ann had climbed a temple once, not a big one, just a little one next to a glass factory near Coyoacan, Mexico. Russ and I got the window air conditioner blowing again, and with the door open, that cleared a lot of the dust. I thought we should stay by the car. I told Russ, "Look, do you want to get another room?'

He said sure.

He got a key from the office and came back to say good night, but first he had another drink with us. Outside, Gayle Ann shook out the blanket and sheets. It was so pleasant, late, with a breeze, the lamplight and music still on the car radio. I didn't think Russ was going to leave.

After he did, we locked the door and because we didn't want anybody on the highway seeing the outline of a car buried in a wall, we clicked our light off.

Our eyes grew accustomed to the dark and we fixed another drink. We took a while getting our clothes off. The moon shone through the window on the grille. It was caved in like a shark's mouth.

We were feverish. Cool air was blowing but our skins were hot, and dry, and smooth. The moonlight was across our bare feet.

RICK BASS

HEARTWOOD

Two boys, wild boys, in my, our valley—but it wasn't their fault. The valley itself was wild: how could they be otherwise? Victor was tall, massive, a man already—he helped his mother in the mercantile rather than going to school. His friend, Percy, didn't do much of anything. Percy's father, whose last name was Coward, was an alcoholic, and his mother did most of the chores around the house: the wood-splitting and baby-raising, the cooking, the egg-collecting. It was funny how we had already written Percy off, even though he had just turned fifteen.

Percy was short and pale, thin, and he bruised easily. He always seemed to be wiping his nose. One eye went slightly off course when he tried to focus on something. The cabin he lived in was back in the woods, with only propane lanterns for lighting, and so it was always a little dark in his house. His hair was never combed.

When Percy's father was cognizant enough to crawl down the Yaak River Road and make it into the bar, things were okay. But usually his father just stayed at home and drank. When life wasn't going well, he threw things at Percy: chunks of firewood, beer bottles, stones, cats. Mister Coward was a large man who had lost his leg in a logging accident almost eight years ago, when Percy was seven, and even then, Mister Coward had been a drinker. It just got worse after the accident.

What Percy and Victor began to do, when they turned fifteen, was to drive long steel nails deep into the trunks of all the giant larch trees in the valley. A single larch tree, a hundred and fifty or two hundred feet tall, and as big around at the base as a small car, could be worth several thousand dollars to a logging crew. The valley used to be filled with them, a sea of giants, trees that had already been a hundred years old back when the big fire of 1910 came through, destroying everything but those giant larches; but now they were being logged out.

The way that I knew the boys were doing it—spiking the big larch trees—was that they kept their spikes in my hay barn; and they painted murals of their deeds inside the barn, with cans of spray paint, on the barn's old weathered wood walls.

I never spoke to the boys, not once—words did not pass between us. When we met we'd look long and hard at each other—centuries, and forests, of words between us—but we never ever spoke. Why did they choose my barn?

Because they could read my heart, I believe. They were devils, they were cold young men and already wild. Dirt, and fright, and wildness, was in their own hearts. I'm pretty sure that they wanted me to join them.

I loved those trees. I loved wildness, too, but was frightened of it.

The boys met in my barn nearly every night, with a lantern, and painted their pictures—bright red and blue and yellow hieroglyphics of two figures in the forest, pounding spikes into glowing trees. The trees had strange yellow halos—and beneath the paintings the boys told roughly where the trees were: Vinal Ridge Road, Flatiron Mountain Road, Lower Fowler Creek.

I'd watch, from my cabin, their lantern-glow seeping through the chinks in my barn.

The next day, in the safety of daylight, I'd go down and look at the new murals, and I'd find myself sweating. The forests are so lovely up here: they demand nothing of anyone. So safe! Why do they have to cut the biggest, oldest trees? Why couldn't they leave the few, very few, remaining giants?

Then the kickbacks began. When loggers cut into the big spiked trees, the spinning saw blade would touch the spike and snap back with the recoil of a fired cannonball, slamming right back at the sawyer. It ruined the blade, of course, and was dangerous as hell. After only a few kickbacks, when it was clear that evil was at work, the men began to take precautions, testing trees with a metal detector before felling them — but even so, they were often forgetting the metal detector, or they would think, Surely this tree, so far off from anything, hasn't been tampered with: and then they would get hurt, sometimes badly.

No one except me knew who was spiking the trees. It seemed I should do something, something to stop it, but I didn't know what.

One man took four hundred stitches in his shoulder, out in the field, with string and a sewing needle, and almost died. Another had the saw hit his helmet and crack it in half, and they thought he was dead and had taken him home to get him ready for burial, were already building the warming fires to thaw the earth, when he woke up.

He said he felt better than he had in twenty years, that he felt like a kid again, and he spoke of seeing a great white light hovering over him the whole time: a white light that wanted him, but would not have him.

I kept thinking one side would give in. I kept thinking the sawyers would give up, and stop cutting the giants.

Those boys — the loggers would have killed those boys.

The men were, I think, angry, but also strangely *alive* — feeling the edges of life is how I imagined it — and each day they went into the woods as if going off to war, and there was no doubt that if any of them ever saw who was doing it there would be one shot from a 30.06, one crisp shot on a winter morning, and the story would be over.

It was the women whom the spikes bothered the most. They'd play pinochle at the mercantile nearly every day, and get drunk and talk about the things they were going to do, if they found out who it was: castrations, that sort of thing.

I'd dated—"slept with" is the better term, the more accurate words, for this valley—Victor's mother for a while, back when Victor must have been eleven or twelve. I remembered once when I'd been over there, staying the night, wide-assed naked on the bed—I remember what I was doing with Carol clearly, what she was having done—when Victor came into the room, just opened the door and walked right in, and stood there.

Carol leapt up and ushered him out of the room, didn't even put a robe on, or wrap a sheet around herself—just hustled him right back out the door.

Not long after that Carol and I got tired of one another's bodies, and drifted apart.

Sometimes the women would be playing cards at the mercantile when I went in for groceries. They played all day long in the winter—the men out sawing, while I, the nature writer, the nature-boy, hung around town, hung around the cabin—and the mercantile would be blue with smoke. The thing I liked about Carol, the way I remembered her, besides in bed, was how she held her cards, arranging them, and how she let her cigarette dangle from the corner of her mouth. I liked to watch all of the women play as I moved down the short aisles, selecting that day's canned goods: soup, beans, mixed fruits.

"I'll get him," Carol said one day to the other women—deciding to lay her cards down when she realized, belatedly, that she had won. Winning always seemed to surprise her, or any of them, and they'd stare at the cards for a few moments whenever they won, even after they had laid the last card down, as if not trusting their eyes, as if unsure of what they were seeing. "Whoever it is, I'll kill him," she said, and they all nodded.

The women started up a new hand then, and played, I'm sure, late into the afternoon, trying not to look at the clock, trying not to wonder if one of the men was down at that very moment. It was February, and hysteria seemed only a step away, as if they could walk right into it, comfortably, and settle in with no effort at all. They spoke carefully and slowly, trying to help each other, watching for signs.

I saw Carol's hands tremble that afternoon as she held her cards. The man she was sleeping with now was a logger. All of the men were. It was all or nothing.

It was also in February, that year when Victor and Percy were fifteen, that they began riding the horses. Davey Prouder, who ran the saloon, was keeping the horses in my pasture in exchange for my free drinks at the saloon, since I didn't drink that much, and it was one of my jobs to feed them, and to keep the ice from clogging up on their hooves, and to exercise them, if I could. Buck was a sweet line-backed dun, but Fuel was a ferocious cutting horse from Oklahoma who was so mean they hadn't even been able to trailer him—instead, they'd had to ride him all the way up here, and it had taken three months.

But when Percy turned fifteen, he somehow got it into his mind to begin riding Fuel. He'd found out that he could ride him as long as it was dark and cold; and he rode after midnight, after he and Victor got in from spiking trees.

Percy, poor ugly Percy, would slip up on wild Fuel—all the cold stars at their brightest, and every sound magnified, every sound a shout—and Victor would climb up on Buck, the sweet horse, the tamer horse, and the two boys would ride around the pasture at a full gallop, riding the horses through the deep drifts and up through the woods behind my cabin, clinging to the wild, startled horses' necks and shutting their eyes, trying to keep from being popped by frozen branches. I'd watch from the window, still passive, and frightened, and amazed at their fury, their anger. I wanted to get back together with Carol, but she was pretty sweet on her new logger. Things were good between them—you could see that. Why did I want to ruin that? Something about the spikes, and all the trouble in the valley that year, made me want to make love to her again.

I would see Victor and Percy in the store, on weekends, and we'd exchange strange looks—glares, sometimes. Percy would be bruised or cut from where his father had hit him with things. No one liked it; everyone wished the old man would go ahead and die, or rot away, so that Percy and his mother and brothers and sisters could start over. And in April, that is what happened: Mister Coward ruptured something, some kind of bleeding started going on inside him, filling him up with his own blood, bloating him horribly, until his face was black and he was shouting, and Mrs. Coward, hysterical, called the mercantile on the truck's radio.

The pain had to have been horrendous. We could hear his screams all over the valley, and one of the men finally had to pull him outside and shoot him, to put him out of his misery.

I helped bury Percy's father in the marsh, in the cemetery for loggers. It was full of tall, shady larches, centuries old, with fine filtered sunlight that came drifting down, so slowly, through the lacey fernlike leaves of the smaller trees, and the forest floor was covered with larch needles. Granite headstones crept up into the woods, dating back to the early 1800s, with names like "Piss Fir Jim" and "Windy Joe Doggs." A slight breeze was always stirring in that cemetery, and that magic, gold light was always there, with the sound of the river below, even at night. It was the most beautiful spot in the valley, a fine resting spot.

Mister Coward had been thirty-eight. Hardly any of the loggers made it to thirty-eight.

One day, on the mural wall inside my barn, there was a spray-painted picture of what had to be me and Carol, in her bed—me doing what I'd been doing that time three years before. It was as if the boys were daring me, challenging me to hurt them — to turn them in.

There's a life to live; fear and lust are in this life. I went over to Carol's one day when Joe, her logger, was out in the woods and there wasn't a pinochle game going. Victor was gone, too. Carol and I had a couple of beers. I got brave and told her I wanted to get back together again. It wasn't so hard. Carol said we should, but that she wanted to keep it a secret.

Used to be, I wouldn't be much on that action — being secret, seeing her like that. But I was changing like crazy with those boys in my barn. I felt like I was on fire. I felt like burning myself up, like hurting myself. "Okay," I said. "Sure. However you want it."

I'd hike over to her house and make love to her during the day. She stopped going to all of the pinochle games. I'd never known a woman with such fury, such *unquenchable* fury. It was such a strange valley, back when Victor and Percy were fifteen.

Just fury: *ten* men couldn't have done her, and that's a fact. Joe's benign picture — her logger — stared at us from the crowded dresser, as we rutted. Nature boy, I thought, and then I'd think, Nature Boy, you've lived too long, you've gotten too dirty. The world has defeated you, has claimed you. It controls you.

Ten men couldn't have done her. It was better than before. It was wild.

Sometimes she seemed to want me to take her to the edge of pain; and sometimes she would try and hurt me.

Sometimes I let her. I don't know why.

In May, Victor and Percy started getting into fights. Usually, Victor won, quickly blackening one of Percy's eyes or bloodying his nose; but in June, Percy got the idea of jousting, rather than just simply fist-fighting.

At first they went at it up in the woods, chasing each other around on the horses with sawed-off poles, more swatting than any sort of jousting — the horses leaping the fallen logs in the trails, one rider taking his horse down the creek into the mist of the great larches, into

the summer morning fog, then wheeling around and
riding hard back out of the ferns and mist, the sun gold
in the other's eyes, blinded, just a hard-riding dark shape
coming at him fast and then the swat of the pole, knocking one of them off of the bare-backed horse, and landing hard on the spongy rotting carpet of larch needles
and bog.

All that silence around them after that, and the sun
so far above them, at the tops of the great trees, strug-
gling to make it down to them . . .

I would run up from behind the house, up into the
woods, and would crouch down behind logs, following
them, as they galloped and wheeled, and chased each
other through the woods on horseback.

But slowly, through the early summer, the boys'
swats turned to true jousts, and they would lift each
other off the backs of the horses, catching the other rider
under the armpit, or high up in the chest, driving them
backwards, even lifting them up, then, as the horse continued forward, suddenly riderless — and then there'd be
that long, twisting fall, for the defeated rider, back down
into the moss and old dark soil.

It had to be a familiar feeling for Percy. He would
pick himself up, never any broken bones, not at that age,
and would whistle for Fuel, who, I was beginning to see,
was the better fighting horse. Percy would have sugar
cubes in his pocket, stolen from Victor's store, I'd bet,
and it was how he got Fuel to return, and he would slip
them to him, when Victor wasn't looking, would whisper things in Fuel's ear.

What I saw was this: that Percy was letting Victor
knock him off that horse. He was only pretending to
lose.

I don't know why — even today, I can't figure it out.
Perhaps losing, and pain, and stupidity, is simply a thing
that is in the blood.

A man on one of the logging crews was killed by the
kickback from a spiked larch. Everyone had known it
would happen sooner or later, they had just not known

to whom it would happen. I felt immensely guilty. But they would have killed Percy, and maybe Victor. Strung them up if they hadn't shot them.

I dreamed about the dead man's face. More than once when I was with Carol, her body would suddenly look like a man's, in the night — *that* man's — and I'd gasp, and not be able to finish, not want to finish.

A number of men had seen the accident, and the death, and were starting to have nightmares about it. Some who hadn't seen it were having nightmares, too. The women didn't know what to do about this. None of their men had ever had nightmares before. These were strong men. But now they were going into the woods without joking, without joy. They were gaunter, less interested in their wives, their girlfriends, in hunting and drinking, in anything. The June sun climbed higher in the sky earlier, and stayed up above them all day, hanging, shining white and warm, but it did not seem like spring to them, did not seem like anything.

Another man caught a kickback on the top of his helmet two weeks later, and he lay there unconscious for two hours in the ferns by the spring creek as the men splashed water on his face, trying to revive him, and when he came to he spoke of seeing the same white light hovering just above him, just out of reach: seeming to want him, but unable to take him — seeming sad, disappointed.

The boys moved out into the meadow with their jousts. They began to use longer poles, too: heavy lodgepole, with pillows lashed to one end, like a boxing glove, and heavy steel garbage can lids for shields — and the horses were running stronger, faster, rich on the green June hays and grasses.

The women in the valley began to watch them, in the early summer, bringing picnic lunches and ice chests, which they sat on as if they were chairs. They would play cards, set up umbrellas to protect themselves from the high sun in the thin mountain air — umbrellas and parasols — and they would pour each other glasses of white wine. At that time no one had been injured, had not even seen a kickback, in almost a month. It was rumored that all of the spiked trees had been cut down.

The women would place bets on the two boys, bets that increased as the afternoon lengthened, and the wine bottles became empty. Some of the men built bleachers for the wives to sit on, and out in the pasture, every half-hour or so, after resting and watching the horses, the two boys would go at it.

Sometimes Victor won, but more often now Percy would win. I was glad to see that Percy seemed to have gotten hold of himself; that he was not letting Victor win on purpose, that he was no longer just giving himself over to abuse.

They were the town darlings. No one had ever seen anything like it before.

Part of the bets went to Percy and Victor. Percy bought his mother a battery-operated radio, a new dress, some perfume. Victor saved his money. Carol said he wanted to get out of the valley. I think Victor was nervous about the legacy he and Percy had already left, at fifteen, and knew that there were entire forests of spiked trees that had not yet had the first tree felled in them; next year's cuttings, and the year's after that, and the next. I don't think he understood what had gotten into him. It had been Percy's idea, I think, but Victor had gone along with it. Bad luck.

Victor gave me the most murderous looks, in town and at the jousting meets; and later in the summer, as I continued to see Carol, he began to spray-paint murals of my death on my barn wall—pictures of me being dismembered by two boys with chain saws.

I'd stand there in the barn, in the daytime, and I'd know that I should tell—that Victor was *challenging* me to tell, and that Percy was, too. At fifteen, these two boys were simply tired of living, such was the dirt and hardness and emptiness of their lives. But I was too far into it, a man had died, and it was too late; and still, too, I held out hope for victory, hope that the spikes would save the biggest trees. I'm not saying that what I did—or didn't do—was right. I'm just saying I did it. That's all. I got into a bad situation, is all—like the boys—and got swept along by it.

In August, Percy caught Victor in the neck with the pole, and everyone who saw it agreed it was an accident, pure and simple—everyone but me.

It was true that Percy hit Victor with the pole no differently than he had a hundred times before—and no differently than he had been hit by Victor a hundred times—but what I believe now was that it had been a fight to the death all along, that Percy had known from the beginning that one of them would be killed jousting, and that he had determined to himself that he would ride hard until it happened, and just leave it up to luck.

Victor died before he hit the ground; bounced twice. Did he see the white light? It took him. The horse, Buck, kept running, into the trees. I was sitting with Carol and Joe. Carol screamed and leapt up and looked out into the meadow at her son—and then, strangely, looked off at the runaway horse for a long time—two, three seconds—before looking back at her son; and then, finally, she hurried down the bleachers and ran out to the meadow to hold him, though it was too late for that.

We buried Victor where we buried everyone: always, in this valley, it seems, we're burying people.

They were just kids, but I was a grown man. The valley was pretty, but somehow the goodness finally left it. The magic and beauty went out of it, years ago, and that was that, an end of good luck. We did something wrong, somewhere—I don't know what. We might simply have held our breath wrong.

The Kootenai Indians who used to hunt up here believe that luck is like pine sap, like tar, that it's something you step into—and that it can be good or bad, but that once you've stepped into it you've got to wear all of it off of your moccasin, if it's bad, say, before you can have the chance to step into good luck. And vice versa. And I have to agree. My luck's still holding, up here in the woods. But I feel like I've used up an awful lot, being associated with those two boys. I feel like I'm getting really close to the bottom by now, really wearing it out.

I'm here to bear witness to luck. I fell away from Carol once again. Joe lost her, too—she became nothing in her sorrow, a living ghost. They've both drifted to other places on the earth—probably still living, but barely: passive, damned, I suppose. Percy's still angry. Perhaps there was a way his anger could have been softened, could even have been healed, but it did not happen; and even today, as a grown man roaming the valley, cutting trees for the Forest Service, drinking, driving wildly, and getting in wrecks, Percy is still alive, and that anger is still in him, I can see, with his heart wrapped around it, wrapped like wood around a deep spike, a spike that is hidden, and which can never be gotten out.

Those great trees, silent in the high forest, some of them still loaded with spikes, from the year that Percy was fifteen, are still standing. And still a danger.

In the end, it all comes down to luck. We're here, and if we're lucky we're alive. Remember this, and be grateful. And be frightened.

THE AUTHORS

RICK BASS is the author of *The Watch,* a short story collection, and three collections of essays. He lives in Montana and is working on a novel.

MICHAEL DELP is chairman of the Creative Writing Division at Interlochen Arts Academy in Michigan. His poems, nonfiction, and fiction have appeared in such publications as *The North Dakota Review, Poetry Northwest, Gray's Sporting Journal, Playboy,* and *Detroit Magazine.* His first collection of poems, *Over the Graves of Horses,* has been highly praised by Jim Harrison and Charles Baxter.

RICK DEMARINIS has spent most of his adult life in Montana, which he considers his spiritual homeland. His fifth novel, *The Year of the Zinc Penny,* was published in 1989 and his new collection is tentatively titled *The Voice of America.* His collection *Under the Wheat* won the Drue Heinz Literature Prize in 1986. He teaches at the University of Texas, El Paso.

DAGOBERTO GILB was born and raised in Los Angeles and lives in El Paso. His work has appeared in numerous literary journals, and his first book, *Winners on the Pass Line,* was published in 1985. He is the recipient of the San Francisco Foundation's James D. Phelan Award for Literature and a Dobie-Paisano Fellowship from the Texas Institute of Letters and the University of Texas.

LAURA HENDRIE was born and raised in Colorado and now lives in Ojo Sarco, New Mexico. She studied at the University of Iowa and University of Alabama, and has published stories in *Missouri Review, Writers Forum,* and various anthologies, including *Into the Silence, American Signatures,* and *The Best of the West 1.* Her story "What Lasts" is a tribute to her mother, who was stricken with Alzheimer's disease two years ago. It was aired on National Public Radio and also appeared in the *Chicago Tribune.*

EUGENE KRAFT grew up on a farm in western Kansas, the area which is the center of most of his writing. After receiving his doctorate in English from the University of Missouri, he taught in university programs in seven countries—in the U.S., the Orient, and Europe. Kraft is the author of some 55 publications and is currently at work on a collection of stories set in Kansas and on a critical study of Langston Hughes.

DAVID KRANES writes fiction and plays. He is artistic director of Sundance Institute's Playwriting Lab and teaches in the creative writing program at the University of Utah.

MARK LITWICKI was born in the Midwest and has lived most of his life in Arizona. His writing has appeared in *Sonora Review, Pine Knots, The Network,* and in a local English-language newspaper he edited while living in the Tohoku region of Japan. He currently lives and works in the border country of southeastern Arizona.

T. M. MCNALLY teaches English and creative writing at Murray State University, in Kansas, and has recent stories in *Apalachee Quarterly, Northwest Review, Quarterly West,* and others.

ROBYN OUGHTON works as a visiting nurse in rural western Massachusetts. She edits fiction for *Peregrine,* the literary journal of Amherst Writers & Artists. She says, "Four years ago I gathered up everything I had ever worked on (about 25 pounds worth) and threw it away. An Amherst Writers & Artists creative writing workshop gave me the courage to listen carefully and respectfully to myself, and to put it down on paper." One result is "Crazy River." She has stories published in *Plainswoman, Sonora Review,* and *Aura.*

LESLEY POLING-KEMPES has lived and worked in Abiquiu, New Mexico, since 1975. Her first book, *The Harvey Girls: Women Who Opened the West,* was published in 1989. Her fiction has appeared in *Puerto del Sol* and

Writers Forum. She has also worked as a documentary filmmaker and has co-directed and produced a film entitled *Between Green and Dry* about rural New Mexico and its collision with modern America. She has recently finished writing a novel called *The High Noon Cafe.*

LISA SANDLIN has lived in Santa Fe since 1974, but her great-grandparents came to New Mexico much earlier, around 1912, in a mule-drawn wagon. She is a participant in Vermont College's Writing Program and is currently at work on a novel, *Jimmy's Eye,* set in New Mexico.

ROBERT SHAPARD is a Texan who lived in Utah for seven years before moving to Honolulu, where he teaches at the University of Hawaii and edits *Manoa: A Pacific Journal of International Writing.* His fiction has won General Electric/Coordinating Council of Literary Magazines and National Endowments for the Arts awards and has appeared in various magazines, most recently *The Kenyon Review.* Currently he is working on a story collection and a novel.

CHRIS SPAIN earned a degree in agriculture from Colorado State University and was a Stegner Fellow at Stanford University. His short story collection, *Praying for Rain,* was published in spring 1990.

ELIZABETH TALLENT's short stories, honored in *The Best American Short Stories, The Pushcart Prize* anthology, and the *O. Henry Award* anthology, have appeared in the volumes *In Constant Flight* and *Time with Children.* She has also published a novel, *Museum Pieces.* She and her husband and son divide their time between New Mexico and northern California.

CHRISTOPHER TILGHMAN lives in Massachusetts with his wife and two young sons. "Hole in the Day" is part of his first story collection, *In a Father's Place,* published in spring 1990.